THIS WORLD OF CORPSES - BOOK FIFTEEN OF BEYOND THESE WALLS

A POST-APOCALYPTIC SURVIVAL THRILLER

MICHAEL ROBERTSON

EDITED AND COVER BY ...

To contact Michael, please email:
subscribers@michaelrobertson.co.uk

Edited by:

Pauline Nolet - http://www.paulinenolet.com

Cover design by Dusty Crosley - https://www.deviantart.
com/dustycrosley

COPYRIGHT

This World of Corpses: Book fifteen of Beyond These Walls

Michael Robertson
© Michael Robertson 2022

electronic, mechanical, photocopying, recording, or otherwise, without the prior written permission of the author except in the case of brief quotations embodied in critical articles and reviews.

CHAPTER 1

J oni hated secrets at the best of times, but holding this one was like gripping a hot coal with hands of butter. Especially keeping it from Antonia and Ralph. And having Matt in her ear made it worse. He knew too much already and wouldn't shut up.

"I can't help feeling like there's something I've missed."

No matter how many times she'd crawled through these shafts, when she moved at this pace, it always hurt her elbows until they were positively thrumming with bruising on top of bruising. Add to that the deep ache beneath her kneecaps. No matter how adaptable a body, no matter what she'd gotten used to over the years, crawling through the guards' block's maintenance shafts never got any easier.

"Joni?"

She grunted. He needed no more encouragement, and she didn't need Antonia and Ralph asking questions. She might be a little way ahead of them, but with the acoustics in these tunnels, you could hear a mouse fart three floors away.

"Something went on between you and your friend. Pocket Rocket?"

"Olga." Her growl rolled along the shaft.

"But you called he—"

"Her name's Olga."

"Okay, fine. But what did she say?"

Joni shook her head. He'd drop it eventually.

"Maybe you'll tell me another time. How are you getting on down there?"

She rubbed her sweating brow against her shoulder. "Fine."

"I can't see you on any of the cameras."

"We're still in the shafts. Is the garage still clear of diseased?"

"I'm not sure. My view is l—"

"Limited. I know. Just stay alert and let us know if you see anything. Other than that, keep your mouth shut." She could have removed the earpiece and claim it fell out, but he also had the tannoy. Using that would put the entire block on alert. It had to be a last resort, and could she really trust him to make that judgement? Better she tolerated his inquisition. And who knew, having him in her ear might yet prove useful.

The grate covering the hatch close to the ammo store remained open from their previous visit. The blood rushed to Joni's head when she leaned out, her pulse swelling through her ears as a wet throb. Ralph and Antonia caught up with her. "Looks clear, and the tool trolley's still down there."

Ralph watched her through wide eyes, his face glistening with sweat. They'd travelled from the top to the bottom of the building. Both Ralph and Antonia had done their best to match Joni's pace without complaint.

Joni pointed through the hatch. "Make sure you set up your escape before you take supplies." She patted the top of his arm and then hooked a thumb over her shoulder. "And let me and Antonia get in position first, okay?"

"Yep."

Joni crawled away, and Antonia went in the opposite direction. She scrunched her nose against the itch, dust dancing in the light coming up from below. She stopped at the next hatch and leaned close to the thin bars. The underlying reek of vinegar and rot soured the cool breeze.

"How's it looking down there?"

"Jeez." Joni jumped.

"Sorry. Did I startle you?"

"No!" Her heart pounded.

"It's just I sh—"

"Quiet."

"Huh."

"It's looking quiet."

"Too quiet?"

"Why do you have to say that?"

"Sorry."

Joni tutted. "We're on high alert. And until we see a reason to react, then we need to continue with the plan, right?"

"Right."

Wincing as if her tension would somehow mute the sound, Joni struck the grate with a sharp whack. The hinges cackled through the garage as it came to a swinging halt, and a return to silence. Thankfully, Antonia didn't need to do the same. Her hatch remained open from the last time. The hatch they'd used to call the diseased away from the ammo store.

Another throbbing head rush as Joni hung down again. The acrid stench riper the lower she leaned. But still no diseased. And not even the shuffle of dragging footsteps in a far corner. Flipping over onto her front, she slid backwards from the hatch and landed in the cool and damp garage. A concrete floor and steel walls. The place packed with floor-to-ceiling shelves, aisles running between them. Plenty of hiding places for the diseased. Plenty of blind spots to hinder Matt's cameras.

Joni gulped, her saliva thick and stale. She gripped her gun with both hands and turned on the spot. The red numbers revealed the magazine's bullet count. One hundred and eighty-seven. All she had, the rest of the ammo on the top floor with the others. They were coming down here for supplies, no need to bring extra. Besides—she reached down and tapped the handle at her hip—they had knives. And if everything went to plan, none of them would fire a gun.

"What's happening?"

"You can't see up there?" Joni's whispers snaked away from her.

"Not as well as you can."

"It seems clear."

"I concur."

"Then why are you asking me?"

"Just to be sure."

"Can you see Antonia?"

"Yep."

"What's she doing?"

"Similar to you. Pointing her gun and turning on the spot."

"Long may that continue."

Joni stood about twenty feet away from Ralph, Antonia the same distance from him in the other direction. They could have called the diseased to a hatch like before, and maybe they would have had they seen them on the cameras. But before they'd left, the place had seemed clear. Why cause a commotion when you could slip in and out unnoticed? They might need to take down one or two, but they were always better moving like they were invisible. Moving through the place like carbon monoxide.

"Where do you think they've gone?"

"The diseased?"

"Yeah."

Joni kept a tight grip on her gun and sniffed. "Dunno. Not far." She leaned to the right to get a clearer line of sight at the other end of the garage. "But from what I can see, the doors are still locked."

"Joni, you're forgetting something."

"You know me talking down here is putting us all at risk, right?"

The gentle white noise hiss of connection ran through her headset.

"So, rather than cryptic messages, just tell me what I've forgotten."

"*What* would have sufficed? And been much more efficient."

"Prick."

"That'd do it too. Now, I'm no expert, but I've just watched Antonia set up a stool beneath her hatch so she can get back into the shaft in a hurry. Shouldn't you be doing the same? Especially when you took the time to warn Ralph."

Mental note: remember to call him a condescending prick when she got back to the top floor. Joni let her gun's strap catch its weight and darted into the closest aisle, her eyes sore from where she hadn't blinked. She grabbed an empty steel box.

Turning the crate over, Joni rolled it towards her hatch, every turn making the slightest scrape against the concrete. She placed it beneath her hatch. "You still can't see anything?"

"Nope."

A phlegmy snarl lifted the hairs on the back of Joni's neck. Her chest tightened. Drawing deep breaths while she rode out the adrenaline dump, she grabbed her knife. One diseased she could cope with. Stab it. Kill it before it made a scene. A quiet and efficient execution. Nothing to see here. But the discontent came from the other side of the garage. Antonia's side.

A wild scream turned Joni's blood cold. "What's happening, Matt?"

"It's okay. She's running to get back into the hatch."

"She wasn't there already?"

"She went to investigate. But she's getting there. She'll be … Oh fuck!"

"What?" Joni pressed her earpiece, jamming it into her ear. "What's going on?"

"The stool she used … It just broke …"

Joni turned one way and the other. Towards Antonia. Back to Ralph. They'd promised they'd protect him. Both women knew the drill. They could look after themselves, but Ralph would be burdened with ammo. They'd promised they'd have his back.

Antonia's war cry responded to the diseased calls. The burst of bullets being fired.

Silence.

"She's taken it down."

"Are there any more?" Joni panted like she'd fought the thing herself.

"Not at the mo—"

More screams.

"Fuck. How many?"

"Three. Four. Maybe more."

Joni bounced on her toes. Her heart urged her the way of her daughter, but her head pulled her back towards Ralph. "Fuck! Is she getting back into the shaft? Has she found something else to use as a step?"

"No."

"*No?*"

"There are too many diseased, Joni. She doesn't have time."

CHAPTER 2

The angry report of bullet fire cackled through the garage. Both saviour and summoner, the diseased it called replied with wails of their own.

Joni cupped her mouth with one hand. "Ralph?"

"Yeah?"

"Antonia's in trouble."

The bullet fire halted. "I'm not." It resumed.

"Ralph, I need you to get into the hatch. I promised I'd cover you, and I will until you're safe, so please get safe. Now."

"Okay."

"I'll be with you soon, Antonia."

Another pause. "Just do what we came here for. Get the ammo into the shaft. I can look after myself."

"Ralph's nearly safe, jus—"

Bullet fire.

Diseased cries.

"How's she doing, Matt?"

"It's not looking good."

"Fuck!"

"She's on the move. Six to eight diseased on her tail."

"How are things going back there, Ralph?"

Steel clattered against steel from where he loaded the maintenance shaft. "Nearly done."

"Fuck this." Joni ran to Ralph. He'd stacked ammo and weapons on the floor by the shaft and tool rack. She scooped up an armful and passed them to him in the shaft. "Stay in there."

A wild scream to her right. Joni's red target danced on its face. She obliterated its features with one squeeze, the bullets tearing open a diagonal slash. It dropped in a heap. Letting her gun strap take the weapon's weight again, she moved like a piston, bobbing to pick up ammo and throwing it up to Ralph. All the while, Matt gave her a running commentary.

"She's getting away from them. But there are more coming."

"How many?" She grunted with the effort of shifting the weapons. Rifles. Ammo. Grenades.

"Ten. Twenty."

"Which one? Ten or twenty." She lifted a heavy ammo crate onto her shoulder, stood on the tool rack, and slid it up to Ralph.

"Twenty."

"Fuck."

Joni's already sore eyes burned with her sweat. "I'm coming, Antonia."

"That's the bulk of it, Joni."

"What?"

Ralph hung down from the hatch. A few guns and magazines remained on the floor. "Leave the rest. Go and help Antonia."

Joni sprinted towards the madness, her gun gripped with both hands. She ran around a shelving rack and sneered at the shattered remains of the stool that had failed to hold her daughter's weight. Her gun kicked when she shot three diseased in the back one after the other, cutting them down.

"Right."

Joni took the next right down a tight alley between two floor-to-ceiling racks stacked with spare wheels and tyres. She fired on the diseased. Eight to ten of the fuckers, half of them fell before they'd even turned around. She shot the rest.

Her hands throbbed, and her ears rang. She blinked like it would help her see Antonia. Like it would somehow make her materialise from thin air. "Where is she?" She fired on more charging diseased, all three of them dressed as guards.

"Not that right."

"What?"

"You took the wrong right."

"Right isn't subjective." She shot another approaching diseased. A woman. A prisoner. She had black hair and a gaunt face, her bloody eyes bulbous, about ready to pop from her skull. She drew a line of fire from the woman's chest to her forehead.

Six more diseased closed in from behind. She dropped them, Antonia's fire rattling in another part of the garage.

Jumping the diseased bodies, the call of bullet fire closer, but Antonia still hidden from sight, Joni turned left towards her daughter and more diseased. Another eight to ten of them. Too many. "How's Antonia doing?" She fired.

"Losing ground. But keeping them back. For now."

Diseased came at Joni from both ways. She darted up a ramp. A dead end. The garage door closed. She backed towards the steel barrier. Her hands shook. Her throat spiky with thirst, she latched onto the first diseased and fired. A sharp burst. Efficient. Another shattered face. A man with long hair, it flailed in an arc as an extension of his theatrical fall.

The next diseased tripped over its downed kin. She shot it before it got up, unloading into the top of its head.

Two more stumbled into view. One tripped, and one remained on its feet. She shot them both. Five more appeared. A never-ending supply of the fuckers.

"How's Antonia?"

"You should worry about you."

"Don't tell me what my priorities are. How's Antonia?"

"Not good."

"Shit!"

Where she'd used bursts, Joni now kept her trigger depressed, dropping the diseased, each one falling a little closer to her than the previous.

Clack!

"Damn!"

"What?"

"Out of ammo."

"So's Antonia."

"Fuck!"

Joni slipped her gun strap free and gripped her weapon with both hands. Leading with the butt, she charged and smashed it into the nose of the next diseased, driving it back, giving herself an opening.

She left the exit ramp and ran right. Closer to Antonia's yells.

"You can't go there."

"Fuck you, Matt."

"Antonia's done for."

The words robbed Joni's legs of her strength. "They've bitten her?"

"Not yet."

"Then don't tell me that. Ever! You hear me?"

Like Joni, the diseased had forced Antonia into a dead-end exit ramp. Eight to ten of them closed in around her.

And while she fought them back with blows and strikes, they were winning.

Joni grabbed a handful of a diseased's uniform and pulled them back down the slope. The ramp's angle challenged their already weak balance, and they fell. She stamped on the creature's face, the heel of her boot sinking with a *crack!*

Two more turned Joni's way. She screamed louder than they ever could, an owl's screech. Mama bird's here. She drew her knife and ended them one after the other with two hard lunges.

The bulk of the mob remained fixed on Antonia and closed in on her, her back against the garage door.

Joni resheathed her knife and grabbed two more diseased by their shirts. She pulled them away, back down the ramp, tripping them as they stumbled. She dragged another two so they fell across the others.

She dragged another clear and made eye contact with her daughter.

Antonia kicked away the final few diseased and followed Joni in jumping the writhing uncoordinated mound still fighting to get to their feet.

Matt said, "Your crate's the best route out of there."

When Antonia went to turn right, Joni pulled her back. "This way."

Around the next bend, the steel crate she'd positioned remained beneath the open hatch.

Three diseased appeared.

Her throat sore with thirst and grief, Joni's wild cry tore it to shreds. She slipped her gun free, held it by the end of its barrel, and hit the first one's mandible for a home run. She kicked the next one away and brought her gun over her head, slamming it down on the top of the third, burying it in its skull like an axe into a log.

The diseased with the loose jaw jumped to its feet.

"Come on, Mum."

Antonia had already slipped into the hatch.

Joni swung for limp-jaw, caught him with a wild hook, and knocked him on his arse again. She boosted from the box and dived into the maintenance shaft after her daughter.

Face to face in the cold and tight tunnel, surrounded by the echoes of their collective exhaustion, Antonia laughed, her snort kicking up a puff of dust. "You're one badass bitch."

Joni forced a smile. A badass bitch who was lying to everyone. Including her daughter.

CHAPTER 3

After lying on the cold and hard floor for the past few hours, his body so tired he would have lain on broken glass if it meant he could regain his strength, Hawk finally sat up and leaned against the steel wall, shoulder to shoulder with Aggie. His heart filled by her proximity and touch. His stomach filled from their feast. The last time he'd eaten this much, he'd been a hunter in Umbriel. A different life. A different person.

The others lounged about, as stuffed. Between them, they'd barely made a dent in the food on the dining room's long tables. He had room for a little more, but every time he looked at Aggie, butterflies danced in his stomach, occupying that small remaining space. They'd welcomed him to the family as Aggie's partner, but while they held hands, they were saving their overt displays of affection for somewhere more private.

Hawk pushed off from the floor and made for the closest table. He covered the exposed food and open water jugs with clean unused plates. Who knew how effective it would be against dust and flies.

The ominous red glow from the stairwell's emergency lighting spilled in from the other side of the room. The others checked it as much as he had, but the blood-red gloom kept its secrets. At any moment it could birth a stream of diseased insanity into their temporarily tranquil space.

Ethan lay on his back, one hand behind his head, one across his stomach. Lit up by a beam of light cast from the open doors leading to the elevated walkways, he squinted at Hawk with a cocked eyebrow.

"I figured we could make the food last longer if we covered it."

"I don't think it matters." Ethan sat up and rubbed his face. "There's too much to save it all."

Rayne sneered. "No doubt they were planning to turn it to mulch and send it down the food pipe with a gallon of red dye. And who knows what else? Dirty fuckers. I swear"—she pointed at the floor, her cheeks turning pale pink on her pallid face—"if I find *any* of those arseholes, I'll make them pay for what they've done to us."

"Fucking hell." Ethan got to his feet and rubbed his stomach. "I look pregnant."

Knives smirked. "With the stinkiest food baby ever."

"Hey!"

"Don't forget how many times I've shared a room with you after a big meal."

"I have an efficient body."

"Is that what you call it?"

"It's good at getting rid of what it doesn't need."

Knives turned a blade through her fingers, the light from outside glinting off the steel. "More like an oversharing body."

"This entire conversation is oversharing." Rowan sat with his back to the wall, Ash's head on his lap. "So, what are we going to do? Where will we go?"

Moving four apples from one dish and placing them around the edge of a plate of chicken, Hawk used the empty dish to cover the lot. "Well, we have enough here to last awhile."

Rowan scoffed. "That's not a plan."

Aggie appeared next to Hawk and helped him cover the food. "You're right, it's not, but we need to take some time to rest. Then we have quite a job on our hands taking control of these blocks. Who knows how many supplies they have here? Maybe enough to last awhile."

"And then what?"

Ethan rolled his eyes.

"What?" Rowan shrugged.

"You always need a plan. It's fucking chaos, and you want us to get out our diaries and pencil in something for next Tuesday."

"See you next Tuesday."

Ethan flipped Rowan the bird. "Look, all I'm saying is that maybe our current predicament isn't very conducive for planning. Why try to control chaos?"

"Maybe thinking like that is giving up?"

"Maybe it's acceptance."

An uptight man, and someone Hawk avoided unless he needed something built, but maybe Rowan had a point. Maybe they should plan. To aim to get somewhere secure enough for him to spend some time alone with Aggie. He held her hand again, and she squeezed back in return.

"I'm with Ethan on this." Rayne tucked her raven-black hair behind her ears. "We're trapped here for the foreseeable unless we learn to fly." Her eyes glistened with the smirk she denied her lips. "But that didn't go too well for our pregnant friend, did it?"

Ash sat bolt upright. "Don't you care?"

Rayne pointed at the doors leading to the walkways.

"About that turncoat flying rock out there? She simply saved me the effort of throwing her. The fewer of them there are, the better."

"But she was just trying to do what was right for her family."

"So she came here?"

"She didn't abandon her kid, Rayne. She's not your dad."

Ethan drew a breath through clenched teeth. "Ouch!"

Rayne slowed her delivery and eyeballed Ash the entire time. "Would you raise a kid here? Would you make it so their first experience in life is to be subservient to the fucking cretins running this place?"

Tears glazed Ash's eyes. She looked at the floor. "I don't know what I'd do."

Aggie folded her arms. "Something you want to tell us?"

A shared glance between Ash and Rowan. Rowan shrugged. Ash said, "I'm pregnant."

"Shit!" Ethan swiped a hand over his cropped hair. "How pregnant?"

"Very. It's not something that's done by degrees."

"Ha-fucking-ha. You know what I mean. How many weeks?"

"A couple. Maybe more."

"*More?*" Aggie tapped her toe on the floor. "Why didn't you tell us sooner?"

The acoustics in the large room amplified Rowan's voice. "It's still early days. We weren't one hundred percent sure. And would it have made any difference?"

Ash took over. "We needed time to process it ourselves. We figured we didn't need to tell anyone until I started showing. And then everything happened. I didn't want you all treating me differently because I'm pregnant. It wouldn't have changed our need to get away from the camp as quickly as we did. And you didn't need to be worrying about me."

"So"—Rowan spoke to his clasped hands in his lap—"you can probably see why I'm keen to work out what our next moves are. We have to plan to be somewhere in the next few months. And ideally be around someone who knows how to deliver a baby."

"Okay." Aggie punched her open palm, accentuating her point with the *crack* of flesh on flesh. "While we might not have an immediate plan, I promise you we'll make sure we're in a good place in time for this to happen."

Rayne stepped in front of Ash and waited for her to stand. She hugged her. "I'll do everything in my power to protect you. This kid will have a good life. They'll see we have agency in this world." Her eyes filled with tears. "We won't be downtrodden and disrespected any longer. Hell, seven months is enough time for us to get control of the south, and maybe even the shining city while we're at it."

"Steady on," Ethan said.

"Why not?"

Aggie leaned closer to Hawk. "The shining city is way south. It's walled in and filled with tower blocks like this. Think about this collection of blocks and times it by a thousand or more. No matter where else has fallen, I can guarantee you the city hasn't. It's where the most important—"

"Highest ranking." Rayne spat on the floor. "Those wastrel rats aren't any more important than flies around shit. Fucking parasites. They've just managed to crawl on their bellies to the top of their fabricated society. And they've only remained there because no one has knocked them off their perch."

Aggie shrugged. "But you get the point, right?"

Hawk smiled.

"It's protected and locked down." Ethan rubbed his belly again and stretched to the ceiling. "Not an easy place to enter or leave. It would have taken a major screwup for it to fall to the diseased. Besides, they probably had fair warning about what was coming. But whatever happens, we'll make sure we're in a good spot for when you have this child."

Some of the tension slid from Rowan's stocky frame. "Thank you."

Knives tossed the blade she'd been playing with and caught it by the handle. "This kid will have the most badass bunch of aunties and uncles in all the south."

"I just need you all to remember"—Ash laid her right hand on her stomach—"I'm pregnant. I'm not made of gla— you okay, Aggie?"

The back of her hand pressed to her nose, Aggie nodded. "I'm happy." Hawk took her other hand, Ethan halting from where he'd stepped towards her. His face flushed, and he turned his attention back on Ash.

Aggie stuttered with her inhale. "This life has always been about survival. Even in our community we were on the periphery. We didn't belong to any of the larger groups. A bunch of mongrels and orphans. But what you have there"— she pointed at Ash—"and what we have now, for the first time, is hope. *Genuine* hope. A future. It's been a hot minute since I've planned for anything past tomorrow. Thank you."

A burst of bullet fire whipped through the block.

Knives dropped into a crouch and pointed her blade at the stairwell. "What the fuck was that?"

Another round of fire.

Rayne grabbed her gun with both hands. "Well, we knew we needed to clear out this block, so let's start with the fuckers who used to run the place." This time she didn't stifle her grin. "We're exterminators coming to deal with a vermin infestation."

"Fuck yeah!" Ethan high-fived Rayne. "Let's make this block ours." The pair of them headed for the crimson-lit gloom at a jog.

Aggie raised her eyebrows at Hawk. And he agreed. Those two needed to be on a very short leash. Whatever waited for them down there, it wouldn't do them any harm to exercise a modicum of caution.

CHAPTER 4

"**D**oes he even know the meaning of the word *caution?*" Olga double-tapped the smaller screen, transferring the footage of William firing his gun to the main monitor. Over the past few hours, she'd mastered the console's intuitive controls while tracking him through the block. A guardian angel, she watched over him and Hawk's group. She also monitored the guards. She was ready should she need to intervene, but the tannoy had to be a last resort.

William, his backpack bulging with half of their ammo, had checked one room after another, working his way through the tower block. Maybe he'd had the foresight to see he'd need the supplies more than them, but with the frame of mind in which he'd left, he'd probably not given it any consideration. He'd gone down through the block, farther away from Hawk and the others. If only he'd ascended. They would have found one another by now.

Matilda appeared beside her. "I didn't think for a second he'd be firing shots down there." She held her bottom lip in a pinch as the end of William's gun flashed with his next attack and the crack of gunfire burst from the tinny speakers. The solitary diseased stumbled and fell on its back.

Olga threw her hand at the screen. "He knows there are diseased down there. He knows how this works. That amount of commotion is bound to get anyone killed."

"And not just him." Matilda nodded at Hawk and the others leaving the room they'd been in for the past few hours and heading for the stairwell.

"At least the guards haven't noticed." The small army remained gathered on one of the lower floors.

"Yet."

Olga's cheeks bulged with her exhale. "Yet."

Backing down the hallway, his gun raised, William shot two more diseased. Carried forwards by the momentum of their charge, they landed limp and lifeless by his feet. Matilda's cheeks reddened, and she sprayed spittle when she spoke. "What's he playing at? It won't be long before he's being attacked by every diseased and guard in the place."

"Not every guard!" Duncan beamed at them from across the room.

Gracie had remained by Duncan's side, learning how to operate the controls. She shoved him back, his arms windmilling, his clumsy steps slamming against the steel floor. For the entire time she'd been in his company, she'd worn a sneer like his presence left her with a foul taste. "Let's just make this about you for a minute, shall we?"

"I was just saying."

"Next time that pompous little voice in your head produces a vacuous idea, and that idea requires you to express yourself, think about it long and hard, okay? Chances are, it's better remaining in your head."

"But I—"

Gracie shoved him again, and he slammed into the fifth block's console. "I reckon I've learned about all you have to teach me. I only need half an excuse to end you. Give it to me, Duncan, you self-satisfied prick. Go on, I dare ya."

Artan and Nick were at block one's console, following the largest cluster of diseased. They were closer to Gracie and Duncan. The pair of them stood tense, ready to jump into action. Although why any of them considered Duncan worth saving … Olga would gladly launch him from a walkway and savour his scream on the way down.

Nick pointed at his main screen. The camera didn't pull back far enough to capture all the diseased in one shot. "They're still oblivious too."

Matilda damn near spat the words as William continued backing away while firing his gun. "Blind luck, that's all. If he wants to go to war, why doesn't he just go out into the plaza and fight the lot of them? End this suicide mission a lot fucking quicker and without involving anyone else."

Even with more diseased in the hallway, William stopped shooting. Olga rested on the console's cold steel case and leaned closer to the screen. "What's he doing?"

Matilda delivered every word through gritted teeth. "He's run out of bullets. Watching this now, I can't believe there was a time when we relied on his decision-making."

William ducked into a room, vanishing from sight. Five more diseased appeared on the camera.

"So what now?" Gracie looked between Matilda and Olga. "How long before Hawk and the others are on top of him? What if he reloads and shoots them?"

Olga pointed at the main control console. "We could use the tannoy to tell William they're coming. Too many people have died who don't deserve it. Too many kids. We've got to make sure our friends don't kill one another too."

Matilda banged a fist against the desk. "If we use the tannoy, we'll alert the guards. This is on William. He's revealed his location by shooting his gun; if we tell him why he needs to stop, then the guards on the lower floor will find out exactly what they're up against. Hawk and the others will lose their only advantage. Right now, they have surprise on their side."

"Is it a good thing when everyone's surprised? What if William and Hawk fight each other before they realise who they're battling? And how can they be prepared for guards they don't know exist?"

William burst from the room into which he'd vanished and opened fire on the five diseased. As he darted back in again, Hawk and the others arrived at his floor, Ethan and Rayne leading their attack.

Olga walked over to the tannoy. "I'm sorry, Matilda, but we have to warn the others. William's a weapons-grade liability right now; we can't rely on him to see who he's fighting before it's too late. We have no option but to intervene."

CHAPTER 5

Joni slipped from the hatch, and despite the finesse of her landing, most, if not all of the forty or so guards stood in attendance. Were a more subtle entrance available, she would have taken it.

The heady aromas of cooking food sent both a twinge and a rumble through her nauseated stomach. Hungry and sick. Did she need to eat or reveal her secret? Or both?

Her backpack heavy with magazines, she slipped free of the straps and rolled the ache from her shoulders as she placed it atop the pile of guns and ammo they'd transported from the basement.

On their first run, Joni, Antonia, and Ralph had returned with just a fraction of their supplies. Seven guards joined them on the second and helped them bring back the rest. They'd paused a few times in the shafts while members from the cult passed beneath them. Fortunately, the cult were on high alert for the diseased. They didn't seem to even consider looking up. Long may that continue.

Matt remained in Louis' comfy chair. As an ex-member

of the cult, he existed on the group's periphery. He served a purpose; otherwise he might not have a place among them. He gave Joni a thumbs up from across the room and held her stare for a little too long before he spoke into his microphone. "Well done."

She removed the annoying buzz and slipped the earbud into her pocket. He either needed to come out with the accusation or leave her the fuck alone. She didn't have time for silly power games.

Theresa elbowed her way through the crowd, shoving aside a pair of tall and wide guards. She stood over their supplies, her hands on her ample hips, and smiled at Joni. At least, that seemed to be her intention. The grimace sat somewhere between a smile and a sneer. It hovered between congratulations and accusation. A flutter ran through Joni's stomach. Had Matt said something?

"Well done."

"Uh …" Joni lowered her head, her cheeks on fire. "Thank you." She knew about the lie. They all did. Had Olga been in contact again? Had she told Matt the south had fallen? That they had nothing to fight for? And if she had, then what now? The cult needed to be taken down. That hadn't changed. But could she expect them to go to war with their motivation gone? Their loved ones were already dead. The children they'd never met were one of the diseased masses.

"Weapons, water, and food." The same grimace twisted Theresa's face. Regardless of what she said, her demeanour suggested she could turn in a heartbeat. "And safety in these three rooms."

"For now." One of the guards Theresa had shoved aside, a tall man with broad shoulders and an enormous belly, shrugged. "What? We can't afford to get complacent."

"I agree." Joni's cheeks went from fire to inferno. She

slowed down her delivery to counter the warble in her words. She'd spent decades on her own. She didn't do crowds. "We've gotten off to a good start, but we still have a long way to go."

Theresa dipped a nod and grimace-smiled again. "Very true. I also want to say how impressed I am with your fighting." She flicked her head towards Matt and the bank of screens. "You took no prisoners."

"You should have seen it close up!" Antonia beamed. Her mum fought like a lunatic. "I'm pleased she's on our side. She's formidable and someone we can all rely on."

As long as they weren't relying on her to tell the truth.

"I saw." Theresa fixed on Joni again, and her eyes narrowed. Had Matt told her something? Was this all part of a little game to make her squirm? "And I agree. We're lucky to have you."

Ralph stepped from the crowd, taking the room's attention. He flung a hand towards the pile of ammo. "Not only is she responsible for helping arm us for this war ..."

Joni shook her head and swayed from side to side like she could work away her discomfort. The shaft hatch hung open above her. She could still run. Go back to the old life. Nutty old Joni living on her own in a hole in the ground. It had been good enough for years. "It wasn't just me, Ralph. Getting the ammo was a team effort."

"True. But you're also the reason we'll be able to get everyone south when this is done." He turned back to the guards. "She's going to make sure we have the tactical advantage in the block because of her knowledge of the network of shafts. We can't do this without her."

And maybe they wouldn't do it without her. But surely they all wanted to take down the cult. Why wouldn't they? And who knew, their loved ones might still be alive.

Matt's chair squeaked as he leaned closer to the monitors. "Uh-oh!"

Never a good sound, but at least it took the attention from her. Having held her breath for the entire time, Joni let it go as she raced to be at Matt's side.

"The cult have gone down to the basement." He pointed to the second screen in the lower right. "Look."

Joni squinted, the glare itching her tired eyes. "It looks empt—"

Two cult members appeared. Both of them with their guns raised. Both treading lightly as they scanned the garage. One fired off-screen, his gun's barrel lighting with a flash.

The other guard joined the attack. A diseased fell face-first into shot, but three more charged. Then another five. The guards only dropped two more before the mob reached them, tackling them and dragging them from the camera's view.

More diseased raced in after. They soon slowed to a halt.

The monitors lit Theresa's face. "Why have they stopped?"

Ralph patted her on the back, and she nearly headbutted the screen. She tutted, but he cut her off before she could launch into a tirade. "They're g—"

Two diseased dressed as guards stumbled into shot. They both carried guns slung across their fronts. Blood glistened on the face of one from a deep gash along their hairline. Rivers of claret ran down his features. Baptised in his own essence. Welcome to the congregation.

Theresa's cheeks puffed with her exhale. "That escalated quickly."

"Saved us a job." Antonia looked around her and shrugged. "What? It did."

The small steel room amplified Theresa's voice. "Right,

we need to take this moment to get ready." She pointed at the pile of ammo. "Take that lot through to the control room. How are the chefs getting on?"

One guard at the back peered into the control room before giving Theresa a thumbs up.

"Okay." Theresa clapped her hands. "Looks like lunch is ready. Let's get this ammo moved, and then we can eat before we take this block from those lunatics."

The guards went to work moving the pile of ammo and guns from the observation room to the control room. Theresa had said it. They wanted to take this block from those lunatics. They needed to get control of the place first. Anything that challenged that would be an unnecessary distraction. Who knew what the future held? For now, they needed to focus on the task at hand.

Joni followed Ralph and Antonia into the circular control room. Six modules stood like pillars around its edge. Each one a different colour of the rainbow, the main door painted red to complete the set. They stood out against the dull grey surroundings. She'd shut down the implant triggers in this room, opened the main gates, orchestrated the prison break by using the warning lights to tell the prisoners when they could and couldn't cross the white lines.

With most of the guards distracted, Joni's nausea subsided. Three guards stood behind the heat rings they'd brought from the kitchen when they'd raided it for supplies. Each chef stirred a steaming pot.

Theresa showed Joni, Ralph, and Antonia the food with a sweeping arm. "You three first. You're the reason we have something to eat."

Antonia smiled. "Thank you."

If only they could have gone last when the guards were focused on their meals. Surely one of them would spot Joni's lie.

"Aunty Mary!"

The woman behind the first pot beamed back at Antonia. About five feet seven inches tall, she had a round face and a kind smile. "Hey, sweetie. How are you doing?"

The familiarity speared Joni's heart, but she straightened her back and swallowed it down.

"As well as can be expected in the circumstances. But things will get better. We'll get control of the block and head south."

Mary reached over her steaming pot, offering Joni her hand. "Hi, I'm Mary. Antonia stayed with me for a while when she was a kid."

Her words had barbs that could catch in her throat, but Joni forced them out. "Thank you for looking after her. And for keeping her away from Louis."

"She was a pleasure."

"That's good to hear."

"So." Antonia lifted a bowl and peered into the pot. "What's in there?"

Mary beamed at her. "What else?"

"No. Really?"

"Of course."

Antonia grinned. "Mary's stew is the best I've *ever* tasted."

Mary clasped her hands in front of her and bounced where she stood.

Thrusting her bowl at the woman, Antonia beamed. "Fill her up, please."

Ralph passed Mary's stew and moved along to the next cook in the line. Joni's mouth watered, but she followed Ralph. She'd try something else, thanks.

Still leading them despite already having selected her meal, Antonia spoke to the next chef of the three. More for the benefit of the room. A way to introduce the menu for those waiting. "Hi, Jay."

33

"Antonia." A portly man in his thirties, he had sallow cheeks and black bags beneath his eyes. His thin lips twitched with his smile. The light shone off his bald head, his skin like highly polished leather.

"What's in there?"

"Parsnip soup."

Antonia leaned closer and sniffed. "Oh my. I might have to come back for seconds."

While Ralph passed his bowl to Jay, Antonia moved onto the third man in the line. In his late twenties. Slim and with tightly cropped hair.

"Winston! I didn't know you could cook."

"There's a lot you don't know about me."

"You sure you're not doing it to avoid fighting with the rest of us?"

"Fuck you, Antonia."

Joni gripped her empty bowl, ready to launch it at the man, but she held back. Antonia had had a lifetime of people being scared away because of her overprotective father. She didn't need Joni filling that role now he'd gone.

The pair of them broke into laughter.

"So …" Antonia dipped her head with a bow. "What delights have you cooked for us?"

"Well, you may or may not know this, but when I first came here, I apprenticed as a chef. I spent the first few years working in the kitchens. The man who taught me was a wonderful cook, and this was his speciality."

Although Jay held Ralph's full bowl of steaming soup towards him, Ralph fixed on Antonia and Winston's conversation, his mouth hanging open. He spoke in a whisper. "Dhal?"

Antonia's smile fell. Joni rested her hand on Ralph's broad back.

"Um …" Ralph looked back down the line at the stack of bowls. "Uh … I'd like …"

Joni took the soup and handed Ralph her empty bowl. His hands shook as he took it from her, and his weak voice cracked. "Thank you." He passed it to Winston. "I'll take the dhal, please."

"This is just as he taught me to make it." Winston used a ladle to deliver Ralph a generous portion. "The first recipe Warren taught me. Simple but—"

"Effective." Ralph took the bowl in his still shaky hands. Joni stopped short of offering to carry it for him. "Thank you."

The other guards had formed a queue behind them. Ralph walked away and sat down beside Antonia. Joni followed.

Steam rose from Joni's spoon. She blew on it while Ralph ate the dhal with his head bowed and his brow locked.

IT TOOK Ralph twice as long to finish his meal. He ate as if every mouthful were a last moment with Warren. Joni and Antonia sat in silence, each of them resting a hand on either side of his broad back.

The scratch of his spoon against porcelain, Ralph drank what remained and stared into the now empty bowl with glazed eyes.

He turned to Antonia first and then Joni, nodding at each of them just once before he got to his feet and returned to Winston. All the other guards had already been served and were sitting around the circular room, eating in small groups. "That was wonderful. Thank you."

Many in the room stopped what they were doing and watched the conversation. How many of them knew Warren?

Did any know about his and Ralph's connection to one another?

Winston pressed his hands together, palm to palm in front of his chest. "Thank you. Although I'm sure it's nothing compared to what Winston used to make."

Ralph's eyes pinched at the sides. "I disagree. If he tasted this, he'd be proud."

CHAPTER 6

Hawk descended the stairs with Aggie, Ethan, and Rayne ahead of him, Knives, Ash, and Rowan behind. Ash said she didn't want protecting, and they all agreed to not treat her any differently. Regardless, Knives stayed close to her, constantly checking back, each time making out she saw something behind. A pretence she'd surely abandon soon enough. Whether irked by her attention or not, Ash couldn't ask for a better bodyguard.

They trod a treacherous path in the gloomy stairwell's poor light. Rayne and Ethan raced ahead, dictating their pace. They were too eager to end their oppressors. They needed to keep their heads. But even they halted at the next round of bullet fire. Even if only for a second or two.

Hawk tapped Aggie's shoulder and leaned close. "You need to get them to slow down."

Grabbing Ethan just as he reached the floor to which they were drawn, Aggie showed him her palm. He halted and pulled on Rayne, dragging her back into the stairwell.

The group above and below, Hawk backed into the wall,

the handrail against the small of his back. "We need to be more cautious."

Rayne's laugh ran away from them. "Be quiet like them, you mean?"

"It's their noise we're following, Rayne. Hardly an example we should look to emulate, wouldn't you say? And do you really think we should go in shooting first and asking questions later?"

"I say we make the most of their noise. Use it as cover to mask our own. And yeah, shoot first. Fuck them up. All of them. I don't need to ask questions."

Knives tossed a blade so it spun in the air, and caught it by the handle. She checked Ash again. "I quite like Rayne's approach. Get in and out. Get it over with. Cut a few throats. End of."

Hawk tutted. "Or get shot in the face."

Using the height advantage of being a step above him, Knives rested the sharp cold steel of her blade against his throat. "Are you saying someone with a gun will get the better of me?"

Obviously! But his confidence withered in the face of her ferocious glare. "Probably not."

"*Probably* not?"

"They are *bullets*. And even if they don't get the better of you, they'll get the better of the rest of us." The pressure on his throat eased, and she stepped back. She checked Ash again, who rolled her eyes when she returned her focus to Hawk.

"Come on, Knives. Surely there's a better way?"

Although she damn near thrummed with fury, Rayne lowered her voice. "Do you really think those people might not deserve to die?"

"What if they don't? What if it's not who you think it is? What if they're—"

"Vampires? Is that what you're going to say? First, don't use that fucking word! And second, if they're in this block with the guards, then I refuse to spare them!"

"*Kids*, Rayne."

"Huh?"

"What if they have kids with them? How would you feel then? Would you still refrain from asking questions?"

"He's right." Aggie forced her way past Rayne and Ethan to the bottom of the stairs into the hallway's bright glow. "We need to work out who the enemy is before we attack. And you're angry, Rayne. You might be unable to make that split-second decision right now."

"I'll be all right."

"How would you feel if you shot a kid? *Any* kid?"

Despite opening her mouth, Rayne had nothing.

"Okay." Aggie led them into the hallway, walking on her tiptoes, her gun raised, the red carpet muting her steps.

Both Ethan and Rayne tutted at Hawk when he forced his way to the front. But Aggie smiled, reached back and squeezed his hand.

Eight diseased lay dead, the brighter lights revealing each one's gruesome end. Their stench added to the stomach-churning presentation. Several had deep holes in their faces. One had had her eye bored out; a black tunnel drilled through her face. Pus glistened on their wounds. They'd been infected before they fell.

The sodden carpet squelched with their progress. They stepped over the corpses, one at a time, Hawk swinging his gun into the empty guards' rooms they passed, ready to get the shooter before they got them.

A scuffling came from a room up ahead on their right. Scratching and rustling like a directionless diseased. Oblivious to what came down the hall towards them. Maybe the person who'd fired the gun hadn't gotten away.

Aggie gave Hawk and the others a thumbs up, which they all returned. They were ready. She led them on, and Hawk gripped his gun tighter as he followed close behind.

The remaining rooms between them and the shuffling stood empty. They reached the doorway, and Aggie stepped away from the wall by about a foot. Hawk slid next to her, leaning against the cold steel just inches from the open door. They both aimed their guns at the floor, the red dots of their laser targets dancing on the stained carpet.

Taking a deep breath, Hawk rolled his shoulders to lose some of his tension. They were in control here. Now they just needed to wait for the diseased to emerge.

Ash heaved. She clapped her hand to her mouth. Close to the mound of dead diseased, she closed her eyes.

The rustling in the room stopped. Aggie mouthed to Hawk, *Ready?*

Like he had a choice.

CHAPTER 7

"Why's she covering her mouth like that?" Matilda held her chin, her eyes narrowed on the main screen.

Over by the tannoy, Olga stood on her tiptoes like it would help her see across the vast room more easily. "Who? What are you talking about?"

"Ash." Artan pointed at the bank of screens. "She's covering her mouth. There are dead diseased in the hallway. As much as they're a part of our lives, she's not used to them yet. And, to be fair, their reek is something else."

Gracie sighed. "I'm sure she'll adapt. Not like she has a choice after what we've done."

"Not us." Olga wagged her finger at Gracie. "This is on Louis."

"Not as far as everyone in the south is concerned. The truth's irrelevant if no one believes it."

Olga hovered over the tannoy's button. An inch from pressing it. "Shall I call them?"

Even Duncan had joined the others around the console

for the second block, his stupid hair wobbling with his movements. "It's all quiet at the moment."

Nick shot him a glare. "I think you should call them, Olga. It's on a knife edge. The second William comes out of that room, it's going to kick off."

"There's no way of avoiding that?"

"They both have their guns ready, so, no, I don't think so."

"Then I need to put the call through, right? It doesn't matter what happens next; this is too urgent to ignore?" Olga's hand shook. "Right, Matilda?"

Matilda fixed the monitor with a glassy stare, her mouth half-open. The bravado of only a few minutes ago had well and truly gone. She might be pissed off with William, but she couldn't lose him. She patted the side of her head, tracing back to the tight plait Gracie had tied.

"Artan?" Olga moved her finger closer to the button.

A carbon copy of his sister's anxiety. Pale. His brow locked in a hard scowl.

"I'm going to call them. I can't let anyone else die."

"I didn't mean what I said." The screen's glare reflected in Matilda's wide eyes. "I was angry, but I didn't mean any of it. We need to save him. We need to save them all. Do it, Olga."

Pressing the button so hard it stung the tip of her finger, Olga leaned close to the microphone. "William! Hawk, Aggie, and the others are outside your room. They think you're a threat. Hawk, that's William in there. And only William. There's no danger. Both of you, lower your weapons. Don't shoot. I repeat, don't shoot."

At least she'd done it without giving them away. Of course, the guards now knew they had a threat in one of the blocks, but without a location, what good would it do? They could be anywhere.

Nick's eyebrows lifted and met in the centre of his creased brow.

"Nothing?"

He shook his head.

Olga tried again. "Hawk! William! Pull back. You're about to kill each other."

Nick now leaned close to the screen and shrugged.

"Fuck!" Olga jabbed the button. "Fuck! Fuck! Fuck!"

His eyes aglow with self-satisfaction, Duncan smirked. "It's not working, Olga."

"And you think that's funny?"

He backed away. "No."

"Then take that stupid fucking look from your face."

To combat his own arrogance, he turned his lips down in a trout pout. It made the clown of a man even more ridiculous.

Gracie shoved him aside and jogged to Olga. She pressed the button and leaned into the mic. "William? Hawk? Stop what you're doing."

"You literally just saw me do that, Gracie."

Matilda headed for the door. "We need to go to them!"

"Tilly, wait!" Artan reached out to her. "There's no point in us going down there. They'll be shooting each other before we even reach the stairs."

The momentum left her, the purpose stolen from her strides. She slumped, and her shoulders sagged. Her weak voice barely made it past her lips. "Then what?"

Olga filled the space made by Artan when he went to comfort his sister. She rested on the cold steel console and leaned closer like the screen might reveal something the others hadn't noticed. But they'd seen it well enough. Like she'd pressed the button well enough. It didn't matter how they looked at it. How they pressed it. How they reframed it. Hawk, Aggie, and the others were gathered outside William's room. All of them armed. All of them ready to go to war.

William stepped from the room and into view. The clack of gunfire burst from the tinny speakers.

Olga clapped her hands to her face as William's body snapped back from the shot, and he fell into the darkness. She shook her head, but held onto her scream.

"What?" Matilda's sharp tone cut across the room. "What is it? What's happened? Was that gunfire? Olga? What's happened?"

Artan clung tighter to his sister while Gracie, who remained by the useless tannoy, laid her palm against her chest, pressing her mum and dad's wedding rings.

CHAPTER 8

"William!" Hawk reached out like he could retract the bullets Aggie had already fired. He knocked her gun so the barrel pointed at the ceiling and blocked William's door. A red dot came from over his shoulder and danced on the opposite wall. "Shit!" He dived aside as a line of sparks lit up the steel, tearing through the space he'd just occupied.

Aggie tried to go again, and again Hawk batted her gun away. This time, she levelled it on him. "Will you stop doing that?"

His back against the wall on the other side of the door, Hawk's shout hurt his throat. "William! Stop! It's me, Hawk."

Rayne and Ethan closed in from the other side, guns raised.

Hawk shooed them back. He pressed down on the air in front of him. They needed to let him handle this.

William stopped shooting. "Hawk?"

"Yeah, it's me."

But Rayne fizzed and spat like a faulty engine. "Then why the fuck's he shooting at us?"

"We shot him!"

"That's right! And I might not be able to use my arm again!"

Aggie lowered her head.

Hawk's ears rang from the gunfire in the tight corridor. The bullets destined for his back had made a mess of the opposite wall. The bright hallway light glistened off the bullets' deep grooves. "William? What are you doing in there?"

"Trying not to get shot."

"How's that working for you?" Still wound up and ready to go, Rayne stepped towards the door again. Ethan thrust out his arm to block her path.

"Who's that?"

"Rayne." Hawk raised an eyebrow at her while he spoke. "It's rare for us to meet someone in these blocks who isn't an enemy. It's been stressful for us all. How are you?"

William grunted as he spoke. "Hurt."

"I'm sorry."

"Who's that?"

"Aggie. I'm sorry, that was me who shot you."

"Why?"

"We heard shooting down here. You appeared with a gun. We thought you were the enemy."

"What are you doing in this block, anyway?" Hawk said. "Had we known you were here, we would have been more cautious."

"I would hope so."

"Can we come in?"

"As long as you don't shoot me again."

Hawk waited for Rayne to lower her gun. "We're coming in now."

A wounded animal, William cowered in the room's corner, holding the top of his right arm with his left hand.

Rayne shoved past, and Hawk grabbed at the air, missing

her as she closed in on William. She dropped in front of him, all trace of her fury gone. "Now, keep calm, and keep pressure on it. On the count of three, I'm going to take a small look at it and work out the best fix, okay?"

Veins stood out on William's neck, and sweat glistened on his brow. He turned away from her and gritted his teeth. "You don't think you've done enough?"

"I'm sorry, William." Aggie pressed her hands together, palm to palm. "This is all my fault."

Hawk put his arm around Aggie's shoulder and pulled her close.

"Now stop being a baby and let me look." Rayne pried William's hand away. She tore his shirtsleeve open where the bullet had already ripped a gash.

Ethan and Knives stepped back out into the hallway. Ethan led with his gun, and Knives gripped a blade in each hand.

"Right, you can cover it again." Rayne grabbed a pillow from the bed and removed the white case. She used her knife to make a cut and tore away a strip about two feet long and three inches wide. She crouched down again and forced eye contact with the sweating William. "On the count of three, I want you to take your hand away again, okay?"

He stared at Rayne through the wide eyes of a confused child. He needed someone else to take charge.

"One. Two. Three …"

William pulled his hand away. Blood leaked down his arm, soaking his shirt and the white bedsheet beside him.

Ash ran to the corner and vomited while Rayne tied the strip of fabric around his arm, William wincing and gurning as she pulled it tight, tying the knot against the underside of his biceps.

William flicked his head towards Ash. "What's her problem? I thought I was the one who'd been shot."

Rowan stepped forwards, fists clenched. "She's pregnant!"

Aggie shoved Rowan back and shook her head. The thickset man let his hands unfurl and returned to Ash's side, rubbing her back as she remained hunched over.

"So, the good news is it's only a flesh wound. The bullet didn't stay in your body. It grazed past you and tore a gash."

"*Grazed*? Like a kid falling over and scraping their knee? She did more than fucking *grazed* me."

What had happened to William in the time they'd been apart? Where had their leader gone? The calm head. The decision-maker. Hawk cleared his throat. "Are you okay, William?"

"Do I look okay?"

"The point is"—Rayne removed another pillowcase, scrunching it into a ball and gripping it in her right hand—"it should heal. We need to get upstairs and wash it out, rebandage it, and take care of it. As long as it stays clean, you should be fine."

"I'm sorry again, William." Aggie reached out and held his bloody hand. "We're a bit jumpy, and I made the wrong split-second decision."

Rayne raised an eyebrow. But she'd have done the same had she led them. Even after Aggie realised her mistake, she'd wanted to shoot.

Ethan and Knives remained on the door, leaning out into the hallway. Hawk joined them and checked both ways. "It looks like we're good to go?"

Knives nodded. "I reckon. And with the noise we've made down here, I'd say the sooner the better."

CHAPTER 9

J oni jumped aside as Theresa pumped the air with her hand holding her gun. "Wooooo!"

There were six dead diseased on the floor from their encounter. They'd been lucky to get so many of them shut off in the confined space, turning the narrow corridor into a shooting gallery. Fish in a barrel.

Theresa aimed her gun at the closest diseased corpse and flipped it onto its back with her foot. It stared up at them through glazed crimson eyes. Its mouth hung open. "They're not so scary when they're dead."

Although the stark reality of what the virus did to its host still sent a shudder through Joni. "Here's to many more reduced to the same state."

"Hear, fucking hear." Theresa kicked the fallen beast in the face, connecting with the crunch of cartilage. "You know, before we came into this corridor, I felt nervous. Obviously I've seen the diseased. Louis made sure of that. But I've never really had to deal with them. He always let me get away without doing clean-up duty. He must have liked me."

"Feared you, more like." Si snorted. A small man with floppy hair and a wonky smile. He had pale skin and yellow teeth. His mirth fell away, melted by the ferocity in Theresa's glare.

She paused long enough to make him squirm. "And the prisoners were always easy enough to control." She rubbed the back of her neck like she had her own implant. Her eyes lost focus like she felt remorse at being a part of the regime. She joined Joni beside the door to the medical room. "But you know what helped me just now?"

Joni shrugged.

"I thought about you down in that basement. How can I not be confident going into battle at your side when I've seen how you fight these fuckers? That display made me realise I'd follow you into hell."

"You're about to." Antonia had locked the medical bay door from the top while she secured the other side of the room. It would have been easier to lock it and forget about it. A Pandora's box never to be opened again. But this room gave them access to more beyond, and to the stairs leading to the block's roof. An access they could well need.

Si and Barry had followed them into the hallway. So far, they'd not had to do much. They were backup, the corridor too narrow for the four of them to be shooting at the same time. They both stepped back when Joni turned to them. "This room's going to be a bit more challenging."

"You can say that again."

Joni rolled her eyes and pointed at her ear. "Matt, you've given me all the information we need. Can you now please shut up?"

"Sorry."

"So, the medical bay, as you know, has four aisles. We need to cover one each. There are four rooms down the side of each aisle, and many of them have diseased inside."

"At least half, I'd say."

Joni's fingers twitched with the need to remove her earpiece. But sometimes he had useful information. "Matt reckons half the rooms have diseased in them."

Barry pulled back his shoulders and lifted his chin. Tall. Broad. Stoic. Si swayed from side to side. His skin had gone pale, his lips tight. But he filled his lungs and swiped his floppy hair back from his forehead. He jumped when Joni shouted, "How we looking up there, Antonia?"

The shaft's grated hatch birthed her tinny reply. "Hang on. Nearly done. It looks like half the diseased on this floor have ended up in this room."

"See," Matt said.

The swish of fabric against steel announced Antonia's approach. She freed the door to the medical bay with a gentle *click.* "You're good to go, Mum."

Theresa grinned, punched the door's button, and stood aside for Joni to enter first, Si whimpering behind her.

Moving to the left side of the room, Joni covered that aisle. Theresa came in next, then Barry. Si entered last.

Eight clinic rooms for each aisle. The opaque walls hid which contained diseased and which didn't. Each had a flimsy door. They couldn't lock any of them from above. Nothing else for it but to meet the fuckers head-on.

"What's happening?" Matt's tinny voice pulled the muscles in the back of Joni's neck taut. "I'm projecting the footage from the room for everyone else to see. They'll be able to hear what you say, Joni."

"Bit busy to give a running commentary, Matt."

"That's fine. I just wanted to te—"

"Ooo-weee!" Theresa's shrill call rang through the room.

Joni raised her gun, snapping the stock into her shoulder. She closed one eye and laid her red target on the wall by the aisle's exit. She sank three bullets into the face of the first diseased, turning its features to mincemeat. The fucker fell before it had left the aisle.

Bullet fire to her right. A diseased stumbled from Barry's aisle and crashed down, falling to their knees and then landing flat. Theresa and Si took down theirs next as Joni shot her second and third. The rattle of their four guns in the enclosed space made her ears ring. With the number of indoor firefights recently, the tinnitus whine rarely stopped. She fired again, painting the walls with the creatures' blood.

A small woman sprinted from Theresa's aisle next. Fast. Slight. Wiley. And seemingly impervious to Theresa's aim as she darted left and right.

Joni rested her target on the woman's face.

"Don't even fucking think about it." Theresa shot the diseased woman from her stomach to her forehead, tearing her open. The woman ran two more steps and fell, landing about six feet from the pair.

Theresa nailed the next diseased the second it appeared. "Ooo-wee, motherfuckers! Mama's back!"

Another diseased ran from Joni's aisle. A man. A guard. Someone she might have known in a previous life. Hard to tell. And what did it matter? That person had long since gone.

"And you get shot in the face!" Theresa sent another burst at the next diseased from her aisle. "And you get shot in the face!" More came from her aisle than any other, the bodies piling up, tripping those charging out from behind. "And you get shot in the face."

"Uh, Joni?"

"What, Matt? Can't you see I'm busy?"

"You're about to get busier."

"Stop talking in riddles."

"Look right."

While the rest of them fired, Si had frozen. He pointed his

gun at the diseased guard, but he hadn't pulled the trigger. And Barry had too many of his own to help.

"Si!" Joni shot two more diseased. "What the fuck are you doing?"

Backing away as quickly as the diseased approached, Si shook his head. "I can't. I can't shoot Jack."

The creature crashed into him, carrying them both into the back wall.

Joni shot another diseased without looking. "Cover my aisle, Theresa."

"And you get shot in the face!" Theresa pirouetted and took down the next diseased charging from Joni's aisle.

Joni ran behind Theresa and Barry, let her gun fall to its strap, and slammed the diseased attacking Si with both hands. It stumbled and tripped. She shot it before it got back up, kept her trigger depressed, and took down the next three closing in from Si's aisle.

Barry made room for Joni, three of them managing four aisles while Si curled up in a ball in the corner.

CHAPTER 10

Joni opened and closed her jaw like she could work away the ringing in her ears.

Charged, her eyes wide, Theresa kept her gun aimed at the aisles. "You're sure that's all of them?"

"Matt tells me it is."

"It is! Every clinic room has a camera."

"He just said it again. And he can see into every room. Just like Louis could when he broadcast your personal procedures to the south." Many were fighting to get to their loved ones. If they found out the truth, they might need another reason to continue this war. No harm in reminding them what Louis had done. She offered her hand to Si to help him stand and led them back to the circular control room.

Ralph stood in the corner next to the orange console. The one that controlled the implant chip triggers by the prison's white lines. He hunched over a bowl of water, washing the dishes. The least he could do after Winston's meal.

Thanks to Matt, the rest of the room had seen everything, and for those who hadn't, he now had it on replay. Joni flinched when faced with her own projected image. Her twisted features. Her gritted teeth. But they were in the business of killing. And no matter which way you sliced it, killing was ugly.

"I'm sorry." Si addressed the floor but spoke loud enough for the entire room to hear. "I don't know what happened. I lost my head."

"You need to remember"—Joni rested her hand on Si's back, his shirt damp with sweat—"when they're infected, they're not the people you once knew. And in that moment, one of you has to die. That's the only agency you have. But we won. That's the main thing."

"Yeah, we did." Theresa stamped her foot.

Boots hung down from the maintenance shaft. Joni reached up and tapped them before clearing a space for Antonia to land. She'd taken a woman with her called Pearl. Wiry, but strong. Much like Joni, she had the perfect build for a shaft-rat.

"Why don't we try to work with the cult?" The second he'd asked, Si returned his attention to the floor.

Although Theresa's jaw fell wide, some of the other guards in the room nodded, emboldening him. "I mean, I couldn't even shoot a diseased guard. How good will I be when faced with someone I know who hasn't been turned? I was friends with half of those in the cult before all this nonsense."

"I'm sorry"—Antonia leaned towards him—"but are you mad? You've seen what they're like. You think you can trust them?"

Joni stopped herself from nodding along. What right did she have to lecture anyone on who they should or shouldn't trust?

Si stepped back. "I'm sorry, miss. It was foolish of me."

Antonia cocked an eyebrow at Joni. "Miss?"

"Most people have been taught to fear you, Antonia."

Theresa turned her hand in the air. "Come on, Si, speak your mind. Tell her how you feel. Daddy isn't here anymore to hand out punishments for unsettling his princess."

Instantly puce, Antonia's lips tightened.

Si kept his head bowed. "I just … with all due respect … think there might be a chance to *negotiate* with the cult. To save any more bloodshed."

Theresa slapped him so hard on the back he stumbled. "Well done. See, you don't have to fear her. But Antonia's right. Are you fucking mad? Do you have a short memory or something? Think about what Andy and his band of nutters did when they lured us into Louis' quarters. They promised to help, but instead they separated and killed us. Whittled us down one or two at a time. We were trapped and scared. You want that again? Huddling in a room, being force-fed their nutty rhetoric about Louis until you either yield or are murdered?"

Si shrugged.

"And you want to go back to the old ways? Where the cult continues sending footage of our most personal moments to the south? You're all right with that?"

He shrugged again.

Another reason Joni couldn't tell them the truth about the south. Half of them already had one foot out the door. They needed to be saved from themselves.

"Right!" Joni clapped her hands once. "We've just taken down the worst room on this floor. The rest should be relatively straightforward. And Antonia's shown Pearl how to lock the doors, so you only have to tackle one room at a time. I suggest we double the number of people we're using to clear this place out. Send eight through to each room. That way, half can fight; half can wait in case—"

"Someone's dick shrinks." Theresa raised her eyebrows at Si.

"In case we need the backup."

"That too."

The man in his forties who'd talked about his kid stepped forward with several others. "I'll go with them. Anything to get to Jacob sooner."

Theresa grinned at the team of eight. "Welcome to my kill team."

Antonia balked. "Your what now?"

"We need to kill the diseased fucks. Do you have a better name?"

"No."

Joni smiled. "Pearl, are you all right doing the doors on your own?"

"Sure. Where are you going?"

"I need to see what the cult is up to."

"And I'm going with Mum."

Joni pressed her finger to her earpiece. "We'll keep in touch through Matt."

But Matt had disconnected. His voice came through from the other room. "Hello … Pocket Rocket?"

CHAPTER 11

Olga threw her arms around Matilda and clung on like she could squeeze the anxiety from her trembling body. Her stoic dam had well and truly burst. William had been a weapons-grade moron to walk off like he had, no one could deny that, but it didn't stop her or anyone else in that control room from caring about him and his fate. She leaned close to her ear. "He's safe now. Hawk and Aggie will look after him."

Matilda's vigorous nod shook them both.

"I'm sure he just needed some time on his own. And if he needed a jolt to bring him back to reality—"

"There aren't many better methods than being shot in the arm." Matilda let out a brief laugh. "What a moron." She looked from one of Olga's eyes to the next, her gaze flitting left and right like she couldn't decide upon which eye to focus. "But what if he hasn't? Got his head straight, I mean? We've seen this before. What if we've lost him?"

Like she'd lost Max. Olga gulped, her words weak. "We won't. Never again, Matilda. We've learned from the past. We won't make that same mistake. We'll stand by him till the end."

Matilda grabbed Olga's arm. "You did all you could for Max."

Tears itched Olga's eyes, and her jaw tightened. She could have done so much more. "Never. Again."

Matilda rested her forehead against Olga's. Close enough for Olga to track the capillaries marbling her sclera. "Never again."

The others watched on. Several of them nodded. On this they were united. And William was with sounder minds than his own. If they couldn't be there for him, at least he had Hawk. Their victories were more often than not minor and hard fought, but they should be celebrated all the same. Olga hugged Gracie, Artan, and Nick one after the other. Each one squeezed back, and each of them moved on to offer Matilda words of comfort. They were in this together. William's wound would heal, and they'd all be reunited.

All the while, Duncan had stood at the group's periphery. Closer to Gracie than the others. When she turned his way, he beamed his signature moronic grin, threw his arms wide, and stepped towards her. She drove both palms into his chest, sending him back with a bark-cum-cough. Red-faced, tight-lipped, he rubbed where she'd hit him, his eyes glisten-ing. He turned away and headed for the main console in the centre of the large room.

An instinct to comfort the man rose and died in Olga. The right thing to do were it anyone else. But it wasn't, and those kids would still be alive were it not for him. Him and his vile self-aggrandising rhetoric and utter scorn for the less advantaged. He'd clearly had more smoke blown up his arse than a chimney. His self-esteem so pungent, just sharing a space with him left a nasty taste in her mouth. But maybe he could do with a distraction. "Duncan."

"What?"

Olga pushed her tongue into her right cheek and took a second. "I've cut throats for less than that."

"Less than what?"

"That tone."

"What do you want, Olga?"

"I need your help."

He folded his arms, and his hair wobbled with his twitching head. "So now you need it."

"You'd be dead if I didn't."

His arms fell to his sides.

"And I'm still questioning if your help is worth the cost."

"I've not charged you a thing."

"All of us are paying a proximity tax."

His nostrils flared. His eyes narrowed.

Gracie stepped towards him. "Something you want to say?"

Olga caught her and pulled her back, Duncan recoiling from her advance.

"I need you to connect me to Joni again. I need to see what's going on. If we can get the message out that releasing the diseased wasn't our fault"—she pointed at the room's exit —"it might half the number of enemies we have out there. It might help William and the others in trying to get back to us if the guards don't want to kill them."

Holding the headphones towards her, Duncan flicked three switches one after the other. "If we get the footage, I can help send out the broadcast."

Olga put them on, the foam soft against the sides of her head, the microphone bent around in front of her mouth. "Hello?"

"Hello …" A man's voice. "Pocket Rocket?"

CHAPTER 12

Barging people aside, Joni ran for the observation room. "Hell—"

She ripped the headphones from Matt's head and put them on.

"Hey!" Matt stood up, but she shoved him back into his seat. Over six feet tall, he landed hard and rolled away from her and the desk.

"Hello?"

"Joni? Hi. How are you doing?"

"All right. But you don't sound great."

"It's not good here. The south's a mess."

"You said."

Matt glared at Joni, hanging on her every word.

"But you should see the state of it. There are diseased *everywhere*. We've been separated from Hawk and William, and we can't get to them."

"Uh …" Joni turned her back on Matt.

"We're the ones being blamed for the south falling. So not only do we have the diseased to deal with, but every person on this side of the wall hates us. Listen, do you have proof that Louis caused this? If you do, you'd be doing us a massive favour…"

And hopefully shut her up about it, too. "I can try to get some footage of what Louis did." She had some in her old home. Of Louis going into the warehouse with guards, and coming back out again as diseased. She could slip out when they went down to see the cult.

Matt stood up, but Joni shoved him back again. He tutted at her. "They have recordings in the warehouse. They're not on the same network as those in the block, so I can't access them, but they should be there and should be accessible."

Like she was going to the warehouse anytime soon.

"Okay." Olga's tone settled. "Please get the footage if you can. I'll be back in contact soon. I can talk to that man if you're not there."

"No, don't talk to anyone but me."

"Hey!" Matt grabbed his armrests like he might try to stand again, but Joni's scowl pinned him to his seat.

"I don't know who we can and can't trust. I'll get the footage for you."

"Thank you, Joni."

"You're welcome. We'll speak soon, yeah?"

The line went dead, and Joni handed the headphones back to Matt.

"What was that about?"

"What?"

"You don't know who you can trust?"

Maybe she should tell him and be done with it? Tell them all. But half of them wanted to join the cult. That would be enough to end their chances. "What if the cult intercepts the call, and Olga, thinking it's someone she can trust, accidentally gives them information?"

"They won't. She'll only get me."

Joni raised her eyebrows.

"What?"

"Look, Matt, I don't fucking know you."

Several guards had come through from the control room and stood in the doorway. "And what I know of you shows me you're someone who will do whatever it takes to benefit themselves. Like join the cult."

Matt pointed at her. "That's not fair."

"It's not?"

"You're hiding something."

"Stop deflecting, you prick. You need to prove you're not with them before I trust you. And you can start by monitoring what's happening, and make sure you keep me updated, okay?"

The guards in the doorway walked off.

Matt slouched in his seat. "Fine. Whatever."

What if she only told him? He'd understand her reasoning. But what if he sold her out? Used it as leverage.

Joni passed Antonia on her way out of the room. "Come on, let's go and see what the cult are up to."

But before Joni climbed into the shaft, a man grabbed her arm, stopping her in her tracks.

"Next time you talk to your friends, can you please ask them to put out a call to Shannon Smith? Can they ask her how her kid's doing?"

For a second, Joni lost her words. She gulped. Shannon and her kid were more than likely diseased freaks by now. But in a world of so little hope, could she really take what he had left? Her reply caught in her throat. She coughed to set it free. "Sure."

CHAPTER 13

Olga handed the headphones back to Duncan. "That's the best we can do for now. From here, I sa—"

"Uh-oh …" Nick leaned over the console for the second tower block. He double-tapped a smaller screen, turning it into the primary image.

"Oh no." Matilda leaned on the console. "That's just what we need."

They made room for Olga and Gracie. The guards were on the move. They entered the stairwell, heading up towards William, Hawk, and the others. Thirty to forty of them. All of them armed.

Artan said, "They're being cautious, which should buy us some time. How quickly do you think Joni will get the footage to us, Olga?"

"Not quickly enough. If at all."

"I'm going out there." Matilda pointed at the door. "I can't just stand by, doing nothing while it all goes wrong." She fixed on Olga. "Never again."

"Okay."

"Okay?"

"I'm coming with you."

Gracie stamped on the steel floor. "We're all going."

"Me too?" Duncan recoiled at his own suggestion. When the going gets tough, this man made himself scarce. He hid in bathrooms. Under rocks. And even if he'd wanted to come, he wasn't the one you wanted beside you when you went into battle.

Gracie looked him up and down. "We could use you as bait?"

The man whimpered.

Olga pulled Gracie back, her entire frame coiled like a cobra ready to strike. "You're not coming, Duncan. We need someone watching over things here. Is there any way we can stay in contact with you so you can keep us informed as to what's happening in the block?"

Duncan opened a drawer in the main console and pulled out a small earpiece. He handed it to Olga. "We'll be able to talk to one another through this."

Olga popped it into her ear and flinched at Duncan's loud voice. "Check-check. One-two-three. One-two-three." He said it with the authority of someone who wanted to believe they had some, but didn't possess a shred. "Earth calling Olga, come in, Olga." His shrill titter ran so deep it struck her bones. "Can you hear me?"

"Yep."

Gracie slapped Olga's back. "Good luck with that." She spun Duncan around, shoved him into the console, and patted him down. She took his knife, and although his argument played out on his features, he kept his mouth shut. "You can lock the door. Why do you need a weapon?"

"But what if you don't make it back?"

She waved his knife at him. "Think of this as an incentive to make sure we do. Otherwise, you'll be punching your way to freedom, sunshine. Your survival superpower doesn't work with the diseased."

"S-survival superpower?"

"Acquiescence."

Clack! Matilda slapped the door's button.

Whoosh! The door opened.

Olga followed them out, Gracie a step behind. Hopefully, an irritating Duncan would be about as bad as this trip got. As much as she wanted to believe that, the sinking dread in her stomach told her things were about to get a lot worse.

CHAPTER 14

"I still think you're hiding something from me."

Matt's whining buzz drilled into Joni's skull. An annoying fly she couldn't swat. "This isn't about you, Matt."

"No, it's about you and what you're hiding."

Turning the next corner towards the dining room in which the cult currently resided, Joni exhaled hard, birthing a cloud of dust. She paused at the next hatch to let the eight to ten diseased below stumble from earshot. She shifted her gun so it sat more evenly on her back. Loaded and nearly full. The only ammo she had. Antonia the same. Enough to get out of a tight spot, but nowhere near enough to fight a war. "Why don't you help us for once and keep an eye on what's going on down here? We could really do with your attention on the screens."

"My attention is on the screens. But I still want to know why you won't let me talk to your friends."

"I wasn't clear enough? I share the opinion of many of the guards up there."

"Which is?"

"You're a fucking snake. A turncoat. I don't trust you."

His petulant whine turned the muscles in her back tight. "I'm not!"

"Of course you'd say that, but until I'm satisfied that's the truth, it's much safer for me to treat you as a liability." The sooner she got that footage of Louis and the warehouse, the better. It would stop Olga asking for it and hopefully move the conversation away from the state of the south, and away from Matt's curiosity. Also, because there were no cameras in the shafts, he couldn't track her movements. She'd only have to reveal she'd retrieved the footage from her old home after the fact. They were currently on the ground floor. Would she have a better chance than this? And Antonia could watch the cult without her. Maybe she should tell Antonia why? Remove her earpiece and explain it all. But she'd have to keep it a secret. With plenty of the guards still thinking they could reason with the cult, there was no way they could tell them the truth. And should she burden Antonia with having to lie to people she'd grown up around?

At the next intersection, Joni turned back and pointed. "The dining hall's that way."

Antonia blinked repeatedly, her azure stare glazed and puffy. She needed more rest, and the dust in the shafts clearly didn't help. "Where are you going?"

"I'm going to check out Louis' quarters."

Antonia and Matt said it at the same time. "Why?"

"Because we have no cameras in there. They used the place once. It might be worth checking again. To be sure they're not hiding something from us."

Antonia's bloodshot eyes narrowed like she could see her secret. It took all Joni had to not turn away. The sooner she sorted this issue with Olga, the better. Maybe she should give Antonia the earpiece for Matt to guide her? But then he'd be in her ear. Distracting her and maybe talking about how he didn't trust Joni. "You'll be okay on your own?"

"Yeah." Antonia smiled. "I'm a big girl now, remember?"

"Sorry."

"I like that you care."

They held hands for a second before Antonia crawled away. Once she'd gone from sight, Joni headed in the opposite direction to Louis' quarters. Towards a grate leading outside. Towards her old home.

"What do you think you'll find?"

"I don't know, but there might be more guards who need help. More guards we can get onside for this coming war."

"You think it will come to that?"

"It won't do us any harm to be prepared."

Joni moved through the shafts like an eel through wet mud. The sooner she got the footage, the sooner she could get back to her daughter.

The outside breeze cooled her sweating skin. The light from the late afternoon spilled in. The aimless diseased chorus snapped a shudder through her. When the mob had nothing to chase, they stayed put. Where else would they go?

Until she shoved open the grate and poked her head from the shaft, she'd have to guess at how many of the fuckers hung about outside. How many she'd have to avoid. And by then it would be too late because the act would make her the focus of every diseased in the vicinity.

"Are you there yet?"

Joni pinched her earpiece. She could leave it in the shaft. But what if she needed him? And she could reveal this secret if backed into a corner. Her friends needed the footage. She went to get it for them and would have told him and Antonia, but they might have contested her plan, and she didn't need the argument. She held her palm towards the closed grate and pulled her arm back. The second she whacked it open, the clock would be ticking.

Three …

Her hand shook.

Two …

She drew a calming breath.

On—

"Joni?"

She dropped her hand. "No, Matt. I'm not there yet."

"You need to get to Antonia. Now!"

Her stomach twinged. "What is it?"

"It's not good."

"Just fucking tell me."

"The cult. In the dining hall. They've just dragged another guard into the room. And they don't look like they want to welcome her to the group."

"You're projecting the footage to the others in the control room?"

"I should do that?"

"Of course. Half of them still think they can reason with the cult."

"There's no need."

"Huh?"

"There's no need."

This man couldn't get to the point if his life depended on it. "To project the footage?"

"What else?"

"Fuck knows. It could be anything with you. Why don't you need to project the footage?"

Someone screamed beneath her. She scooted back and peered through the closest hatch into the room below. Diseased gathered around the projected footage of the dining room. It showed the cult surrounding a woman.

"They're doing it themselves."

"I can see that now."

"They're filming like they did before."

"Yep. Can still see it."

"They've taken over all the screens in this building, including the one in the control room."

"Jeez, Ma … You know what? Forget about it. Can they broadcast outside the prison? To the south?"

"You just said forget about it."

"Can they?"

"No, it's a local network. It's for our eyes only."

"Lucky us."

"Joni, it looks like shit's about to get dark real fast. I think you should be with your daughter."

What did he know? "Don't tell me what to do."

"I don't think she should be on her own to witness this. She needs you at her side."

Of course she shouldn't be on her own, but Joni needed to get that footage.

"It's jus—"

"Jeez, Matt. Shut the fuck up, yeah? I'm going, all right?" Joni turned to the hatch leading to the plaza outside. She inhaled the cool and slightly curdled air. Olga's footage would have to wait. She'd told her not to talk to Matt. Hopefully that'd be enough to keep her secret safe.

CHAPTER 15

"It's good to see you, William." Hawk inhaled the fresh breeze coming in from the two doors leading to the elevated walkways. It helped rid his nostrils of the diseased reek of putrefaction.

Sitting against the wall, his bag of ammo at his side, William forced a smile that switched to a grimace when Rayne poured more water into the gash on his right arm. He kicked out, his feet scraping over the steel floor.

Rayne patted his shoulder. "Nearly there."

The first strip of white pillowcase she'd used to dress his wound had turned entirely red and sat discarded on the floor. She pinched the freshly cleaned gash and flicked her head for Hawk to join her. "Keep it closed while I bandage it again."

Hawk squatted down beside his friend and pinched the wound shut, William's blood turning his arm slick. "It's okay, it's nearly done." He moved to the side to give Rayne access and stepped away the second she laid the bandage against his skin.

Rayne wrapped it tightly and tied a knot against the

inside of his biceps. Spots of blood leaked through, but for now, the bandage appeared to be doing its job. At least, it held up better than the first dressing. Progress, if nothing else.

Washing her hands with what water remained in the jug, Rayne dried them on her trousers.

His face coated with a sheen of sweat, William forced a weak smile. "Thank you."

"It's the least we could do."

William perked up and opened his mouth as if ready to agree, but clearly thought better of it. For the sake of ingratiating himself to the group, whether he felt like he'd been wronged or not, he needed to move on. Fortunately, even through his suffering, he had the wherewithal to read the room. Although, judging by Ethan's scowl, he'd clocked the unspoken resentment like Hawk had.

"Well," William adjusted himself where he sat, "of all the people I could have run into in these blocks, I'm pleased it's you lot. There aren't many friendly faces around right now."

"Can you blame them?" Ethan stepped closer. "You expect a welcoming party when you created this?"

"Easy, Ethan." Hawk reached out to him. Too far away to touch, but the gesture stayed the boy's advances. "I've already told you this isn't on us."

"You think the rest of the south will believe that?"

"So, she's pregnant?" William gestured towards Ash.

Still pale from throwing up, she recoiled as if his question were an accusation.

"And what of it?" Rowan struggled with his ego's need to be the alpha male at the best of times. Now he had a pregnant woman to protect, his machismo clung to him like stink to the diseased.

"You're a couple?" William snorted a weak laugh. "Obviously you're a couple. I have met you before. What I mean is, it's yours?"

"No, I loan her out to the highest bidder each night. Who else's would it be?"

"Rowan …"

The man turned on Hawk. Coiled.

"Go easy on him, yeah? He's just asking."

"He should pick his questions more carefully."

William's eyebrows rose and pinched in the middle. "I was just going to say congratulations. It's nice to have some hope."

"That's what Aggie said." Hawk held her hand. "A future, right?"

She offered a weak smile and then threw a glance at William.

Shifting where he sat, William winced again. Blood glistened on his bandage. More spots rose to the surface. "So what's the deal?"

"The deal?" Rowan's tension returned and locked his stocky frame.

"Look, man, I'm just trying to take my mind off the pain. Jeez, talking to you lot's like pulling teeth." He flashed a facetious smile. "Like having a gouge torn from your arm. I'm just trying to get to know you all better. Tell me about yourselves. What's your story? Where did you come from? How did you meet? Tell me something sweet. I need to hear it."

"Well, I'm sorry to disappoint," Rowan said, "but we're vampires, remember? Our histories aren't very *sweet*."

"You think you need to tell that to someone from the north? In Edin, they send eighteen-year-olds outside the city's walls to be slaughtered. But that doesn't mean we live entirely without hope or happiness. I met Matilda in Edin."

Fixing William for a few more seconds, Rowan relaxed a

little, and his voice softened. "I was raised in the shining city. Do you know much about it?"

Using his one good arm as support, William adjusted how he sat. "Very little. What's it like?"

Hawk's stomach relaxed. They had a clear line of sight towards the two neighbouring blocks and the crimson-lit stairwell. They were all quiet. For now.

"Hell on earth." The intensity left Rowan's glare. "I was taken from my family and sent there. I don't remember much of my childhood before that. I think I have siblings." He laughed a little too loud, the deep boom escaping the room through all three exits. "*Had* siblings. No one's survived this mess, have they?" A hint of accusation sharpened his words.

William's cheeks bulged with his quickened breaths. He grimaced. "How old were you?"

"Five. Just how *he* liked them."

The words struck Hawk like lightning. He jumped when Aggie touched the base of his back.

A glance from Hawk to Rowan, William leaned closer to the stocky man. "He?"

"My owner." Rowan's features turned to stone. "That's all we are in this world. Commodities to be consumed by those in power."

Rayne spat on the floor. "Fucking cretins. I'll cut the throat of every one of them."

"I was kept in a bedroom for years." Rowan's glistening eyes cracked his stoicism. "Fuck knows how long. Long enough. Too long. They made sure I was fed and cleaned, ready for my owner whenever he wanted to visit." His laugh died. "Presentable."

Hawk trembled, and Aggie stepped closer, wrapping her arm around his waist.

"And I made sure I was ready." He jabbed a finger at William. "I was ready all right. They were so confident in their right to me as a person, they didn't even consider I had agency over my destiny. Every time they fed me, they gave me metal cutlery. Driven with enough hatred and anger, even a butter knife can tear open a jugular."

Hawk rubbed his scars.

"I'd left the city before all the blood had drained from his body, let alone before they'd found him. And I headed north."

Rowan blew out with every inch of his broad frame. He played with his hands, twirling his fingers over one another. "I stopped at every vampire community on my way up the country, looking for my family. Hoping they were still alive. They said they'd sold me. That they willingly gave me up, but I don't believe that. How could anyone willingly give up a child?" He cast a glance at Ash, who rubbed her stomach.

"I got as far north as I could and found nothing. I was left with a choice: head south again and search from the top of the country down, or stay. By then, I'd met Aggie. Soon after, I met Ash and the others. I'd found a family. After years of being alone. After years of feeling nothing but acute apathy, I suddenly had something I wasn't prepared to lose."

"And we're glad you stayed." Aggie beamed at Rowan. The man physically grew by a few inches.

"What about you, William?" Aggie said. "Why are you on your own? What happened?"

He spoke to the floor. A scolded child revealing a dirty secret. "I wanted to help. I wanted to clear the block of diseased."

"On your own?"

"I wasn't any use anywhere else."

"What do you mean?"

"It was my dream to head south. To find something better. And we did it. I got everyone south."

Hawk's laugh fell dead in the large room. "It's not like we didn't want to come. The north had little to offer any of us."

"But now we're here, I don't know what to do. It's not what I'd hoped it'd be. And then things got worse. The diseased came through. We got trapped in a basement. I didn't know what to do. For the first time in my life, I didn't have a plan. For as far back as I can remember, I've always had a goal. From wanting to be a protector—"

"A what?" Ethan said.

William shook his head. "It's not relevant anymore. Some stupid shit from Edin. It meant the world to me back then. I had no idea it would become so insignificant. But after that, we set our sights on coming south. And now we're here … I dunno what I am or want to be. I don't have any purpose." He finally looked up. "And were it not for Matilda, Gracie, and Olga, we would have died in that basement."

Aggie frowned, the snap of her accusation whipping around the room. "Why's that a problem?"

"It's not."

She pulled away from Hawk and closed in on William. "Sounds like it is. Three women come up with a better idea than you, and you have a meltdown? Throw your toys out of the pram? Weaken them by leaving them one member short." She gestured at his bag beside him. "And steal half their ammo while you're at it?"

"I didn't *throw my toys out of the pram*."

"Then what are you doing here? Why aren't you still with them?"

"*You* shot *me*, remember!"

Hawk stepped closer to the pair.

"So, because of an accident, I can't question you? Believe me, I'm eternally sorry for what happened, but do I now have to accept everything that comes from your mouth? Or is it because I'm a woman? I should be quiet? Know my place?"

"No. My mum's a woman."

Rayne clapped her hands once, the single crack running

through the room and out of the three exits. Her face slack, she spoke as if addressing a child, and a particularly stupid one at that. "And you met a vampire once, so you can't be prejudiced, right?"

"What?"

"I think you need to look inside, William."

He turned back to Aggie. "What's that supposed to mean?"

"I think this is about you not being the big man anymore. This is about your fragile ego."

"That's not how it is."

"That's how it looks."

"Well, you're wrong, you—"

"Careful, William." Hawk stepped closer.

"You're on her side? Seriously?"

Ethan joined in, "It's hard not to be." He pointed at William. "She's saying you need to wind your neck in, you misogynist prick."

"Come on, Hawk." William grimaced with the effort of getting to his feet. "Tell her."

"Tell her what? Aggie's only expressing her opinion."

"You've changed. What's happened to you?"

Jamming his thumb against his chest, Hawk laughed. "What's happened to me? I think if either of us has changed, it's you. When did you get so bitter? So insecure?"

William threw his bag of ammo over his left shoulder. "You know what? I was doing all right on my own."

"You really weren't."

"Your *girlfriend* shot me! *I'm* the victim here!"

Rayne tutted. "And don't we fucking know it?"

"Imagine if we were guards. They're not all gone, you know? If one of them recognised you, they wouldn't have saved you like I did."

"So you want me to thank you now?"

"William, what's gotten into you? Stop being—"

"A baby!" Aggie folded her arms. "Stop being a little baby and grow the fuck up!"

"Fuck this! I'm out of here."

William headed for the stairwell. Rayne and Aggie raised their eyebrows at one another. What could Hawk do about it? William had to take responsibility for his own actions, and how much time could he waste trying to reason with the unreasonable?

Just before he vanished into the crimson gloom, William froze. He turned back to the group. His malice had gone. He pressed his index finger to his lips, pointed down, and mouthed just one word. *Guards!*

CHAPTER 16

"What the hell is he doing in there?" Duncan tutted. "He's been ages."

Olga rolled her eyes.

Gracie gave her a thumbs up. "You okay?"

She rolled her eyes again. After five minutes of Duncan's wittering, she'd had enough. The past ten had dragged into a lifetime. Who knew what it would feel like by the time he'd served his purpose and she'd severed their connection? And if the talking wasn't already bad enough, not replying to him only made him worse. The man couldn't cope with silence. He had to fill every second like a nervous child. Olga had turned managing him into an art, dragging the pauses out for as long as possible, and getting in just before he spoke again. A slight scratching on the other side. Agitation. An inhale. She caught him on his first syllable. "He needed a moment. Allow it, yeah? How are things looking for the others?"

"I can't see much because the guards are in the stairwell, and there are no cameras there."

What he couldn't see. Helpful. If she rolled her eyes much

more, she'd lose her balance. Gracie watched on, her lips tight, her nostrils flared. But Olga had this. "Well …"

"What can I see?"

A pause. A moment of peace. Stretch the silence until it snapped. "Yep."

"I can see them through the cameras in the rooms they're closest to. Activity on the stairs. They're going up and down with weapons. A shitload of weapons. Although, it looks like just guns. Guns and ammo. Bags of ammo. And maybe a few grenades. And I'm sure they have knives. Everything I don't have."

"Brains and good sense too?"

"Funny."

Another pause, Olga stood with Gracie, Matilda, and Nick, all of them gathered outside the bathroom door, waiting for Artan. "So they're preparing for war?"

"That's certainly what it looks like."

"And the diseased?"

"The large mob are still in block one. There are a few in the other blocks, and there are a shitload still in the plaza, but the broken ramp means there aren't any more coming. It also means the ones down there aren't going away anytime soon. There are some in block two, some in block three, some in block four, som—"

Olga cut him off by clearing her throat.

"The bu—"

"Bulk of them are in block one. I get it."

Gracie frowned at Olga like she felt her pain. "What's that prick jabbering on about? Promise you'll let me be the one to end him when the time comes?"

Artan emerged from the bathroom. His hair dishevelled, his eyes puffy and swollen. Nick wrapped him in a tight hug.

"What's wrong with him?" Duncan tittered. "He did such

an evil shit he needs to be comforted after? I've had ones like that. Too much steak and patatas bravas. It plays havoc with the old digestive system."

Olga focused on Matilda, who squeezed her brother's shoulder. "Are we okay to move on now?" She hooked her thumb towards the ballroom with the mirrored floor. "We need to make sure we're in place in case they need us."

Artan rubbed his puffy eyes. "Yes, sorry."

"Don't be. Duncan will tell me when it kicks off down there. The diseased are in another block, and the guards are yet to attack, so we're all good at the moment. I just want to make sure we're in place for when we're needed."

Normally a job for Gracie. The tactician. The warrior. But because it required having Duncan in her ear, Olga led the way through the ballroom, holding her gun across her front, the red target scribbling on the steel floor.

The wind hit Olga from the right the second she stepped out onto the elevated walkway. She gritted her teeth like it might help temper her shiver. It only made it worse. The grey rain clouds denied them the late afternoon sun's heat. The plaza and surrounding blocks still blinked red. As did the blocks in the distance. Unrelenting. A maddening warning pulse several hours too late.

"How is it out there? I used to enjoy walking the walk-ways. I'd often take a stroll on my own after dinner. I never had a girlfriend, you see. My mum said I was always too fussy. That I had my pick of all these wonderful women. I could be anything I dreamed of, and be with anyone. But I never made the move, you know? She said I denied them my shining light."

The walkway's railing came up to Nick's abdomen. He bent over it and peered down. "What the …"

Olga joined the others, the handrail level with the top of her chest. The diseased in the plaza stared back. Some of them reached up like they could close the impossible distance with sheer will. The broken ramp penned them in. At some point, they'd have to kill every last one. But they were a noisy distraction, nothing more. A frame around the broken and twisted pallid corpse of a vamp … of one of the people from beneath the blocks.

"What's going on, Olga? I can only see along the walkway. What are you all looking at?"

"Staff from before the collapse?" Gracie said. "Thrown off or jumped?"

The blinking tiles stung Olga's tired eyes. "Let's think she jumped. That she made the choice. We don't know any better, so we can choose the narrative, and the last thing we need to consider is someone's running around doing that."

The edges of Gracie's mouth turned down like she tasted Olga's suggestion. "That makes sense."

"What are you talking about, Olga? I can't see anything. This isn't fair. I'm telling you what I see. Now you need to tell me what you see. It's the least you can do. I am keeping you all alive, after all."

Shame they couldn't say the same for the kids and other guards. But Olga held her tongue. Again. She led them into the neighbouring block. A large round table dominated the plain steel room. "What is this place?"

"A meeting room. See. I tell you that. I give you the information you need."

"Meeting room?" She fed it back to the others, Matilda's mouth closing when she got the answer to her silent question. "Sounds awful. What did they do here?"

"Have meetings."

"So the only time you decide to be succinct is when you're mugging me off?"

"What more do you want? I was never in on any of the meetings. The people running the blocks would get together and discuss how they managed the place. They'd confer with, and learn from, those running the other blocks. They talked about what was happening on the farms. How they—"

"All right. I get the point. I think I preferred being mugged off." Olga led them across the room. A similar layout to the block they'd just departed. Gracie entered the toilet on their left, the elevator and stairwell on their right. But they had no control room here, just a dead end where its door should be.

"So what's the plan? They're still loading up the ammo down there. They're preparing for a massive war. This will be nasty. Bloody. I hope you all come back. Especially Gracie."

"I'll tell her you said that."

"Said what?" Gracie came out of the toilet. "What's that prick saying? Has he finally taken a long hard look at himself and decided the best thing for everyone is for me to launch him from a walkway?"

"Don't tell her, Olga. It was a joke, honest."

"So, this is where we're going to stay." Olga pointed at the floor. "William, Hawk, and the others are still two floors below in the dining room. We'll wait until Duncan tells us it's kicking off."

"*If* he tells us." Gracie rolled her eyes.

"She thinks I won't tell you now? That's what I'm here for. And it's not like I can run away because she's taken my only weapon. And then wha—"

"*When* Duncan tells us the guards are attacking, that's when we go down these stairs and open fire from behind. They outnumber us, but I'm hoping if we catch them by surprise, that might even it out a little. Especially as we'll be in the confined stairwell."

"As long as they don't let off a grenade. Or set the stairwell on fire. Or—"

"Shut up!"

The others frowned at Olga. "I was talking to Duncan."

"Why don't you just go down now?"

Nick pointed at the door. "Why don't we just go down now?"

"That's what I said."

Gracie shook her head. "It's not up to us to start this war. We need to be on standby. What if the others decide to run? What if they have a better plan? It's their call, not ours."

"Ohhhhh! That makes more sense. I get it now. I was wondering what you were playing at. Why I'd led you over there for you to just stand about and wait. I just …"

Duncan in her left ear, Olga pressed her right to the stairwell's cold door. But she heard nothing through the two inches of cold steel.

The others fell silent. So silent it lifted the hairs on her arms and the back of her neck. It dragged her attention from what might be going on two floors below, to what they had going on with them up there.

The others had already turned to face it. Canted. Snarling. The red dot of Nick's laser sight danced across its red eyes. Its torn face, its top lip ripped open, the bloody gash in its cheek revealing the white of its teeth. Dressed in the finest fabrics, her hair still half up, the once woman wore the sneer she'd no doubt brought with her across the void. A permanent disgust for everyone and everything around her. Especially Northerners. Northerners and vampires. Her utter disdain so strong, it appeared to even overpower the urge to spread the virus. The sole purpose of every other diseased they'd encountered. Olga spoke from the side of her mouth. "What the fuck, Duncan?"

"What?"

"You could have told us the diseased were coming."

The creature in a dress—an improvement on the monster she'd once been—screamed.

Artan pushed down Nick's gun and sprinted towards her.

"Damn!" Duncan's voice rose in pitch, and his words ran one into the next. "I was watching the others. Watching the army like you told me to. They were on another screen. I didn't see them coming. I wasn't watching block one. I was …"

Artan ducked the woman's weak slash and stepped aside so she stumbled past him. He lunged and buried his knife in her temple. She turned limp and crumpled. Dead. The best version of herself.

Her face red and her plait swinging with her shaking head, Gracie pointed at Olga. "I swear, Duncan, if we die up here, you pompous moron, I'm going to come back from the grave and make you pay!"

Olga winced in anticipation of a whining reply that never came. "Duncan?"

Gracie cocked her head to one side.

Pressing against the earpiece so hard it hurt, Olga tried again. "What is it, Duncan? Why aren't you saying anything?"

Having peered into the meeting room, Artan pulled back. The colour had drained from his face. He mouthed two words. *Fuck!* And *Diseased!*

Gracie pointed at her own eyes and kept her voice low. "Have they seen us?"

Artan shook his head.

"I'm sorry." Duncan burst to life again. "I was so busy watching the guards, I didn't look at the other block. I should have seen them coming. I'm sorry."

"Have they all come across?"

Gracie raised an eyebrow, waiting, like Olga, for Duncan's response.

"That's what I was trying to tell you. I'm sorry, Olga. I really am."

"Fuck."

Throwing a sequence of air-punches that ended with her spinning on the spot, Gracie stamped her foot, halting before it made contact with the floor. Artan peered back again.

Gracie pointed at the meeting room.

He held his hand out flat and wobbled it in the air.

They were good for now. For now.

"From what Duncan's saying, there are too many to fight."

"Send Gracie back there to take them on."

Olga rolled her eyes.

Gracie snarled. "What did he say?"

"Don't focus on him right now."

Pulling the knife she'd taken from Duncan from her belt, Gracie wedged it through the door handle leading to the stairs, locking the door from their side. She spoke in a whisper, "The diseased won't be able to get through now." She pressed the call button for the elevator.

While the others stood silently waiting, Duncan spoke faster than ever. "So what's the plan? What are you going to do? What will Gracie do to me when she gets a hold of me? Will you tell her this isn't my fault? That I didn't see it coming. That I couldn't have seen it coming because I was making sure William and your other friends were okay, like you asked. That's what you asked me to do. That's what I was doing. I want to follow orders. I want to help you. Will you—"

Ping!

The arriving elevator went off like a hand grenade. Artan's shoulders snapped up to his neck.

Wild. Uncontrolled. Furious. The diseased in the meeting room had heard it too.

"Fuck!" Gracie shoved Nick, Matilda, and Olga into the

elevator and waited outside for Artan. She kept a foot in the door so it didn't close too soon, and aimed her gun towards the meeting room.

Duncan went off in Olga's ear like a siren. "They're coming, Olga. They're coming. They're coming."

Like she needed to be told.

CHAPTER 17

A ntonia jumped when Joni tapped her feet. Matt had given a running commentary all the way.

"They're tying her up."

"I'm here now, Matt."

"Okay."

Paler than when she'd last been with her, Antonia climbed over the hatch to the other side, making room for them both at the grate. Her puffy eyes had grown more bloodshot, and the light coming up from the room below reflected off her loaded tears.

They had a woman in her forties gagged and bound to a cross.

"They're fucking crucifying her."

"I'm here now, Matt."

Andy turned to look up.

Both Joni and Antonia pulled back.

The cult's hymn started a second later. Andy's maniacal whine skimmed along the top. "In Louis we trust. And his spirit we will honour."

The cult repeated Andy's mantra.

Joni gave Antonia a thumbs up. They were all good. If Andy had twigged they were there, someone would have opened fire on them by now. Fish in a barrel. Diseased in a corridor. Shaft-rats in a shaft.

Andy stood before the bound woman, his gun hanging from him by its strap. He clung to a twelve-inch knife with a curved blade. He slid the tip between the buttons on the woman's shirt and snapped it away, ripping it open and exposing the woman's white bra. He cut that next. It fell to the floor, leaving her naked from the waist up.

He stood still save for his left hand, the hand without the blade. It remained at his side, but his fingers worked like they were kneading something soft. Fleshy.

Snapping from his daze, Andy spun towards the camera, his long piss-blond hair flicking out with his turn. He either didn't know about the bulge in his trousers, or more than likely didn't care. Enlivened by the ritual and mugging like his idol used to when presenting his horrors to the south, he gesticulated with his blade. "We will rid our community of those who seek to belittle everything Louis stood for. We will cull those who've strayed from the flock, for doubters will either return poisoned, or as wolves. We are strong, and we are many. To stay that way, we need to remain vigilant to external threats. And we need to live our lives guided by the teachings of Louis."

In one fluid movement, Andy spun around with his knife. He moved so fast, Joni almost missed it. But the woman's cry and the gash in her left breast removed any doubt. About six inches long and a few inches deep, it ran straight through her nipple and birthed a river of blood that ran over her dark skin.

The woman bit on her fabric gag and yelled at the ceiling, but Andy's cackling laughter drowned out her pained cries. He turned to the camera again, and for a second time, he morphed into Louis. He'd studied the man. No doubt mimicked him in private. And now he had the chance to step into his shoes. He'd only get out of them again if they were surgically removed. If someone cut him off at the ankles. His greasy hair fell across his gaunt face when he leaned towards the camera, forehead first, looking down the lens from beneath his brow. "I will strike down those who oppose us and stand in our way. They say you shouldn't offer the swines your pearls lest they trample them. But this isn't a cautionary tale for us. We offer our pearls freely, but those who trample will be destroyed. We are in desperate times, friends. We don't have the luxury of leniency. You're either with us, or you die." His grin spread, and he spun again, slashing the woman's other breast, the second cut running from her shoulder to her sternum.

The woman howled.

Tears streaked Antonia's face like the blood streaking the woman's stomach. Another guard she knew. Another casualty of the cult. Hopefully those who thought they could reason with this lunatic were bearing witness. "You still getting all this up there, Matt?"

"Yep."

"And how do those look who wanted to side with the cult?"

"Pale and shocked."

Antonia trembled like she had hypothermia. Her voice wobbled, and her lips bent out of shape. "We've seen enough."

"I'm going to send Antonia back up."

"What will you do?"

"I'll stay down here a while longer. Keep track of them." And then get the footage for Olga.

Antonia frowned.

"You've seen enough."

The thought of an argument played out in her expression. "Matt, she'll be back to yo—"

Andy yelled as he cut the woman's throat, dressing her in an apron of her own blood. She bucked and twisted like slaughtered livestock. A few seconds later, she fell limp, her weight supported by her bound wrists and ankles. Joni closed her eyes, but opened them again when Antonia grabbed the back of her hand. She pointed down at the grate.

"I've seen enough too."

But Antonia pointed again.

Andy left the room alone, blood dripping from his blade, which he held at his side.

"Change of plan, Matt."

Antonia nodded.

"Huh?" Matt said.

"Andy's just left the room on his own. This might be the chance we're looking for. The chance to cut the head off the snake. If he falls, hopefully he takes the vile rhetoric and passion for the way of the cult with him." And with the end of the cult, Joni could finally tell everyone the truth. "Will you try to track him from up there? When we have him cornered, I want the entire block to witness his demise."

CHAPTER 18

J oni took the lead, Antonia on her heels as they crawled
through the shafts in pursuit of Andy. He reached a
door and punched the button, his act of machismo
undermined by his weak strike. On the other side, he opened
and closed his hand like he'd hurt himself and plugged a
device similar to the one Joni used for hacking into the jack
by the door's button.

Antonia crawled close to Joni, both of them leaning over
the hatch. She kept her voice low. "I didn't know they could
lock those doors."

"Another privilege reserved for Louis."

"What is?" Matt's voice stabbed into her ear. If only the
earpiece had a volume control.

"One of many. One rule for him, one for everyone else."
Antonia gritted her teeth. "You can be damn sure half the
people in the south haven't seen *him* naked in the shower."

Andy passed beneath them, chuckling to himself.

Joni led them on, tracking him by his steps and stopping at every hatch to keep tabs on him. If only he'd
walked down the middle of the hallway. She'd have ended

him by now, sent the rest of her magazine into the top of his head. But she'd have to open a grate to get to him, and in a contest where the quickest draw survived, she'd be giving him too much of an advantage. She passed over the next grate in the same way she had all the others, stretching and balancing her weight while she moved, like a lizard across a scorching desert. Antonia kept pace behind.

"Joni?" Matt's sharp tone speared her ear. Almost worse for his periods of silence. "What's going on? Are you all right up there?"

"We'll let you know when we need you. If you're following Andy, it's safe to assume we're close. I'm sticking to the man like I'm his shadow."

At the next hatch, Joni paused. Instead of passing through the door at the end, Andy headed for one of the block's many bathrooms.

She crossed over to give Antonia space to see. "This could be it."

Antonia's eyes remained swollen, her cheeks damp with fresh tears. That woman must have meant a lot to her.

Matt laughed. "You can catch him with his pants down."

"We'll jump on him while he's pissing."

"That's what I just said."

"But Antonia can't hear you, can she?"

"What the …?" Antonia rubbed her eyes and leaned closer to the hatch.

Andy had stopped short of going into the small bath-room. Instead, he unbuttoned his flies and pissed all over the door's button.

"Jeez!" Matt said. "Are you seeing this?"

Antonia's mouth hung open. "What a sick fuck." She flinched when he turned around, his penis exposed and erect. She clapped a hand to her mouth.

Hands on his hips, Andy thrust his pelvis forward and arched his back.

"You should have ended him by now, Joni."

"That's your strategy, is it? From all the way up there in your comfy seat?"

"I'll never unsee that, you know. Get down there and end him. Do the world a favour."

Joni gripped her knife's handle and reached over the grate. In a contest where the quickest draw survived, maybe his exhibitionism had just given her the edge.

"No." Antonia still covered her mouth with her hand. "He'll shoot you before you've slipped from the hatch. We have to be sensible."

"I'm faster and stronger than that febrile half-wit. And will we get a better opportunity than this?"

"I don't think you will."

Joni sighed and rolled her eyes at Antonia. "Matt has too many opinions for his own good."

Antonia smirked. "Sounds like Matt."

"I heard that."

Joni rolled her eyes again.

Lying on her side to peer through the shaft, Antonia went from pale white to slightly green. She heaved.

"What is it?"

Matt said, "I'm not sure you want to see."

The steel cold against her cheek, Joni took Antonia's spot and angled her head to get a better view.

Andy, his penis still fully on display, stroked the button that now glistened with his piss. He sniffed the tips of his fingers, inhaled with all he had, his appendage flexing as he huffed in his own urine. He licked his hands all over. From his wrists, up his palms, he licked all the way to the tip of each finger. Joni's stomach churned.

Dropping to his knees, his nose an inch from the piss-soaked button, Andy clung to himself with a tight grip and groaned all the way to completion.

"Fucking hell," Matt said. "Do you still think I'm with this lot? Look at the state of him. Jeez."

Crack! Whoosh!

The door at the end of the corridor opened, and footsteps stumbled through. Five or six diseased. Maybe a few more.

Andy swiped back his piss-blond hair with his piss-soaked hands, bit his blood-coated blade, and buttoned his flies. Facing the oncoming diseased, he stood with his feet shoulder-width apart and swayed from side to side. Maybe his position of power had filled him with a false confidence. He could wank where he pleased, but he still punched like a frail old man. Maybe the diseased would do them all a favour and end the slippery fuck right now.

But like he'd killed his sacrifice in front of the cult, Andy attacked the diseased with the same speed and grace. The *whip* of his blade cut through the air as he twisted away, avoiding the first beast while it fell dead on the floor beside him, a rictus grin of a slash lining its throat. He brought his attack around and stabbed the next creature in the face with a sharp jab, his blade going in and out of its eye, dragging a trail of blood with his withdrawal.

While she had nothing but seething hatred for the man, Joni lay mesmerised by his balletic aggression as he worked through the group of six, ending every one with a single strike. When he'd finished, he pressed his hands together, palm to palm, and bowed at his fallen foes. "Namaste." He returned to the bathroom door, striking the button and this time entering the small room.

"Well, that was unexpected," Joni said. "Are you ready to follow him?"

"I ... I think so."

"But?"

"I worry that, after what we've just witnessed, about what it is he feels he needs to go into the bathroom for? Do we really want to see that?"

"You need to get in there, Joni. End this fucker right now."

"Maybe even Andy uses a toilet to shit. Come on, this might be the opportunity we've been waiting for." Joni rested her hand on the back of her daughter's. "Let's catch him with his pants down and finish this." And let her finally tell everyone the truth about the south. Joni headed for the intersection and turned right, following the shaft towards the bathroom.

Their path came to a dead end, but a hatch led into the small room. It sent up the reek of mould, bleach, and stale farts.

Joni reached the hatch before Andy, who locked the door behind him again. He passed beneath her and went to the stall in the corner. Out of sight. He closed the door, securing the lock with a *click*.

"You think this is a good idea?" Some of the colour had returned to Antonia's face.

"Do you think we'll get a better chance to end this?"

"What's happening down there, Joni?"

"No cameras in the toilet?"

"Not in this one. I get the impression Louis was much more into broadcasting people showering than shitting. Even he had his limits."

"He didn't. Trust me." If only the fucker were still alive. She'd love the chance to kill him with her own hands. The disease was too good for that snake. She grabbed Antonia's arm and forced eye contact. "I think we should do this."

"You want to go down there?"

"I don't want to. But we should. This is our moment."

"I agree," Matt said.

"No one asked you."

"Right. Just here to give information. Not have an opinion."

"Not when you can't even see what's going on." Joni held her hand over the hatch, fixed on Antonia, and tilted her head to one side. Should she?

Antonia paused for a moment and then nodded.

Joni whacked the hatch, forcing it open. But before she slid down, Antonia caught her arm.

"What?"

Antonia pointed into the bathroom and cupped her ear.

"What is it, Joni? What's going on? The suspense is killing me."

Andy ran beneath them and cackled with wild laughter, his gun rattling as he shot the shaft. Columns of light punched up from below. He moved slowly closer, spraying bullets, closing them off in the end of the blocked hatch. "What, you think I didn't hear you when we were sacrificing another non-believer? And that I didn't hear you follow me down here? You're not fucking quiet up there. Why do you think I've led you to a dead end?"

The hatch shook from his attack. "This is something I should have done a long fucking time ago. And now I have a chance to end Louis' whore and her mistake of a child."

CHAPTER 19

W hether William believed he hid it, Hawk knew him well enough. A wince on his usually stoic face. The slight flicker at the corner of his left eye. The almost inaudible grunt from the effort of holding his gun with both hands and resting the butt in his shoulder. The slight sway of his weapon, his wound impairing his usual accuracy.

Focused on the crimson-lit stairwell, ready to fire, William backed across the room towards Hawk and the others. The hellish mouth about to vomit, as yet, an unquantifiable enemy. Be it diseased or guards, little good came from that dark orifice, which consumed the laser target that would at least offer some guidance to his unsteady aim.

Knives, blades drawn, moved closer to Ash and guided her away from the stairwell towards the elevated walkways. Rowan assisted, looping his arm through that of his pregnant partner's and leading her away.

Ash might not have wanted special treatment, but her condition had made her special. In a hopeless world, she'd become precious cargo, and every one of them would die protecting her. Hawk included.

Joining Aggie, Ethan, and Rayne, Hawk charged to William's aid. He and Aggie to one side, Ethan and Rayne on the other. They ran forwards only to back away with him. To make sure William didn't get left on his own. They kept their weapons aimed at the stairwell. Turn their backs for a second and they might get shot. Or even worse … someone might shoot Ash. But with all five of them ready to attack, the guards didn't stand a chance of getting the jump on them. The narrow doorway rendered their numerical advantage useless.

A woman appeared. Aggie stopped and laid her target on her face. "Stay there! Keep where we can see you and lower your weapon."

Hawk halted with the others. He added his laser target to the quad of glowing red dots. One wrong move and they'd tear this woman to shreds.

The guard watched them through narrowed eyes before she finally let her gun fall, the weight of it catching on the thick strap and resting on her belt buckle. She slowly raised her hands in the air, her attention on Aggie the entire time.

Aggie restarted their retreat. Ethan had to tug the back of Rayne's shirt to get her to join them.

Slow and steady, they moved closer to the elevated walkways. Closer to getting out of there. They could hold them back and lose them in the blocks. Regroup and turn from prey to predator. Why go to war when they could stalk them from the shadows? Hunt the guards and whittle their numbers with minimal risk to themselves. They might be outnumbered, but they'd just survived where thousands hadn't. This war would rely on more than just numbers.

"And to those still hiding." Rayne's cheeks glowed, but they were too far from the stairwell for it to be from the artificial light. She shone as crimson as her desires. Her words ragged with the force of her shout. "We know there are more of you in there. Come out with your weapons lowered and your hands raised."

The dining room stretched about four hundred feet from the walkways to the stairwell. They were only about a quarter of the way across the large room when a man's voice boomed through the vast space, birthed from the scarlet gloom. "We just want to talk."

Keep them occupied for a minute and they'd be out of there, following Knives, Ash, and Rayne to another block.

"Like fuck you do." Rayne sprayed spittle with her reply. She snapped away from Ethan's grip on her forearm.

"Calm down, Rayne."

If she heeded Aggie's caution, she hid it well. She worked her jaw like she chewed on her seething resentment.

Aggie shrugged at Hawk. Rayne, the wildcard. The volatile substance in this delicate formula.

Rayne lifted her weapon higher, the stock squished against her cheek. "Besides, you say you want to just talk, but you've had plenty of time for that. Lifetimes. The time for talking's done. You have but one choice here. Fuck off and leave us alone, or die, motherfuckers."

Hawk's heart sank. They were only about one hundred and fifty feet from the stairwell. Closer to the enemy than freedom. Inciting them wouldn't give them the time they needed to get out of there.

Aggie and Ethan copied their aggressive friend. They too snapped their guns higher. If you can't beat them ... And with someone like Rayne, who came from the womb marching to her own beat, you most certainly couldn't. Hawk did the same, the cold stock against his warm cheek.

The woman in the doorway visibly trembled. Caught in the middle, she clearly shared Hawk's plummeting dread. This could only go one way.

"You've had your fun." The man's derision came with a

pompous twang. "Now it's time to take a back seat and let the adults handle this. I'm going to step into view in three …"

Rayne halted, the others continuing their retreat.

"Two …"

They were nearly halfway across the room.

Aggie and Ethan paused next.

Hawk stopped too. With too far to run, they only had one choice.

William halted.

"One."

The man's head appeared on the doorway's right side. Rayne screamed and fired. The bullets blew a hole in his brow, blood and brain matter blowing out behind. He fell to his side with a thud.

The female guard screamed, turned, and ran. Rayne fired on her too, but she ducked, tripped, and fell down the stairs. The shots aimed for her birthed a series of sparks in the scarlet gloom.

Voices called to one another. Tens of voices. Maybe a hundred or more. An army. The time for negotiation had passed.

Rayne turned to Aggie and threw up her thin shoulders. "What?"

"Did you have to?"

William stamped his foot. "They said they wanted to talk."

"To vampires and the people who brought the diseased to the south? Are you brand new?"

Hawk, William, Rayne, Ethan, and Aggie continued their slow retreat. Focused on the stairwell and now closer to the walkways. Rayne fired again.

Aggie snapped her gun up and fixed on the scarlet shadows. "What was that for?"

"We have enough ammo. We need to show them the second they appear, we shoot. Also, it's too narrow for more than a few of them to come at us at a time. They have to expose themselves to advance. Expose themselves and they're dead. We just need to hold our nerve and we've got this."

Adrenaline turned Hawk's legs weak and his steps unsure. If he'd seen a better plan, he would have voiced it. Hopefully they could get out of there before they went to war. And what else could they have done? Give up? Hand themselves over to the guards who hated him and William more than they hated the vampires? Rayne had done the right thing. And with the narrow doorway covered, the army, no matter how large, didn't stand a chance.

CHAPTER 20

A ntonia shoved Joni toward the dead end and crawled back to the hatch.

"You're not going down there." Joni boosted off the wall and caught her daughter. She paused and then kicked back against the wall again. The dead end gave off a hollow tonk. "Cover me. But don't go down there, okay?"

"What are you going to do?"

"Promise me!"

"Okay!"

Joni spun around.

"I want to know too," Matt said. "What's happening?"

Aiming her gun at the dead end, Joni made herself as big as possible, filling the shaft as best she could. If any of her shots ricocheted, she'd take the bullet. She paused, her finger hovering over the trigger.

All the while, Andy restricted the space in which they had to hide, laughing as he fired on the shaft. "One, two, Andy's coming for you …"

Joni pulled the trigger and closed her eyes. She opened them again. She'd filled the dead end with holes. Light came through from the room on the other side. She kicked the panel, bending it with her attack.

Unloading again on the wall, Joni drew a line of fire along each edge of the small square and flinched from every expected ricochet. Antonia pressed against her from behind. Not much space left in which they could hide.

"Three, four, kill Louis' stupid whore …"

Joni kicked the wall again. It buckled, but not enough. "I need you to buy us some time, Antonia."

"How?"

The room below turned dark.

"Matt? Was that you?"

Andy yelled.

"Matt?"

Dead air.

Screaming even louder, Andy fired on the shaft again, the bullets closer than before.

Antonia leaned down through the hatch and shot back.

"Fuck!" Andy yelped. A stall door slammed shut with his retreat. "You have to come back this way sooner or later."

"What are you waiting for, Mum? Get us out of here."

"Did it work?" Matt breathed heavily in Joni's ear.

"Yeah, it did. Thank you."

"Welcome."

Firing on the dead end again, the counter on Joni's gun dropped past one hundred. When they ran out, there were none left. Hopefully they had enough ammo. This was supposed to be a recon mission. Recon and getting the footage for Olga.

She kicked the panel again, and this time it burst open, punching away from the wall, flooding the tunnel with the neighbouring room's light. Their escape a jagged steel hole, Joni ripped open her shirt, the buttons pinging off the inside of the shaft. Stripping down to just her bra, the steel cold against her bare skin, she placed the shirt around the edge of the hole and went first.

The sharp and jagged steel nullified by her shirt's thick fabric, Joni spun around and slid backwards into the room. She landed and trembled instantly like she'd dropped directly into the past. Racks on the wall. Harnesses. Handcuffs. Gags, whips, and chains. The snap of leather cracked through her mind. The sting of it hitting her skin. But only against the parts of her body she could cover. No one else could know what he did to her. Tracing a deep scar on her hip and one across her stomach, she jumped when Antonia landed next to her.

Her skin still pale. Her eyes still swollen and puffy. Her jaw loose. "Mum? What the hell is this place?"

"I can't see," Matt said. "Whatever it is, I'm guessing Louis wanted to keep it private."

"He did."

Antonia cocked an eyebrow.

"Sorry." Joni pointed at her ear. "I was talking to Matt. Do you really want to know? It's somewhere your dad would bring his … girlfriends … although that suggests it was a two-way thing. His—"

"Captives? Victims?"

Joni lowered her head.

"I'm sorry, Mum." Antonia took Joni's hand and led them across the room at a jog, slamming her palm against the door's button with a *crack!*

The door opened onto a hallway like many others in the block. Bright white lights. Too bright. It had steel walls, ceiling, and floor. Doors ran down either side, and a crowd of about eight to ten diseased congregated about one hundred and fifty feet away. Joni sighed and raised her gun. Just under one hundred bullets. Hopefully it would be enough.

CHAPTER 21

"Come on, girls, you've got this."

"Easy for you to say." Joni aimed at the charging diseased, her gun's red target prophesying their demise. She peeled the skin and flesh from their faces, exposing and shattering the bones beneath. She attacked in efficient bursts. Four or five bullets for each diseased. All head shots.

Beside her, Antonia dispatched the creatures with the same deadly efficiency. Dropping them as they ran. Ending them before they'd begun. Before they'd even considered beginning. Nine diseased in total. No match for this mother and daughter pair.

Joni angled her gun to read the top. Seventy-three bullets remained. Her cheeks puffed with her exhale.

"Well done, girls."

"What's with this *girls* shit?"

Antonia shook her head.

"How old are you, Matt?"

"Twenty-eight."

"I'm old enough to be your mother. Show some respect."

"Sorry."

Antonia smirked.

A diseased burst into view at the end of the hallway a few hundred feet away. It ran, clumsy with its charge, its arms hanging as limp as the strips of fabric that had once been its uniform. While everything else about it teetered on the edge of its balance, the once-guard held a steady glare, fixing Joni and Antonia with unwavering crimson hatred. Its mouth widened. Impossibly wide. It hissed like a bag of angry snakes.

Still a few hundred feet away, but Antonia's target rested on its face. She pulled the trigger. Its head snapped back, and it fell. A groundswell of charging steps called to them from around the bend. Beside her, Antonia closed her eyes. A futile search for calm before the madness.

The diseased raced around the corner, many falling from where their coordination couldn't cope with the sharp turn. Ten, twenty, thirty of them. They kept coming. Seventy-three bullets wouldn't even make a dent.

Louis' sex dungeon behind them. The maintenance shaft above. A corridor ahead on their left leading back towards Andy and the bathroom. The hatch to get into the shaft halfway between them and the diseased. They wouldn't get to it in time.

"Andy's heading your way."

"Shit!"

"What?" Antonia said.

"Andy's heading our way."

"That's what I said."

"I'm telling Antonia."

"Oh."

The diseased two hundred feet away. They packed the width of the corridor. They fought one another to be the first to reach them. Crimson glares. Stretched mouths.

Joni froze. In her mind she turned back towards Louis'

dungeon. Back the way they'd come. She flinched at Antonia's hand on her forearm.

"We'll find another way."

She'd already put her daughter at risk once on this trip. She'd sent her to watch the cult on her own while she slithered off to protect her lie. If they didn't go back the way they'd come because of her and her stupid hang-ups, this would end them both. Joni hit the door's button and ran back into the room she never thought she'd visit again.

They reached the torn entrance to the shaft as the first of the diseased ran into the room. Her present terror slammed into her tormented past. Her brain slipped. But she bent down and linked her fingers, offering Antonia a boost. The need to protect her child shone a fog light through her fugue state.

Antonia paused.

"Get in the shaft now!"

"Andy's in the corridor and heading towards you," Matt said.

Antonia stepped on Joni's hands and climbed in. She spun around and shot the diseased, those at the front falling and tripping the ones directly behind. She hung down and caught Joni's hand, pulling her up just as the diseased crashed into the wall where she'd been seconds before.

Matt laughed. "Oh, shit!"

"What?"

"Andy wasn't expecting that."

Joni replied with Antonia in mind. "Andy's met the diseased?"

"Yep."

"Are they giving chase?"

"Yep."

"They're giving chase."

"That's what I said."

"Antonia can't hear you, numb nuts."

"Oh."

"We need to get going." Antonia led the way back through the bathroom shaft, over the cheese grater of bullet holes and over the section of hallway where Andy had relieved himself in more ways than one. Antonia quickened their pace.

At the intersection, Antonia turned left, but Joni paused.

"What are you doing?"

Joni pointed right. The door that way led to the diseased corridor they'd just vacated. She pressed her earbud. "How close is Andy to getting back into this corridor?"

"A hundred feet. Maybe less."

Joni only had to travel fifty to reach the door. She could make it.

"Eighty feet."

She took off in the opposite direction from Antonia. An eel through mud. A snake in the grass. She'd get there before him.

"Sixty feet."

Grunting with the effort of the crawl, the crack of her elbows slamming against the shaft, her feet slipping as they propelled her on.

"Forty feet."

Finish Andy and they finish the cult. They'd finish her secret. She could tell the guards the truth.

"Thirty feet."

Joni reached the door and the screw to lock it.

"Twenty feet."

Her hands shook as she drew her knife. She lost her grip, sending it skittering away.

"Ten feet."

Joni boosted after her blade, caught it, spun around, and locked it in the screw's groove.

Clack! Whoosh!

"He's through."

"Fuck!"

"And he's looking up. He knows you're there, Joni!"

"Shit."

"He's locking the door with his device."

The shaft shook with the diseased hitting the other side of the door.

Joni took off, shouting ahead of her, "Go, Antonia, go!"

Turning around, Antonia led their retreat.

Quicker than she'd ever gone through these shafts, Joni still struggled to keep up with her daughter.

The clack of bullet fire below.

The slap of Andy's steps as he tracked them from the ground.

Antonia passed over the door Andy had locked earlier.

The shaft shook with the man's attack. Bullets whined as they punched through the steel and died against the ceiling. One ran through Joni's legs and fell dead against the base of her back.

She crossed the locked door.

"He's stopped to unlock it."

Joni, covered in sweat, half-naked, and gasping for breath, shooed Antonia on with a wave of her hand. "Let's get out of here while we still can."

CHAPTER 22

"He must have given up following us by now." Joni tapped Antonia's feet. "I said—"

"I heard. I think you're right."

The cold steel pressed against Joni's sweating skin, and her trousers clung to her. "There's a wider spot in the shaft ahead. I think we should stop for a break."

"Sure. But hang on a minute." Antonia whacked a hatch so it swung open on its hinges, and slipped out.

"Where are you going?"

She vanished, landing on the bed in the guard's room below. She pulled open a wardrobe and removed a fresh top. Jumping back on the bed, she clambered in again and handed it to her mum.

"Thank you." Joni clung to the soft cotton.

"You can't go back to the control room like that."

"No. Thank you."

"No problem."

The next junction had a vertical shaft leading to the next floor. Slightly wider, but now they stood, they were still just a few inches from one another, and it took all of Joni's dexterity to make sure she didn't whack Antonia while she changed. The diseased moaned as they passed beneath them.

"Joni should have locked that door."

Antonia frowned and tilted her head.

"I." Joni opened her right hand, her fingers splaying. She resisted the urge to whack herself. "*I* should have locked that door. I got there in time."

"We did what we could." Antonia rubbed Joni's upper arm. "It all happened too quickly."

She held up her betraying hands. "But if I hadn't dropped the knife, I would have had time to end his life. Strife. Wif …" Joni inhaled the shaft's dusty air and shook her head like the action could banish the madness. "Had we stopped Andy, it might have also stopped the cult."

"Sooner or later, if nothing else, Andy will fall victim to his own hubris. The man's more of a monster than those things. He's going to get his."

"How have you lived with him in your life for so long?"

"I didn't have a choice. But it made going away to live with all my different aunties much easier."

"And …" Joni shuddered, and her toes curled. "What the fuck was that about in the bathroom?"

Antonia still wore the bloodshot glaze of grief from the sacrifice. Reliving what Andy had done deepened her glaze, like she'd retreated even further into her own skull. "He knew we were watching. What a fucking creep."

"Lik—"

"Like my dad? Is that what you were going to say?"

"I'm sorry. It's just he—"

"No, you're right. Dad was a creep, no matter how much I wish he weren't."

Since they'd left Andy behind, Matt, save for the occasional sniff or squeak of his chair, had been silent. Maybe he'd finally learned to read the situation. "Matt, did you broadcast *everything* Andy did?"

"I did. I heard at least half of them heaving."

"I'm not surprised. Can you send it to the entire block? Show the rest of the cult? Let them better understand the man they call leader."

"I *could* ..."

"But ...?"

"They'll know where it's coming from. We'll give away our location. Like if we use the tannoy."

"Shit! Okay, that makes sense."

Where Antonia had wanted to be in on their conversation before, she now remained glazed. Lost. Withdrawn. Like a panel of frosted glass separated them. She flinched when Joni touched the back of her hand. "How are you?"

"What?"

"After the sacrifice?"

Antonia drew a breath and paused. The frosted pane thawed. Joni flinched. Naked grief from the same azure glare that stared back at her in the mirror. "I'm sorry, but I don't think I'm ready to talk about it. Not now. Not here. We have too much else going on. I can't go there right now."

The words stung, but Joni hadn't been in her life for long. How could she expect to be her support at that moment?

"But thank you."

Joni forced a smile. "Of course. Any time."

"And there's no one I'd rather have beside me right now."

Not even Aunty Mary? Drop it, Joni. She pressed her lips tight. "Thank you."

"I'm proud to call you Mum."

"Please, Antonia, this isn't about me and my feelings. You need to do what you need to do. And I want you to know I'm here. Always. Okay?"

"Thank you."

But how could she talk to her daughter about opening up when she hadn't told her the truth about the south? Maybe she should tell her. Matt too. Get it out of the way. Off her chest. Help them see the need for secrecy. They'd agree, wouldn't they? Secrecy, for now at least. "There's something I nee—"

"The kill team's in trouble."

Joni pressed her finger to her earpiece. "Did you just say the kill team's in trouble?"

"You need to get back now. They're in a bad way, Joni."

"What's happening?"

"I don't know. But come. Quick!"

Antonia pulled back against the shaft, giving Joni space to lead.

Jumping where she stood, Joni opened her legs and arms, pinning herself in the shaft. She climbed with Antonia close on her heels.

CHAPTER 23

Already in the elevator, blind to Artan's struggles, Olga could only judge the situation from Gracie's taut face and from the way she remained in the hallway, her gun pointing towards the chaos. From the way she looked at her foot when it stopped the doors closing and returned her focus to the meeting room. From the way she chewed on her bottom lip like someone caught between two impossible decisions. Run into chaos and let the elevator drop, or hold tight and hope Artan made it. All this from Gracie. And then she had Duncan in her ear, his panic rattling along, one word tripping over the next.

"He's fucked, Olga. You need to get out of there. Leave him. The diseased are on him. There are too many of them. He's got no chance. He's a fox, and the hounds have his scent. They won't let him go now. Get away while you still can."

Olga jumped aside as Gracie and then Artan dived into the elevator, the pair of them tripping over one another and crashing into the back wall where she'd just been standing. She pressed the button to take them to the next floor down. William and the others were two floors below. They needed to be close enough to help, but not so close they started a war their friends might not want.

The diseased descended on them.

"There are too many, Olga. You need to get out of there."

Her fingertip sore from repeatedly pressing the button, Olga said, "What do you think I'm doing?"

"But you need to be quicker."

"What's that prick saying?" Gracie picked herself up from the floor.

"Not now, Gracie."

The first of the diseased overshot the elevator, stumbling past.

"Doesn't she know I'm trying to help? I can see up here, you know? That's why you have me. And I can tell you, the diseased are coming. You need to get away."

Olga jabbed the button so hard the tip of her finger turned numb. "But you're not fucking helping!"

"I swear, I'm going to end him when we see each other next."

"Not helping either, Gracie."

Ping!

Dirty hands, their fingernails coated with dried blood, caught the closing doors and pulled them wide.

Olga kicked the diseased in the mouth, driving it back. But the damage had already been done. They'd already reopened the doors. Yelling, she fired her gun and jumped out into the hallway, opening up on the mob.

"What are you doing? You can't fight them all."

"Watch me." Like she had any other choice.

Every shot landed. Arms snapped away from bodies; heads flipped back; legs gave way as kneecaps shattered. Foreheads and faces obliterated. But there were too many.

Gracie stumbled into Olga, slamming her aside, making room so she could join the fight. Twice the firepower. It helped. Extinguished the imminent threat, but it wasn't enough.

Matilda, Artan, and Nick came out shooting, forcing Gracie, and Olga by extension, farther away from the elevator. They dropped the diseased. Killed many, and those they didn't became a squirming carpet of incapacitation. A tricky sea for the others to cross.

"So what now? What about when you reload? What then? What will you do? And what about me? How will I get out of here with no weapons? Gracie did this on purpose to screw me over."

"This isn't about you, you prick."

The diseased charge unrelenting, they swarmed around the bend. They'd dropped twenty to thirty. Duncan had said there were a hundred or more.

Four of them continued shooting while Artan reloaded, swapped his gun with his sister's, and pulled back into the elevator, reloading the next weapon.

Olga stepped farther out into the hallway for a better angle. She straddled a corpse, the floor slick with blood. The red counter on her gun dropped with the discharging bullets, the falling numbers a blur.

"You're going to run out of ammo, Olga. Olga!"

"Olga!"

A gun flew towards her from the elevator. Dropping her own, the strap taking its weight, she caught Nick's and fired again.

Matilda slipped into the elevator next, leaving just the two of them out there as Artan swapped weapons with Gracie.

Olga shot the diseased as they appeared. Many hit the wall to her right from where they couldn't manage the bend. One or two crashed through the bathroom door and vanished from sight.

"Gracie, get in the elevator."

"No, you need to go in before her. We want to keep you alive. Gracie doesn't matter."

Gracie shook her head. "You first."

"Stop being a hero." Olga stepped back over the mound, closer to the elevator, and shoved Gracie, sending her in with the others.

Ping!

The doors started to close.

Her trigger finger sore, the tendons in her wrists aching, Olga took down three more. The trio, like so many she'd already shot, wore the ridiculous garb of those from the tower blocks. Silly dresses. Loafers, trousers, and ties. Fucking ridiculous.

Five more appeared.

One, two, three down. Olga jumped, turned sideways, and tripped over her own feet on her way in. She fell, struck the side of her head against the elevator's internal wall, and slid into a heap, her ears ringing as the diseased beat a hammering attack against the now closed doors.

The elevator descended. The banging fists grew distant. The five of them panted.

"Olga! Are you alive?"

She shook her head at the man's intrusion.

Gracie tutted. "He's still jabbering in your ear? Fuck off, Duncan, you fucking turnip-faced buffoon. Born with a silver spoon in your mouth and one wedged firmly up your arse."

Matilda, her brow damp with sweat, snorted a laugh. A few seconds later, Artan joined in, then Nick.

Holding her hand down to Olga to help her stand, Gracie pulled her to her feet and hugged her. "Well done." She raised her voice. "And I'm not talking to you, Duncan, you bothersome little cretin."

119

The others laughed harder.

"Well, I don't think it's very funny. I don't see why she has such a problem with me. I'm just trying to help, and all I get is abuse."

Olga joined in, snorting with her laughter and quickly losing control.

"Where would you be without me? You should all be thanking me. I'm the reason you're still alive."

Trying to catch her breath while she guffawed, Olga bent over and rested her hands on her knees. It might only be temporary, but they'd evaded the diseased again. They should enjoy it while it lasted.

CHAPTER 24

Now closer to the doors leading to the elevated walkways than the stairwell, but Hawk and his friends were still about one hundred and fifty feet from their escape. They might have been in control, five guns trained on the narrow exit, but make no fucking mistake, things were in the balance.

They remained as a line of five. Aggie on Hawk's left and William on his right. Rayne on the far right moved slightly slower than the rest. Clearly reluctant to step away from all-out war with these motherfuckers.

The army had been quiet, and had Hawk not witnessed the guard vanishing into the stairwell, he would have taken it to be abandoned. The one dead guard lying on his side in the doorway merely the aftermath of a past conflict. The man tracked their retreat with the glazed apathy of the recently deceased. Far worse than the diseased's scarlet rage. That they could hate. Something to fight against. But the guard, rendered useless by Rayne's bullets, his head blown apart from the brow up, stared at them in accusation. He'd fought to survive the infection he and his friends had brought to their world, and this was how it ended.

William grunted with the effort of keeping his gun raised. Hawk bit his tongue. Was he okay? Of course he wasn't. Aggie had shot him. But they had it covered … even if only four of them had the faculties to defend their escape. The red glow consumed their laser targets as they searched for a surface on which to rest. A face. A torso. A forehead. Long may that search be in vain.

The shuffle of feet and the beating of steps called to them from the gloom. Hawk raised his gun higher, but the stairwell kept its secret. They'd see what the guards were up to when the guards decided.

One hundred and twenty-five feet to the elevated walkways. Hawk's throat dried and pinched with his gulp. He blew out hard, like he could drive away his anxiety.

Shunk!

A small metal sheet flew from the darkness, tossed out from the stairwell. It slid across the steel floor. A foot tall and wide, the hand that had shoved it vanished as quickly as it had appeared.

Five laser targets rested on the metal invader, one swinging in larger circles than the rest with William's unsteady aim.

"What the …?" Rayne halted.

Bang!

The sheet exploded, the thud running through the floor as it quadrupled in size. Four feet tall and wide. They kept their targets on it.

Aggie's eyes narrowed. "What the hell?"

Hawk jumped when Rayne fired, her bullets missing the guard darting from the doorway as he slid behind the sheet. It held firm despite her continued attack. "It's a shield."

Ethan's mouth hung open. "I've never seen anything like it."

Hawk stepped back. Aggie, Ethan, and William followed. But Rayne held her ground. She'd come here to fight, and with her she'd brought a vengeful thirst from generations past. A thirst she finally had a chance to quench. These fuckers had to pay. For what they did to her parents and her parents' parents. They'd amassed a debt that could only be settled by their eradication, and Rayne had come to collect.

Shunk! Swish!

Another shield birthed from the darkness. Sent into the dining hall by another hidden soldier. Their arm retreated as quickly as it appeared.

The man behind the shield caught the second one and sent it out to his right.

Shunk! Swish!

The arm in the stairwell sent out another. To the left of the first shield.

Bang!

Bang!

Three shields. The first one the tip of the arrow, the other two set back a little. Together, they provided cover for those exiting the stairwell.

The second soldier dived from the stairwell and hid behind the right of the three shields. Another soldier ran to the final unoccupied barrier.

Shunk! Swish!

Bang!

More shields. Spreading out. Taking control of the space.

Hawk stepped towards the elevated walkways, and the others followed. Even Rayne. They couldn't fight here.

Bang!

Shields popped up in an ever-widening fan from the stairwell's exit.

Bang!

The guards doubled like bacteria.

The first man behind the first shield yelled, "You have no right being here."

Rayne halted again and scoffed. "So, what, you're going to issue a warrant for our swift removal? Your old ways are as dead as this world. As dead as every one of you fuckers will soon be."

Shunk! Swish!

Bang!

Bang!

"Dream on. We have vampire scum and the reason the south has fallen in our sights. You're mad if you think you're getting away from this."

Rayne spat on the floor. "You have no fucking idea just how mad."

Shunk! Swish!

Bang!

"We're going to take back what you've stolen from us—"

"Stolen from you?" Rayne fired on the first shield. It ate her bullets, sparks and a few scratches the only evidence of her attack. "You stole lifetimes from us, you fucks. You claimed this land like it was your fucking right."

"Natural selection, you vile rat. You're too weak to thrive, so you look for someone to blame."

"Hard to thrive when you have a boot heel on your neck! And I'll fucking prove it." Rayne stepped forwards, but Ethan caught her. Seventy-five feet to the elevated walkways.

"Oh, stop being such a victim."

Shunk! Swish!

Bang!

"But however aggrieved you feel, we will make sure you pay the price for what you've done. You need to be annihilated like the vermin you are. All of you. We should have burned the vampires a long time ago. Fucking parasites leeching our food from the food pipes. Fucking vermin!"

Rayne widened her stance and rested the butt of her gun against her cheek.

Hawk leaned closer to Aggie. "We need to keep going. This isn't a fight we can win."

"So we let them get away with that?"

Shunk! Swish!

Bang!

"Look, I get it. We should punish them. I'm not saying we shouldn't—"

"Sounds like it."

"But we should do it on our terms. They're baiting you for a reason. If we take too much longer getting out of here, we won't be leaving at all."

Rayne smiled. "Neither will they."

Aggie's lips peeled back. "This is an opportunity, and you're calling for calm heads? You don't know what we've suffered."

"I don't, but I get it."

A raised eyebrow, Aggie cocked her head to one side.

"I can empathise with how you feel."

"How good of you."

"Look what they're doing to us, Aggie. We're on the same side."

"Are we?"

"Please, I love you."

The fury fell from Aggie's face like creases from a silk sheet. "You …?"

"I know it's really soon to be saying that, but I've been on this planet long enough to know what this is. I love you, and I want us to survive this. And I want to help you punish them for what they've done. But only when we have a chance of walking away after."

"Yeargh!" Ethan opened fire and charged at the shields.

This time, the roles reversed, and Rayne caught him. The jolt of his sudden stop sent his line of bullets streaking up the back wall and into the ceiling.

Shunk! Whoosh!

More shields appeared all the time.

Bang! Bang!

Rayne grabbed Ethan by his shoulders and spun him around so he faced her. "Hawk's right. I can charge in when it's just me, but seeing you attack … we can't win here."

Ethan glanced at Hawk and then at Aggie. The fire left him.

They quickened their retreat as more shields sprang up.

Fifty feet to go.

The tinkle of two metal spheres played against the steel floor.

"Grenades!" William grimaced as he shot them both before they got anywhere near them. The heat from their combined explosion warmed Hawk's face.

"Let's go. Now!" Aggie led their retreat, the rip-roaring blast of another grenade behind them as they burst from the dining hall onto the walkways.

They sprinted with all they had, the wind strong, the *ting* of bullets hitting their surroundings.

While Ash waited for them at the other end of the walkway, Rowan and Knives busied themselves inside the next block.

Aggie reached the neighbouring tower first, Hawk behind her. Another dining room, wrecked from what must have been an earlier skirmish. The vinegar rot of diseased curdled the air, and blood glistened in pools on the floor. Tables lay on their sides, and the leg of an upturned chair held a lump of rotting flesh like a spoiled kebab.

As William, Rayne, and Ethan entered the large room,

Rowan and Knives rolled a massive round steel tabletop across the doorway. They braced table legs against the underside, the feet locking into the floor's grooves and pinning it in place.

"Well?" Knives threw her arms wide, her gaze shifting from Aggie to Rayne to Ethan.

Aggie stared at the floor. "There are too many of them. We need to take the fight deeper into the blocks and be smarter about this. If we stand toe-to-toe with them, there will only be one winner."

CHAPTER 25

J oni landed in the observation room, and Matt spun in
his seat. She pointed at the furore in the control room.
Crying. Screaming. Shouting.

"No. It's—" Matt's voice came through the earpiece and
from directly in front of her.

No time for him to explain. She ran to the control room
as Antonia dropped in behind her.

The guards were reacting to the footage of the madness
on the other side of the door just feet away. The kill team
was penned in in the corridor leading to the medical bay.
They'd been driven back by an ever-increasing number of
diseased. Some came from the other end of the hallway,
while others came from the medical bay's open door. The
crowd remained fixed on the screen, blocking Joni's access to
Theresa and her crew. She shoved and pushed. "Get out of
the fucking way!"

Many were so lost in their own grief they barely saw her.
She shoved those harder than others. Passing the pile of
ammo, she picked up four magazines and tossed two back to
Antonia, who followed in her wake.

Crack! She slammed her fist against the button to open the door.

Crack! She whacked it again.

"You've locked the door?"

Pearl appeared on her right. A shaft-rat like Joni. Her face twisted, her eyes bloodshot. "We need to protect everyone else. Have you seen how many diseased are in there?"

"You don't think there are enough of you to fight them?"

"We got scared."

"Fucking hell."

Antonia had already cleared a route back to the open hatch. She dropped to one knee and linked her fingers, offering Joni a step.

Joni ran. A woman stumbled across her path. She hit her shoulder, the woman spinning away. She stepped on Antonia's hands and pulled herself into the shaft.

Sliding like she'd been greased up, Joni slithered to the grate above the carnage. She spun her legs around in front of her and yelled, "Hold your fire." She dropped into the hallway and rolled into the open door of the medical bay on her right. Antonia followed her in.

The kill team resumed their attack on the diseased while Joni and Antonia covered the four aisles, the diseased bursting from different ones at different times.

Joni's gun bucked and kicked. She dropped three more diseased and had eight bullets left in her magazine. She ejected it while Antonia covered her.

Reloading, Joni resumed her attack, the diseased no match for her and her daughter.

With no more diseased, Joni turned to Antonia. "You good?"

The kill team continued firing in the hallway.

And then the shots halted.

At the door, Joni paused. "Theresa?"

"Joni?"

"You okay?"

"There are no more diseased out here, if that's what you mean? You?"

"I think they're all down. What happened? We secured the medical bay?"

"Clearly not well enough. And I think these fuckers came from beyond the medical bay."

"Shit!"

"Wait there; we'll come to you."

Joni counted the kill team as they entered. Theresa led all six through, Jacob's dad at the back, the only one of them staring down. "You all okay?"

They nodded. All except Jacob's dad.

The others backed away as Joni drew closer to him. Her voice and hands trembled. "I said, are you all o—"

He looked up, and Joni gasped. She stepped back and held her gun.

His brow pinched in the middle, and he whined, "It's just a scratch."

About three inches long, the red line running down the left side of his neck damn near throbbed with infection.

"I'm fine. It's just a scratch. I'm fine. I'm going to see Jacob soon. Nothing's going to stop that. Nothing." While he spoke, his sclera turned red. His top lip twitched as he clearly wrestled against his instinct to snarl.

Joni shooed the others back. "Clear some space."

"I said—" The man's voice morphed into a rasp. "I'm o—" He snarled and hissed. He charged.

Joni shot him on his second step.

The man fell flat at her feet, his arms limp at his sides. A halo of blood surrounded his head.

Theresa clapped a hand to her mouth. "Shit!"

"Are you okay, Joni?"

She pressed her finger to her ear, Matt still connected through the headset. "You saw that?"

"We all did. I'm sorry."

"Someone had to do it."

"Still …"

"Yeah." Joni sighed. "Still …"

CHAPTER 26

Olga sighed as the elevator came to a soft halt, the chime of their arrival cutting off the tail end of the others' laughter.

The elevator's whirring door servos called into the silent room. Olga pressed her earpiece and, cowed by the atmosphere, kept her voice low. "We're getting out on the next floor." Even her whisper ran away from her, desperate to reveal them to anyone who cared to listen. Diseased or otherwise. A massive screen dominated one of the room's walls. Seats had been lined up to face it, but some at the back were turned around like they'd been recently used. "It looks like a theatre."

"Cinema room."

"Huh?"

"It's a cinema room."

"Okay. How's it looking down here?"

"So you want my help now?"

"What?"

"After being horrible to me."

The screech of chair legs across the steel floor sent spasming tension through Olga's back.

Artan winced and mouthed, *Sorry.* He lifted the chair and wedged it in the elevator's door.

"Of course we need your help."

Gracie tutted. "What's he saying now? Stupid prick. He needs some backbone beating into him."

"Like that would work." Duncan scoffed. "You need to put a leash on your friend."

"You can try if you like?"

Gracie squared up to Olga. "What did he say?"

Olga pressed her finger to her lips. She pointed at the stairwell to the lower floors on the other side of the room. An army of guards somewhere inside.

"Duncan, focus on the task at hand, yeah? Where are William and the others?"

"On the floor below you. Still."

"They're safe?"

"For now."

"And the diseased?"

"The floor above. Still. Oh …"

"What?"

The others all fixed on Olga.

"There are more diseased in block one. On the middle floor of the top three. On the other side of the elevated walkway."

"Shit." Olga sidestepped across the room. The walkway stretched from her to block one, but the shadows inside the building made it impossible to see the threat. She chewed the inside of her mouth.

"What?" Matilda said.

"Diseased." Olga pointed. "In block one on the middle floor."

Nick first, Artan followed. They lifted some of the disturbed chairs from the back of the room and laid them in the doorway. They placed them gently, stacking them higher, knitting their legs together to form a fence that would hopefully withstand the diseased's pressure.

While Nick and Artan finished, Olga led them out to the walkway leading back to the third block. The block with the control room and the mirrored dance floor. "So, what now?"

"The others are safe for now." Duncan clicked his tongue while he paused. "You know what? I think the best thing you can do is to get the diseased away from the tower you're in."

"But we've blocked the door and the elevator so they can't get down here."

"But what if your friends end up in the elevator in this room, unblock it, and go up? The second those doors open on the top floor, they're screwed. Or what if they bust open the door at the top of the stairwell? If you won't start this war with the guards, you need to at least give them a chance to escape."

"And you're sure they're doing okay beneath us?" The crimson-lit stairwell was quiet. Not even the scuff of guards' steps.

"Yep."

Not a single strand out of place in her immaculate plait, Gracie squeezed past Matilda and leaned closer to Olga. "What? What is it?"

"William and the others are beneath us still, locked in a stalemate with the guards. They're doing all right for now." She pointed at the scarlet glow. "Duncan said the stairs are packed." She led the others to the walkway back to the block they'd just left. "The best thing we can do is get the diseased above back over to the block we were in. Get them into the mirrored ballroom so they're out of the way. Help William

134

and the others remotely by removing that threat should they need to escape."

"But we've blocked the door and elevator."

"They could bust down the door. Or make it up here and free the elevator."

Gracie scowled. Anything to do with Duncan left her sour.

"Unless anyone has a better plan?"

Artan shook his head. "Nope." He stepped out onto the walkway, the day getting darker as they moved towards evening. He leaned on the railing and peered at the bridge below. "Why's that door barricaded down there?"

"Duncan?" Olga said.

"Huh?"

"The door at the end of the walkway below us is barricaded shut. In the block we're heading for."

"So?"

"What do you mean, so?"

Gracie tutted again. "Fucking idiot. Fool needs some sense beating into him."

"There are plenty of barricaded doors in these blocks, Olga. The place has gone to shit. People are scared."

"Okay."

Artan perked up. Only privy to one side of the conversation, he raised his eyebrows. "Well, in the absence of any other plan, let's bait some diseased."

Matilda took the lead, running along the elevated walkway.

The fresh and strong breeze stung Olga's tired eyes.

Matilda led them through the dusty sports hall, the worn wooden floor and faded lines marking courts for games Olga didn't know and didn't care to know. Probably gentle non-contact nonsense where everyone got a prize and they all celebrated afterwards with a rich meal and fine wine.

Into the crimson-lit stairwell, they headed up the stairs two at a time.

Kicking the door open so hard it cracked against the wall on the other side, Matilda ran out into the ballroom with the mirrored floor, the glare as dazzling now as ever. When you wanted the attention of a hundred or more of the fuckers, there was no time for stealth.

The walkway to the second block was clear. The meeting room on the other side filled with diseased. The most interesting thing to happen in that room for decades.

Matilda reached the doorway, and Olga held back with the others. It only takes one to bait a room filled with diseased.

Stood with her feet shoulder-width apart, Matilda fired at the creatures. A burst of three shots. They met her aggression with their own. A wail, no matter how familiar, still turned Olga's blood cold.

The creatures shoved one another in their desperation to get onto the walkway.

"I'd say that's done it." Olga led their retreat. Back through the mirrored ballroom. Back past the bathroom where they'd found the kids Duncan had killed. Past the elevator, probably still inactive because of the tool trolly jamming the door in the basement. Duncan at the end of the hallway in the control room, but they ducked into the stairwell. The poor light compared to the bright ballroom demanded her full concentration so she didn't slip and break an ankle.

Matilda, the last one in, pulled the door shut behind her and wedged her knife in the handle.

Crack! Crack! Crack!

The diseased tugged against the other side, the small blade holding for now. It made Duncan's logic about their friends forcing the door open in the other block far less logical.

"It's done?"

Olga jumped. The first thing Duncan had said in a while. "Yeah, it's done."

"Good work. You've just given your pals the best possible chance at survival. You should be proud."

CHAPTER 27

Hawk kept his voice low and gestured towards the stairwell. "Well, I guess that's our only way out." The one in this block glowed with the same ominous gloom as the stairwells in the others. Hardly inviting, but compared to facing the guards and their shields, or running across the walkway to the block in the other direction, shooting practice for the guards, what other choice did they have?

Aggie's cheek bulged from where she pressed her tongue against the inside like it helped her think. "It looks that way." She pointed up and then down. "So, which direction?"

Using a blade, Knives let the sharp tip hang down. "If we go lower and get trapped, we're fucked. We have no escape. At least high up, we have the elevated walkways to get us into a different block."

Hawk nodded along with the others.

"What do you want to do, Ash?" Aggie said.

Stepping back like the question had given her a hard shove, Ash scowled. "Whatever the group decides. I'll do whatever's required of me."

"I know, I just wa—"

"Whatever's required of me, Aggie."

Aggie pursed her lips, breathed through her nose, paused for a few seconds, and then led the way, Ethan shoving past Hawk so he walked a step behind her.

The silence from Ash's retort remained with them as they climbed the steel stairs. A red highlight from the bulb on the wall between floors glinted off the very edges of each step, the horizontal crimson bars guiding their ascent.

At the middle floor of the top three, Aggie paused. She pressed her finger to her lips, weaving from left to right, meeting the eye of every one of them in turn. She then pointed up and cupped her ear, pushing back her curly hair. Hushed conversation. More guards. Banging and snarls. More diseased.

Knives snuck past her, blades drawn, and climbed the next flight to the plateau between floors. Any farther and she'd reveal herself to the guards. She made a cutting motion with her hand across her throat.

Aggie led them again, into the large sports hall with a wooden floor. Hawk scrunched up his nose from the dust in the air. This room clearly hadn't seen much use in a long time, the faded lines marking out areas in which they'd played sports now long forgotten.

Two doors led to the two elevated walkways out of there. One back to the block they'd just left, with the guards in, and one to a block they were yet to visit.

Outside, afternoon gave way to evening. The air had turned slightly gritty with the grey of encroaching night, the transition almost tangible. The choice seemed clear.

"I say we go back." Ethan pointed at the block they'd just left.

"What?" Hawk clapped his hand to his mouth. A bit too loud.

Knives faced the stairwell, blades ready in case the guards heard them.

Hawk raised his hand at the others and mouthed, *Sorry.*

The large room threatened to amplify Ethan's whispers, but he kept his voice just low enough. "That block is the last place they'll expect us to be."

A sadistic grin split Rayne's withdrawn face. "And we might get the jump on them. Attack them from behind in the stairwell. End the threat." Her smile broadened.

"Exactly." The same wildness that had possessed Ethan in the dining room remained. The wildness that had sent him charging down to William. His eyes shimmered with the kind of mania that birthed many poor decisions.

Knives leaned towards the group. "I agree." She turned back to the stairwell door.

"Me too." Ash's tanned skin had turned several shades paler from where she'd been sick earlier.

Aggie raised an eyebrow at Hawk, William, and then Rowan. Did they have anything to say? Hawk had already said too much, and the others kept their thoughts to themselves. "Okay. That's what we'll do, then. Ethan"—she swept her arm in the walkway's direction—"will you do the honours?"

Ethan took off like Aggie's words were a starter's gun. Rayne a step behind him, Ash next. Knives followed Ash, Rowan behind her. William, then Hawk, and finally Aggie took up the rear.

Hawk shivered, the lower temperature hitting his adrenaline-filled body. The sun had set, but only just, a small amount of light still holding out against night's inevitability. The Earth's rotation one of the very few constants left in this mad world.

Impossible to move both quickly and in silence, they

opted for speed. Hopefully the wind would disperse their steps before they found the ears of the guards in either block.

Ethan slowed to a walk and entered the middle room. The cinema room.

They'd been in this room before, but someone had at least passed through here since their last visit. A chair blocked the elevator door to prevent it from closing. More had been stacked in the doorway leading across to the next block. Knitted together to form an impromptu fence. No chance they could pull it down without raising a din. It looked clear in the neighbouring tower, but they'd blocked it for a reason.

Holding up his right index finger, Ethan lifted his ear. Footsteps in the stairwell. Coming up to meet them. The guards from the floor below.

Aggie said it best when she mouthed the word, *Fuck!* So much for catching the guards unaware. She led them back the way they'd come at a sprint. The wind might have buried their steps, but it wouldn't hide them from sight if the guards emerged from the stairwell.

At the other block, Aggie slowed before entering the sports hall. She cupped her ear. The guards were coming from the other way. Down the stairs towards them.

Back out onto the walkway. The cold wind cut into them. The walkway for the floor below about ten feet beneath them and down to their left. Diseased filled the blinking plaza. Their fallen guide from earlier lay lifeless and broken amongst the madness.

William turned one way and the other. Guards in both blocks. "So this is how it ends."

CHAPTER 28

Dragging her feet, her head down, Joni entered the control room last, the guards parting, making way for the diminished kill team. The automatic door closed behind her, followed by Antonia scrabbling above, securing it from the top with the definitive *click* that must have been missing somewhere for this shit show to have happened.

If the room grew any quieter, Joni would probably be able to hear her own organs functioning. She kept her head bowed until a woman stepped directly into her path.

Round-faced and ruddy-cheeked, she had sharp eyes and mousy-brown hair. A smile played with her lips, like she got off on the chaos. "Proud of yourself, are ya?"

"Wha …" Joni blinked back her tears. Her eyes burned. Dust. Exhaustion. Grief.

"I said—"

Antonia slid from the hatch and stepped up to the woman, shoving her. "What's your problem, Sarah?"

Sarah's thin lips drew back. She pointed at Joni. "Her. She's my problem. She killed Malcolm." She flashed Joni a facetious smile. "That's his name, by the way. Although I'm sure you don't care."

"Of course I care." Joni grew hotter. Her pulse raced. The room's attention made her skin itch. She could get into the shaft. The only way out of there. The only place she felt comfortable.

"Hang on!" Antonia tugged Sarah's shoulder, spinning her around so she faced her. "What did you expect her to do?"

"Don't think I fear you anymore, *princess*. I've held my tongue for too long, but now Daddy's gone, you'd best believe I'll speak my mind." Some of the other guards nodded along with her. They'd all held their tongues too long.

"While I'm pleased you feel liberated about being able to embrace how much of a poisonous arsehole you are, Sarah, and by the way …" Antonia cupped her mouth in a mock whisper. "You never held your vicious tongue, as much as you might think you showed restraint. How about you stay on track here rather than airing all your resentments? Unless this is about you instead of Malcolm?"

"It's about Malcolm."

"Then what do you think Mum could have done to help him?"

"Do I really need to answer that?"

Antonia folded her arms across her chest.

"She could have given him time. Made sure he was going to turn before she killed him."

Theresa's whip-crack of a tut commanded the room's attention. "He was haemorrhaging through his fucking eyes. A second longer and he would have infected the lot of us."

Swelling with the venom of her reply, her cheeks redder than before, Sarah's eyes narrowed. She opened and closed her mouth, but she had no words. She drew breath again, and for a second time, her reply abandoned her.

Antonia shook her head at the woman and turned to

Theresa. "What happened anyway? Why were you having to fight so many diseased?"

Sarah retreated into the crowd.

"Dunno." Theresa shrugged. "They came from nowhere."

The guards surrounded them. No choice with so many bodies in the tight space. They watched Joni, Antonia, and Theresa. But Pearl, the shaft-rat, didn't stand among them. Joni took two steps to the right, giving her a line of sight to the observation room. The slight girl sat beside Matt in the hard plastic chair at the bank of screens. She needed that moment away. The truth would come out soon enough. "I think we all need to rest for now. Take a moment. Let our emotions settle and then work out what to do next."

The crowd parted for her. She found a space against the wall beside the green console, the one that controlled the prison's main gates. Antonia and Ralph joined her, and the rest of the guards dispersed.

Aunty Mary came over with three steaming bowls of stew. She handed one to Joni, one to Ralph, and, finally, one to Antonia. She kept hold of it for a second. "You okay?"

Grief disturbed Antonia's features like a slight breeze on a still lake. She pressed her lips tight and took the food.

Joni's first mouthful caught in her throat. She couldn't change the relationship Antonia had with this woman. A bond that, were they alone in that moment, would have seen Antonia talk about what had happened with the sacrifice. The person she most needed when the chips were down. Her protector. Whether through blood or not, her mum.

But at least she had someone to fulfil that role. God knows Louis didn't. She'd needed it growing up. Swallowing harder than before, her throat sore, Joni nodded at the bowl in Antonia's hands. "You should eat."

"I'm not very hungry." Her eyes watered. "Aunty Carly looked after me for about six months too."

"That was her name? The woman down in th—"

"Yeah. She was kind."

Ralph sighed into his stew, steam kicking up from his exhale. "She was a good woman."

Antonia smiled. "She always put me first. Allowed me to be a child. She even taught me to sew."

"Wow. You'll have to teach me some time."

Antonia scratched her face with a shaking hand. "Lying there. Watching what we saw and not doing anything about it …" She looked up at the ceiling and blinked away her tears, her voice weak. "It was one of the hardest things I've ever had to do." She rubbed her eyes, laid her bowl on the floor in front of her, and stood up. "I'm going back into the shafts to see if I can work out what happened and make sure it's safe up there."

"Joni can come with you?"

Only subtle, but Antonia threw a glance at Ralph. "No. I'd rather be on my own. *Joni* needs to rest."

CHAPTER 29

"You trying to eat the porcelain too?"

Joni scraped up the last of her stew and put the entire spoon in her mouth. "Huh?"

Ralph had a twinkle in his eye. "I think you might have finished."

"Yeah." She scratched her head and put the bowl on the floor. "Sorry."

"You wanna talk about it?"

Before she could reply, Antonia slipped from the open hatch and landed back in the control room. Red blotches covered her face, and she wiped her nose with the back of her sleeve. There had been plenty of times when Joni had done the same, crawling through the steel tunnels, seeing Louis or the way he treated yet another woman held against her will. Although Antonia didn't have to deal with the cowardice of having not acted. Much braver than her mum, she wouldn't have skulked back to a hole in the ground.

Pearl stepped from the observation room. She wrung her hands, and her gaze flitted from Antonia to Joni and back.

"I found it, just beyond the medical bay." Many in the

room were already watching Antonia. "There were two doors leading from the corridor on the other side, and one of them wasn't properly locked. That must have been how they got in."

Clapping a hand to her mouth, Pearl's eyes widened. She shook her head.

"It's all shut down now, and it looks like this floor is relatively clear because of what happened. We've dealt with most of the diseased. Not the most ideal way to approach it, but effective all the same."

"Unless you were Malcolm …"

"Fuck off, Sarah."

Ralph crossed the room to Pearl, but she showed him a halting hand and shook her head. Not here. Not now. She'd fucked up. She needed to own it.

"Theresa?"

The stocky woman flicked her head up at Antonia.

"Are your kill team ready to clear out the rest of this floor? I can deal with the doors from above."

"Yeah." Theresa got to her feet and brushed herself down, breadcrumbs falling to the floor.

"I can go with you?" Pearl had turned puce, and she shook where she stood. "I'll take Malcolm's place. It's the least I can do. I know it's nowhere near enough."

"You can say that again."

Antonia grabbed her knife at her hip and glared at Sarah.

Pearl said, "I just want to help."

Theresa shared a glance with Barry and the others who'd gone with them last time. Barry dipped a single nod. "Fine. Get a gun."

Antonia stood on the chair beneath the open shaft and climbed back in while the kill team mobilised. They lined up before the door and waited for the *click* from above. Pearl stood at the front and whacked the button, leading them in.

147

The door closed behind them, and Antonia secured it with another click before she slid away.

"So that's how it works around here, is it? You kill a man and you get a promotion?"

"Sarah, is it?"

The ruddy-cheeked woman sneered at Joni. "You know it is."

"Well, *Sarah*, I have a suggestion for you."

"I'm sure you do."

"Maybe you should focus on yourself rather than everyone else. Maybe think about how *you* can help the group rather than divide them. How's that sound?"

"What would you know? You're just a nutty old woman who's survived well beyond her use."

Ralph didn't lose his patience often, but when he did, people listened. His deep tone filled the room like a lion's growl. "That's enough, Sarah."

Sarah looked like she might argue, but even she thought better of it.

"Joni's done more for this group since joining them than you have the entire time you've been here. You're always at the centre of the drama. And often, you're the instigator. You think people don't see who you are? Life would be a lot fucking easier if you weren't here. Now wind your fucking neck in and show this woman some respect. She's more of an asset than you could even dream of being."

The lines on either side of Sarah's nose deepened with her sneer. Her piercing little eyes narrowed, but she held her tongue. What would she say when Joni told them all she'd been lying? That Ralph had been wrong to back her. Ralph, Theresa, and Antonia.

"Hello?" Matt talked to someone in the observation room. "Hello? Who's that?"

Joni ran in. She'd told Olga not to talk to him. She

removed her earpiece, laid it on Matt's desk, and ripped the headphones from his head.

"Ow!" He held his ears. "You could just ask for them, you know?"

"Olga!" Joni pulled the mic closer to her mouth. "I told you to only talk to me!"

"What?" A man's voice.

"Who are you?"

"Duncan. And you're Joni, right?"

"Duncan? What? They didn't mention you. Who the fuck are you, and what the fuck do you want?"

"I was bored and wanted to talk to someone. Thought we could be radio buddies."

"Are you simple or something? Every call is a chance for someone to intercept it. Where are Olga and the others?"

"They're clearing out the tower block. It's a mess here. I'm worried they won't survive."

"What do you want us to do about it?"

"I'd not really thought it through."

"I don't suppose you had."

"I'll go, then, shall I?"

"You do that."

As Joni handed Matt back his headphones, Ralph came over. "Everything okay? Are Olga and the others all right?"

Matt leaned closer to Joni. "I'd like to know too!"

"I've just had to kill one of your mates. I've been shot at. Hunted. Watched Andy do what he just did, and have nearly been infected by the diseased. This isn't about you and what you need to know, Matt."

The man had every right to ask questions. Why shouldn't he? But, fortunately, it shut him up. For now.

Ralph took Joni's hand and led her away. "Come with me."

A man of Ralph's stature cleared a path wherever he went. Especially after his outburst. He led Joni through the control

149

MICHAEL ROBERTSON

room. The guards focused on them, but none more so than Sarah. The kind of person who watched from the shadows and took notes. Armed herself with the ammunition to take someone down whenever she felt the need. A snide little shit. Someone to keep at arm's length. If only she'd joined the cult with the rest of the arseholes. Although, what Sarah had done so far had nothing on the lie Joni had been selling to these people. Their loved ones were dead. They had no reason to risk their lives in this fight.

The comms room a redundant space. They'd moved the radio equipment to the observation room. It had several broken chairs and spare equipment stacked on dusty shelves. A glorified storeroom. When the automatic door closed behind them, Ralph turned his palms towards the ceiling. "What the hell, Joni?"

"Huh?"

"What's going on? Matt asked a reasonable question, and you bit his head off."

"Joni didn't. Joni's just trying to do what's right for everyone."

Ralph's features softened. He took one of her hands in his. "Talk to me. Whatever it is, you can't carry this on your own."

"The south's fallen."

"Fallen?"

"It's as bad as the prison. Filled with diseased. Olga told me. They followed them out. They couldn't close the gates behind them. They didn't think they needed to. They didn't know Louis had set the diseased loose. The—"

"Shh." Ralph gripped Joni by the tops of her arms and glanced at the door. He squeezed, the pressure helping ground her. "Slow down. And lower your voice."

"The south's fucked, Ralph. And they're blaming Olga and the others."

"Who are?"

"The people in the south. Joni was … *I* was going to get the footage from my old home and send it down to them so they could prove this is all Louis' fault."

"But why have you kept it a secret?"

"What would those lot out there say? And what about you? You and Warren?"

"I don't want to see Warren. Not after how he left. But it's not about me and Warren. Why keep it a secret from the others?

"Half of them are fighting based on the prospect of seeing their loved ones in the south. This battle is going to be hard enough as it is. What will happen if we take away their hope? Hell, before they saw the sacrifice and what Andy did, half of them wanted to join them. If they know the truth about the south, how many of us will be left to take down the cult? We need to end those nutters, Ralph. Before anything else, we need to stop what they're trying to do." Her breaths ran away from her, and she gasped as she spoke. "And then there's Antonia. And Theresa. And you. You're all defending me. Telling the others I'm here to save them. But Joni's a liar. A cheat and a liar. She's a rat. Someone who can't be trusted. Rusted. Dusted."

Ralph pulled her in for a hug and squeezed her so hard it restricted her breathing. "Oh, Joni. We're in a right fucking pickle, aren't we? But I agree with you. We shouldn't tell them."

Laying her head against his chest, Joni melted into his embrace. She'd not been hugged like this in a long time. "You think?"

"I know all about secrets and holding onto them. I spent the first eighteen years of my life living a lie. When it serves no one to speak the truth, you're better keeping it to yourself."

"But it would have served you."

"Me, but not Warren. I wanted to be with him, and he wanted to keep us a secret. Sometimes you have to make a choice for the greater good."

"You think I've done that?"

"I do. At least until we have the cult out of the way."

"Thank you, Ralph." She leaned into him. "Thank you."

CHAPTER 30

W *hoosh!*
Joni pulled from Ralph's embrace and turned on the door. "What? What is it?"

Theresa's usually stern features softened. "I'm so sorry, Joni."

"What?" Joni turned to Ralph and back again. "What's happened?"

"They've got her, Joni."

"Who?"

"Antonia."

"Who's got her?"

"The cult."

"What?" Joni stepped forwards, her hands balled into fists. "How?"

"We were clearing out a room, and we heard voices above."

"And you did nothing?"

Ralph pulled Joni back.

"By the time we'd reacted, Antonia had already fallen."

"Fallen?"

"We were close to the elevators. Someone must have snuck up on her and dragged her down one of the vertical shafts to the lower floors."

Joni barged past Theresa and ran for the observation room. On her way past, she lifted a gun and her backpack filled with ammo from the pile of weapons. Shouldering her bag, she hooked the gun across her front. "Where is she?"

His elbows on the desk, Matt leaned close to the screens, moving his head as he scanned from one to the next. "I don't know."

Twenty-eight bullets in her gun, Joni ejected the magazine, discarded it on the steel floor, and loaded another. "Then what fucking use are you? The rest of the guards see you as a pariah. We've been trying to look after you, but the one job we give you, you can't fucking do. I thought you could see the entire block?"

"So did I."

Slapping the magazine back into her gun with a *clack,* Joni angled it for a better view of the top. One hundred and ninety-eight bullets. "But you can't?"

Ralph ran into the room behind them.

"I think they've shut down some cameras."

"You can't open them up?"

"I can't get into a part of the system."

Joni shoved Matt aside, propelling him away in his wheeled chair. She'd had her hacking device on her the entire time. She plugged it into control console's jack, the lights turning from red to green.

"What's that?" Matt wheeled himself back over.

"It should give you access to their system. Has it worked?"

Matt divided his attention between his keyboard and the screens. His fingers danced over the keys. The images rotated much quicker than before. Like the screens were trying to keep up as more and more cameras came online. Every four seconds, the images changed. Then every three seconds. All the while, Matt continued typing. Every two seconds.

"How many cameras are there?"

"I had no idea there were this many."

"How many?"

He said it with a sigh. "Hundreds. It might take a while for me to track her down."

"What if she's somewhere there aren't any cameras?"

"That's possible."

"Like Louis' quarters?"

"Maybe. But I wouldn't like to guess."

"I'm going there."

"You don't want to wait to be sure?"

"I need to do something, Matt. They have my daughter. I'll head to his quarters. If you get something in the meantime"—she grabbed the earpiece she'd left on the desk earlier and plugged it back in—"let me know. The others don't think they can trust you. I hope they're wrong." And there she goes again. Like she had the right to lecture anyone about trust.

Ralph moved aside, and the guards in the control room cleared a path to the chair beneath the open hatch. All of them save for Mary. "What's happening?"

"She's gone, Mary. The cult has her."

"You think she'll be okay?"

"I don't know, but standing here talking won't help."

"I'm sorry. I'm worried about her."

"And you think I'm not? In case you've forgotten, she's *my* daughter."

Mary bowed her head and pulled aside.

Joni threw her gun around so it lay against her backpack and dived up into the shaft. She took off towards the elevator and the vertical shaft leading to the lower floors.

Thuds and pops behind her. Joni turned around. "What are you doing, Ralph?"

"Coming with you."

"You won't keep up."

"You worry about you, yeah?"

"I won't slow down and wait for you if I get a sniff of Antonia."

"Nor I you."

JONI REACHED the shaft by the elevator. Although a twenty-foot drop, thankfully it didn't go all the way to the ground floor. But the bottom had been smashed out from where someone must have broken it with their fall.

"What's happening, Joni?"

Maybe more of a hindrance, but she needed him in her ear in case he found something. The useless prick might surprise her. "I think we've found the spot where Antonia fell." Pressing her hands to either side of the cold steel shaft, she hung her legs down and slid, the toes of her boots playing the welded ridges that held the shaft together.

Joni pressed hard to slow her descent, the friction burning her palms. She halted above the hole just as footsteps descended on her location. She dragged her gun around, aiming the laser target at the floor while staring down the barrel. A diseased appeared beneath her. Mouth wide and bloody. Eyes glistening with the crimson grief of the freshly turned. Yet to atrophy, the virile beast stared up at her, its mouth working like it could taste its first bite. But she lifted her finger from the trigger. Little point in wasting ammo.

Thud! Thud! Thud! Thud!

"What's that?" Matt said.

Ralph filled the shaft and slid towards her, barrelling out of control.

"Shit!"

Joni dropped, shooting as she landed. She rolled aside as Ralph hit the floor like a ton of damp clay and groaned.

"Joni! What's going on down there?"

"Just focus on finding Antonia." They were in a long hallway. Diseased descended on them from both ends. Joni turned one way and the other whilst firing. Keeping them at bay. For now. "Get back in the shaft, Ralph. Hurry!"

The big man scrambled to his feet and stared up, the shaft just out of reach.

Joni took down three more creatures at one end. They all fell as they ran. She dropped and patted her knee.

Ralph stood with his hands on his hips. "I can't stand on you."

"You think I'll do a better job pulling you in from up there?"

Two more diseased appeared. She shot one. Ralph the other.

"We've really not got time to discuss this. Get up there, now."

"I've picked you up on the cameras."

"Don't worry about us, Matt. Find Antonia."

Joni grimaced and clenched her teeth against the big man's weight. He stepped on the top of her knee. If he stayed there too long, the pressure would turn her shin to dust. He scrambled back into the shaft, and she stood again, her right leg dead. She took down the creatures closest to her, more coming from either end.

Two large hands hung down into the hallway.

"Joni, look r—"

A door opened on Joni's right.

Three diseased just feet away.

She jumped, and Ralph pulled her in. A diseased grabbed her boot, but she kicked it away. Thankfully, an entire panel had fallen from the shaft; otherwise the torn steel might have ripped her to shreds.

His hot breath on her face, what skin he had on show that didn't have a covering of hair glowed red and glossy with his sweat. "Sorry. I fucked up."

"We're doing all right. Now let me pass, and I'll take us to Louis' quarters."

SEVERAL PEOPLE HAD TOLD Joni they'd heard her coming when she moved through the shafts. Probably not her, but the people she brought with her. She slowed down, forcing Ralph to do the same. She couldn't make him any more agile, but she could make him take his time.

They crossed over the hatch in the hallway outside Louis' quarters. Not as many diseased as before, but they still shambled and stumbled, bashing into one another, waiting for something to chase. It could have been one of many guards, especially with it being a few hours since they'd been here, but one of the diseased wore a guard's uniform and carried a gun. It had to be one of the two they'd murdered earlier.

She passed over the locked door to Louis' quarters. There were people in the room below. They spoke in low voices, but their whispers carried. They must be using the tunnels more frequently. Using Joni's methods to get around this place. And from what had happened to Antonia, attack. Pressing a finger to her lips, she showed Ralph a halting hand and pointed at the screw. "I need you to be ready to turn this."

"How will I know?"

"I'll give you a signal."

"Okay."

Joni slithered on her front. The whispering voices continued, locked in their own conversation. The hatch hung open.

"What's happening?"

Reply to Matt now and she'd blow her cover. Joni inched towards the hatch and slowly peered—

Hands reached up, grabbed the back of her shirt, and pulled her into the room. Her legs flung over her, cracking against the other side of the hatch before she fell and landed on her back, the ammo bag like landing on a mound of rubble.

Winded from the fall and with three armed guards looming over her, she gasped for breath. "Where the fuck is she?"

One guard prodded her cheek with the barrel of his weapon. "You think you get to ask the questions?"

"Antonia. What have you done with her?"

Another guard untied a rope from around her waist. "I don't know what you're talking about. But I know Andy will be pleased to see you."

"What have you done to her, you fucking lunatics?"

The first guard gesticulated with his gun. "Stand up."

"Fuck you!"

"Stand." He jabbed her in the cheek again. "Up!"

She did as instructed. The third guard, the one yet to speak, unzipped Joni's bag and pulled out a magazine. She grinned. "Not only will we be handing him Joni, but we've also scored a decent boost to our supplies."

Matt came through to her. "She's in the warehouse."

"What?"

All three guards frowned at Joni.

"The warehouse, Joni. That's where they've taken her."

"Ralph! Now!"

Click!

Whoosh!

The door opened.

Joni kicked the guard with the ropes, knocking her on her arse. She shoved the one who'd taken her magazine and smashed the other one in the nose with the butt of her gun.

Two large hands hung down into the shaft. A safe and strong grip.

Joni jumped and caught them.

Ralph dragged her into the shaft as chaos flooded the room.

Nose to nose with the big man, she nodded. "Thank you. And thank you for coming with me. You too, Matt. Antonia's in the warehouse."

Ralph moved aside. "Then lead the way."

CHAPTER 31

The diseased beat against the other side of the door, Gracie gurning at them through the long vertical window to hold their interest. Matilda's knife kept the door locked. Olga adjusted how she sat. Her right leg buzzed with pins and needles from how long they'd all been on the cold steel stairs. She pressed against her earpiece. "So what now?"

"Stay there and keep the diseased distracted."

"We've been doing that for days."

"Twenty minutes, Olga."

"Feels like days."

"Right now, your friends are in control. They're ready to spring the guards. If you get involved, you might blow their cover. You don't want to blow their cover, do you? I mean, I can lead you across to the next block if that's what you want? They're your friends not mine."

"For someone who was sulking a minute ago, you sure are a Chatty Cathy."

"Bygones."

"Huh?"

"I don't want to hold a grudge."

"That surprises me."

"I'm not Gracie, you know?"

"So how are things going with that grudge you don't want to hold?"

Duncan's huff distorted from where he blew across the microphone.

The lowest on the stairs, closest to the sports hall on the next floor, Olga tapped Matilda's foot and hooked a thumb behind her. "I'm going to check down there to make sure it's safe."

"Okay. I'll come."

"You don't need to do that. I've already said you're risking your friends."

"But you said they're in the other block. We'll stay in the sports hall. And the others will keep the diseased distracted."

"I've got it covered; you need to listen to me."

"Forgive me, Duncan, but we thought you had it covered when we were in the meeting room. The next thing we knew, we were faced with a diseased army."

"Are you saying you don't trust me?"

"I'm saying I want to see what's going on in the sports hall. Anything to break up the monotony of sitting on these damn stairs." Olga descended the stairs, Matilda behind her, the gentle tock of their steps calling down into the murky depths.

"I'm offended."

In her mind's eye, the whiny man currently stood in the middle of the control room, his arms folded across his chest and his bottom lip turned down like someone should give a fuck about his feelings. But they did still need his help. "Look, I'm sorry you're offended, but I still don't understand why it's a problem for us to go to the sports hall."

"I just think you need to show you trust me. Put some

more faith in what I'm telling you. Or maybe I should give up? Leave you on your own to work it out."

Olga halted on the plateau between floors. The light from the sports hall hit the bottom few steps.

"Yeah"—he grew giddy like he'd surprised himself with his own idea. Invigorated by the power he held over them— "that's what I'll do. The second I see you in that sports hall, I'll know you've stopped trusting me." His whine grew so high in pitch it jabbed into her ear. "And what's the point then? I might as well give up."

"A bit petulant, don't you think?"

"I need to know you trust me. If you're going to ignore my advice, then what's the point?"

"Need to feel important, do you?"

"Just valued. And after Gracie's hatred, I'm feeling light years away from that."

She could go lower on the stairs and peek out without him seeing. Just to be sure. "They're safe?"

"And in control. You interfere and you might force them into a fight too early. Do you want to be the reason your friends die?"

She should have done more to help Max.

"I need you ready, Olga. Wait on the stairs, keep out of the way, and I'll tell you when you need to help them, because, eventually, they'll need you to keep them alive. Now, the question is, do you trust me?"

A small flight of stairs away from getting an answer. An answer that could deprive them of any more. That could be the undoing of their friends. The next time she saw him, she'd kick his arse for being such a baby. But they needed him more than he needed them right now. They needed to know what was going on in the rest of the block. And they couldn't lose anyone else they loved. They'd lost too many already. Olga tutted and pointed back up the stairs.

Matilda mouthed, *Really?*

She rolled her eyes and mouthed back, *Really.*

Although Matilda paused like she might resist, she turned around and headed back up the stairs while shaking her head. Duncan had said they were clear. Their friends were safe. And beyond that, nothing else mattered.

CHAPTER 32

"They're leaving."

Joni paused. "What do you mean, they're leaving?" She quickened her pace, clattering through the tunnels, no doubt disturbing the diseased below. And hopefully only the diseased. What's the worst they could do? Stare up at her and sway like drunkards. "Where are they taking her?"

"She's not with them."

"Matt, for once in your fucking life, please get to the fucking point." Rounding the next bend, Joni kicked off the side of the shaft, propelling herself forward, Ralph on her heels.

"The guards who took Antonia into the warehouse are leaving, but Antonia's not with them."

"And you can't see into the warehouse?"

"I ca—oh!"

"What?"

Joni spun around as she slid backwards, sliding down to the next floor. She landed with a crash. The ground floor. They were close to the warehouse, the air fresher because of their proximity to a grate leading outside.

"They're projecting footage through the prison. Of Antonia. She's tied. She's not moving."

"Not moving, dead?"

"I don't know. But if she was already dead, why would they tie her up?"

Light shone up through the next grate from the projection below. Joni paused and pressed her cheek to the cold steel to get a better angle. Her daughter. Hogtied. On the warehouse floor. Unconscious. "What are they doing to her?"

Ralph tapped her feet. "I'd say whatever it is, the sooner we get there, the better."

Joni rounded the next bend, the grate leading outside up ahead. Propelling herself forwards with her feet, she reached out in front of her and boosted into the steel grille. It bust from the shaft like a cap from a bottle and fell clattering to the ground outside. About four hundred feet of open concrete bathed in silver moonlight between her and the warehouse's entrance. Clear both ways. No guards and no diseased. "How's she doing in there, Matt?"

"Nothing's changed."

Joni slid from the hatch, landing outside with a quiet *clop!* The still evening stood in stark contrast to her rapid pulse. Diseased calls whispered to her from around the front of the block. She aimed her gun in their direction, but they were too far away.

"At least we know where Andy is."

"He didn't leave with the others?" Joni stepped aside to give Ralph space to exit.

"I didn't see him. And someone has to be projecting this footage through the block."

"You don't think he's sending it to the south?"

"Any broadcasts going south have to go through me."

Ralph landed in his usual way. *Thunk!*

His round face a bristly mess. A thick beard and shaggy hair. He glanced past Joni. "Run! Now!"

"Wha—"

A garage door had fallen open behind her. About twenty feet away. Diseased spilled out, clumsy with their charge.

Joni led them across the open concrete. The diseased gave chase. She reached the closest warehouse entrance first, Ralph now about one hundred feet behind, the mob gaining on him. Peering down the barrel of her gun, she laid her red target on the closest diseased and pulled the trigger.

Red mist. Clumsy steps. Downed diseased.

Dropping three more, she stepped aside to give Ralph access to the warehouse, dropped six more creatures, and ducked in after him.

"Antonia!" Her voice amplified by the vast space, Joni ran to her daughter, who lay on the floor, alone in the cavernous warehouse.

She crouched at her side and freed her flaccid form from her bonds while Ralph kept his gun raised.

The first diseased, once a prisoner, ran in, stumbled, and fell before Ralph shot it. They landed face first, spluttered, twitched, and expired.

Matt gasped. "The implants! They can't get in there."

Three more diseased ran in, and the trio dropped like the first.

Ralph lowered his gun. The diseased were drawn to the door like flies to an electric zapper. Buzz! One fell. Buzz! Another dropped. Buzz! He helped free Antonia's ankles while Joni worked on her top half, her daughter only moving from where they manipulated her to make their task easier.

"Joni! Look out!"

A diseased continued running after bursting through the door. Unlike the others, its screams grew louder and its legs stayed strong. In one fluid movement she stood up and blew its brains out, dropping it as it ran. Unlike the others, it wore a guard's uniform. "They don't have the implant, do they?"

"No," Matt said.

Andy's sickly-sweet tones came at them from multiple speakers. "Well, that was close." An image of his pallid face burst to life on one wall. The projection ten feet tall by twenty feet wide. It revealed every clogged pore on his dirty skin.

Joni pressed her finger to her earbud. "Are you hearing this?"

"Yep."

The twisted hymn he'd forced on those in Louis' quarters played in the background. "Now, it looks like our heroes have worked out that while every diseased is vile, furious, and fast, not all are equal." He winked at the camera and swiped his long hair back. Grease held it in place. "In infection, as in life, some are lucky, and some aren't. The guards can enter the warehouse because they don't have implants."

"Unless Louis wanted to prevent them from heading south!" Joni shot another guard as Ralph helped Antonia sit.

Groaning, Antonia rubbed her head and squinted like the warehouse's poor light stung her eyes.

"Now, how many guards will enter the warehouse? Will we run out of diseased before nutty Joni and her two muske-teers run out of ammo? It's almost too exciting. Stay tuned, ladies and gents." His image vanished.

A scream came at them from the other side of the ware-house. Another guard had burst in through another entrance and descended on them. The darkness aided Joni's targeting. She laid her red dot on the beast's face, squeezed the trigger, and dropped it like she had the others. "How's she doing, Ralph?"

"She's okay. A little battered, but give her a moment and we'll be able to get her out of here."

A first-floor walkway ran around the warehouse's perimeter. On it, a small cabin.

Joni slipped off her backpack and passed it to Ralph. She pulled her gun over her head and laid it on the ground beside the bag.

"What are you doing?"

"Andy's up there."

"How do you know?"

"Call it a hunch. This ends now."

"Without a gun?"

Joni tapped the knife at her hip. "Antonia will need it more than me. When she's able, I want you and her to get out of here and get back into the block, okay?"

"Even if you're in trouble?"

"Don't worry about me. Just make sure she's safe. You hear me?"

Ralph's lips tightened.

"I need you to promise me, Ralph."

"Okay, okay."

"Say it!"

"But are you okay?"

"What?"

"Are you all right? Should you be doing this? It's just … earlier, when you started referring to yourself as Joni."

"I'm fine."

"I'm worried about you."

"I'm *fine*, Ralph. Now say it! Tell me you'll look after my daughter. Allow me to do this without having to worry about her."

"Okay, I promise. When Antonia's able, I'll get her out of here."

"No matter what."

"No matter what."

"Good. See you back inside."

"Good luck, Joni."

She snorted. "I don't need luck."

CHAPTER 33

Aggie tutted. "That's not very helpful though, is it, William?"

Hawk positioned himself between the two. She'd disliked William since he'd shown up, and he couldn't blame her, even if he'd wanted to. His motives for leaving the others had been entirely selfish and utterly petulant.

Still turning from left to right, William shrugged. "We're not screwed?"

"It's just not very helpful." Hawk tried to keep his tone neutral. "Maybe you could come up with a solution?"

Next to them, Ash leaned over the walkway's barrier and stared down at the flashing crimson plaza. At the sea of diseased and the dead pregnant woman. From the way Knives stood beside her, she wanted to pull her back, but Ash had been explicit. She expected to be treated like everyone else, and while she couldn't prevent Knives from watching over her, she could reject more overt forms of protection.

William spoke slow and deliberate words. "So, *Hawk,* seeing as you want to get involved with my and Aggie's conversations, maybe *you* could offer a solution? Something really useful like your girlfriend wants? I dunno"—he rolled his eyes—"how about we learn to fucking fly or someth—"

"No!" Knives reached out to where Ash had been moments before, but she'd already jumped.

Hawk crashed into the barrier and leaned over just as Ash landed on the walkway below. She bent her knees with her landing, her hands thrust out to the sides to steady herself.

Rowan followed her, his arms windmilling. He landed with a *thud,* many diseased staring up.

Ethan, Rayne, and Knives went next.

William shook his head. "They're like fucking lemmings."

Aggie raised her eyebrows at Hawk. He shrugged. If she went, he'd follow her.

She jumped, and his heart broke for the second between her leap and landing.

He patted William on the back. "It's not quite fucking flying, but it's close." The others stared up at them.

"You're really going to do it?"

"Come on, man, we've done harder things than this." Despite his body's determination to betray him, adrenaline turning his legs to jelly, Hawk stood on one leg and put his foot on top of the railing. "See you down there." He rolled over the edge and boosted from the walkway.

A moment of weightless freefall. A moment of his stomach in his throat. Bollocks in his brain. A moment to realise he'd jumped too far. His momentum carried him towards the far side of the walkway and beyond, the hard solar-panelled plaza waiting to receive him like it had the pregnant woman.

But Hawk landed with both feet on the walkway's farthest railing, the jolt of his landing spearing beneath his kneecaps. He spun his arms, fighting to reverse his momentum.

Several pairs of hands caught his shirt and dragged him

back. He hit the walkway and fell on his arse, a stinging lightning bolt streaking up his spine to the base of his neck.

The steel bridge shook a second later with William's landing.

Aggie, Ethan, and Ash peered down at Hawk. He laughed. "Thank you."

Both Ash and Ethan set off. Aggie smiled and helped him stand. She held on longer than necessary. "Don't do that again. I refuse to lose you."

At some point, this would all be over and they'd have the time they needed together. And he loved her. He didn't regret saying it. Even if she never said it back.

She turned and ran.

Hawk set off after her.

The dining room free of guards. About twenty pop-up shields littered the floor like sails. Lit by the bright bulbs in the ceiling, they cast deep shadows. The others were using them as cover. Hawk slipped in behind one, next to Aggie. If the guards came down again, they wouldn't see them. Right now, they had the advantage. They'd tear into them before they knew what happened.

Aggie peered around the shield and pulled back a second later. She sat close. Close enough for her warm breath to hit his face. Close enough for him to drown in her deep brown eyes. Close enough to kiss.

"We're going to wait here for now rather than move on to another block."

Hawk pulled back a little. It helped him concentrate on her words.

"Crossing the walkways exposes us too much. And the stairs are a no go. We don't know where the guards are, but at least we know we're hidden here."

Hawk nodded and held her hands.

She kissed his cheek, turned, and ran to another shield.

His yearning pulled him after her. She moved from Ethan, to Knives, to Rowan and Ash, and finally to William and Rayne. They had time, so Rayne had taken another water jug from the table on the side and had torn a strip of fabric from her shirt to re-dress William's wounds. The white pillowcase had turned as crimson as the stairwell, and if she didn't change it soon, he might get an infection.

At that moment, they could only wait. Let the guards make the next move. Bide their time and be patient. At some point, there would be a future where they could rest. Where he an Aggie could finally be alone.

CHAPTER 34

The elevated control room—a cheap portable cabin made from thin steel—directly in front of her. The ladder leading to the walkway on the left. Diseased were many things, but they weren't adept climbers.

Joni flew up the cold steel ladder rungs and paused at the top at the crack of bullet fire.

Taking down two diseased guards who burst through the warehouse's closest entrance, Ralph waited a few seconds. He kept his aim on the doorway before returning to Antonia, helping her to her feet while he looped the spare gun over her head. There's no one Joni would have trusted more to take care of her daughter. He'd get them both away from there. She could focus on Andy.

The control room's door buckled from Joni's kick and crashed against the inside wall. It hung open like it would never close again.

Andy smiled before he gasped and clapped his hands to his mouth. He leaned close to the microphone, his voice coming at her from both him and the warehouse's speakers. "Oh my. You've got me." He sat on a comfy chair. Another one of Louis' thrones. A screen on the back wall showed him the warehouse, Antonia and Ralph heading for the exit.

"Are you taking the piss?" Joni turned so her earpiece remained hidden.

The man tittered and swiped his hair behind his ears. He laughed again. "Ever so sorry. Let me give it another try." He clapped his hands to his mouth for a second time. "Oh my! Fuck! You've got me. Oh no, what am I to do? Help! Help!" He cocked an eyebrow. "Better?"

Matt whispered in her ear, "What's wrong with him?"

Joni pointed at the vile cretin with her knife. More shots outside. Antonia and Ralph stalked across the dark warehouse, heading for the exit, Antonia's steps surer with every passing second. "Did you really think it would be that easy to take my daughter from me?"

"Louis' daughter."

"That sick fuck was no father to her."

Andy's smug face fell slack. "He was more of a parent than you'd ever be." He slammed his right fist against his left palm. "He was a leader. An example. Someone to whom we could only aspire."

"You wish he were your daddy, don't you?"

Andy's green eyes narrowed. The sides of his tight mouth twitched. The control room's poor light shone off his greasy skin. It highlighted the stippled surface of his blackhead-covered nose. He smiled again. "So you've got me. I'm your hostage, and you have a big knife. Although, I'm a little insulted you didn't see the need to bring a gun. Nevertheless, you've won. Clearly didn't need it, eh?"

"You don't seem bothered?"

"The only thing that bothers me is living a life in the spirit of the great man. Upholding his values and methods."

"Even when you're about to die? To be thrown to the

diseased like you tried to do with my daughter? *His* daughter."

"You're right, she's no longer his daughter. Not since she joined you. She came to a crossroads and took the wrong fucking turn."

"Joni?"

She twitched from Matt's aural intrusion. Andy's face fell again. He tilted his head.

Gunfire outside, Ralph leading Antonia to safety. Her gait steadier. And a good job because the diseased spilled in like they were being shepherded towards the warehouse.

"The footage of what Louis did … The footage your friend needs. If you're in the control room, you're close to it."

"So"—Andy clapped his hands—"enlighten me. What awful things do you have planned?"

Joni stepped forwards, but he pushed away, rolling in his chair and staying just out of reach.

"Look for where the cluster of screens are. There should be a switch on the control panel."

Screens and switches dominated the control room's back wall.

"On one side, it'll have an arrow pointing one way, and a double-headed arrow on the other. You need to switch to the double-headed arrow. That will give me access to those computers."

More gunfire in the warehouse. Fallen diseased bodies gathered around the exits. Prisoners who haemorrhaged the second they entered, and guards who fell to bullet fire a few seconds later.

"She's looking stronger." Andy nodded at the screen showing him the warehouse. "She took quite a fall down that shaft. She's lucky we were there to pick her up; otherwise the diseased would have been on her in seconds. Oh, that reminds me. I need to thank you."

"Thank me?" Joni reached the bank of screens, Andy playing his part in their strange dance, remaining just out of reach while she remained slightly twisted, hiding her earpiece. The console was littered with switches. One of them had to be what Matt had described.

"For showing us the way."

"The way? We're nothing like you lot."

Andy's laugh ended with a snort. "Oh, Louis, do you really think you and your faithless life could offer us any teachings? I meant *literally*. You showed us just how useful the shafts are." He dropped his voice to a mock whisper. "If only you could have locked me in with those nasty diseased when you tried. That would have made everything a hell of a lot easier, wouldn't it? It would have avoided all this kerfuffle."

"My failing's regrettable, but don't think I'll make that same mistake twice."

He spread his arms wide and leaned back his chair. "Then what are you waiting for?"

"Huh?"

"If you're here to kill me, then kill me already." He wagged a finger at her. "But I have a theory. I think you secretly like me. I think you want to know the way of Louis."

Antonia and Ralph shook with their firing guns. They continued pressing forwards, the diseased guards landing just feet away from them. They'd have to make a break for it soon.

"Have you found it yet?" Matt said.

Too many switches on the console.

"Also, we knew where you were all along. That's why we remained in the areas visible to the activated cameras. We wanted you to feel you could see everything from the top floor. That gave us the chance to bring little Antonia here unnoticed."

"But we've got her back, you fool. You've lost."

"I'm not lost, Joni-bear. *You* are."

"I said you've lost. Not you are lost."

"I've been found, whatever happens."

She scanned the first line of switches from left to right. About fifteen along the top row. Hard to know what each symbol meant. But she only needed a single arrow and a double arrow. Nothing else mattered. "I think you're talking out of your arse. If you knew where we were, why didn't you come up?"

"How do you think Antonia fell? Do you seriously think we'd try to attack when we could only go through the shafts? That we'd queue up and drop into the room one at a time to be slaughtered? It would have been suicide. Like trying to crawl into a wasps' nest. But as well as giving Antonia a little shove, we unlocked one of the doors. Caused a bit of mischief while we could."

Matt gasped. "Fuck. Pearl thought it was her fault."

The next row of switches. They were all different colours. None of them had the image Matt had described.

"And don't get your hopes up."

"What?"

The right side of Andy's mouth lifted in a sneer. "My *display* earlier. That wasn't for you."

"Display? You shot your load like a filthy animal. I didn't think that was for anyone but you, you sick fuck."

"Maybe Antonia thinks differently. Maybe it gave her a little twinge. Deep down. Of course, she'll never admit it. But what if?"

Joni clenched her jaw. "The woman you've known since she was a child, you mean?"

He beamed a broad and yellow-toothed grin. "I've been waiting patiently for her to flower."

"You sick fu—"

"Remember, Joni. Two arrows. One single. One double. Keep your head. He's trying to rile you."

The next line of switches. Different shapes and sizes.

Andy remained out of Joni's reach, the plastic wheels rolling across the steel floor. "Wanna know why we brought her here? This is Louis' church."

"I didn't say I wanted to know."

"This place is the perfect altar on which to sacrifice his mistake. To repent. She came into this world evil, and no amount of nurturing could steer her true. So it's best for all that we end her, send her soul back to be cleansed."

Ralph handed Antonia a fresh magazine, which she loaded into her gun. They were close. Almost ready to make a break for it. "Well, that's not going to happen now, is it?"

The switch! An arrow. One single, one double. Joni flicked it.

"Yes! That's it, Joni." The clack of Matt's fingers against his keyboard in the background. "Good work! I'll take it from here. Now, he might think he welcomes death, but make sure that sick fuck suffers."

CHAPTER 35

"On your knees."

"What?"

Joni's throat itched with the force of her command. "On your knees. Now!"

Dropping his gaze to her crotch, Andy tucked his hair behind his ears. "I hope you've washed down there."

Joni lunged at the greasy man, but Andy slipped from his seat and threw a wild elbow, slamming it against a control panel on his right, shattering the screen, the keypad below falling down and hanging from wires. He tore the keypad free, ripped the microphone from the desk, and stamped on the lot, turning them to shrapnel.

"Why break them?"

Where he'd giggled with a high-pitched whine, his laugh deepened and bubbled from his throat like air escaping a tar pit.

"I'm nearly there, Joni." The clack of keystrokes accompanied Matt's assurances.

Joni lunged at Andy again. Again, he moved aside, easily avoiding her attack. She had the knife, but he had control.

There were things he kept from her. And unlike her secrets, his gave him power. Or he believed they did.

An influx of diseased had driven Antonia and Ralph back. They fired on the creatures and changed course, heading for an exit farther along. It wouldn't be long before they were out of there. And Andy could only avoid her attack so many times.

Andy giggled again. "The doors."

"What doors?"

"Into and out of the warehouse."

"What about them?"

"They have triggers."

Joni tutted. "I know. The prisoners fall, but the guards get through. Another one of your sick games. Only let a diseased guard kill a guard, right? Like the symbolism has any kind of meaning."

"Symbolism's very important, my dear."

"I'm not your dear."

"Still. But you're right, let the guards kill her. At least, that was the plan …"

"Until we untied her?"

"Yep. But the trigger on the doors had a timer switch. You could temporarily disable them."

"Had? Could?"

Andy kicked the shards of plastic and wires on the floor. "It's what Louis used the last time he came here. It allowed him to infect himself and the prisoners, and it made sure most of them could get out again."

Joni shrugged. "And you've broken that timer. So what?"

Matt said, "I have the footage, Joni. End the fucker now."

But Joni kept a hold of her knife. Kept it aimed at the grinning Andy. "So no prisoners can get in here. Diseased or not."

"If you like."

Ralph and Antonia were closing in on the next exit. Close to making a break for it.

Andy produced one of the buttons they used against the prisoners to activate their chips.

Even now, with many of the prisoners lost to the disease, the button still sent a shudder through her. She slammed Andy into the wall and held her knife against his throat. He stank of stale piss and engine grease. She pulled the trigger from his grip, dropped it on the floor, and stamped harder than he had, the entire hut shaking. Although, if he had one, there were bound to be more. Still, she laughed.

Andy smiled with her. "What are we laughing at?"

"My daughter and Ralph are nearly out. When they're gone, that'll leave just you and me. I might take my time. Especially as you've made it so most of the diseased won't get through. You've made it much easier for me to savour this."

"Easier for you?" Andy grinned again and turned towards the screen with Antonia and Ralph just fifteen feet from their intended exit. They made slow progress, the night concealing what could be waiting for them outside. "You still think you're in control?"

"What are you talking about?"

"See that device down there?" He pointed at a screen fixed on where they'd left Antonia bound in the middle of the warehouse. A small wand of a device lay on the ground close to where they'd found her. "The one that implants chips."

"No." Joni's stomach tensed. "No."

"The second Antonia leaves this warehouse, her chip will turn her insides to mush. And, as you know, there's no way of deactivating it, and now no way of shutting down the triggers."

"You're lying."

"Let's see, shall we?"

Joni drew blood from where she pushed her knife harder into his throat. She gritted her teeth. "You're lying."

Antonia and Ralph were ten feet from the exit.

"You're ready to back that assertion? To risk Antonia's life?"

CHAPTER 36

P opping up from behind his shield again and resting his gun on top, Hawk pointed it at the stairwell's entrance. Movement somewhere in the darkness. His heart beat a steady but forceful pulse. His mouth so dry his saliva had turned into a foam he couldn't swallow. Four full pitchers of water sat on a nearby table. But that would mean exposing himself and weakening their defence as a collective. Even if only for a minute. If the guards appeared at that moment, and if he didn't get shot, someone else might if they tried to cover him. So what if he spent the night thirsty? Better than spending it dead. Or even worse, mourning someone who'd died because of his selfish actions.

The movement ceased. Hawk dropped again and leaned against his shield. Both the floor and shield were cold and hard, and the glare from the ceiling's strip lights burned his tired eyes. Like being in Dout, but at least they had the good sense to dim them at night-time. It had turned dark outside, but the bulbs glowed as bright as ever.

Bugs came into the room. Moths mostly, their fluttering wings caught the light. Many of them landed close to the strip lights. On the ceiling. On the white plastic at either end. The bulbs were clearly too hot, because the ones landing on them fell like autumn leaves.

Hawk rocked the aches from his tired body and fatigue from his weary mind. The movement kept him alert. The fuckers would be bound to show when they least expected them.

The others were close by. Each behind their own shield. Even Rayne had separated from William now she'd re-dressed his wound. Now she'd poured all that water onto the steel floor. Hawk swallowed another spiky gulp.

The night had stolen Hawk's view of the room they'd left at the other end of the walkway. The one with the barricaded door. The towers blinked red from where they remained in emergency mode, but like the stairwell, the scarlet glow did little to reveal their surroundings.

Aggie crouched behind a shield over to his right. He popped up from behind his, and the others did the same, taking his lead. When he ran across to Aggie, Ethan tutted, shook his head, and ducked back behind his barrier again. The others followed suit, albeit with less derision.

Aggie kept her voice low. "What are you doing?"

"It's dark out."

"I can see that."

"But you can't. That's the point."

"Huh?"

"What if some guards get onto the walkway now? They could hide in the shadows and have us surrounded before we know it."

Aggie chewed on her bottom lip, her eyes flitting between the two exits. "*If* they know we're here."

"True. Or if they discover we're here at some point."

The others watched on.

Aggie waved them over.

Ethan reached them first. The others followed, the shield just about wide enough to protect their congregation from the stairwell.

She pointed at the doors leading outside. "Guards could get down onto those walkways without us seeing. They could attack us before we know they're there."

Like Aggie before them, the rest looked from one exit to the other. Rayne turned her palms to the ceiling. "But we don't know if they know we're here. And if we leave now, we're exposed on the walkways."

Rayne sneered. "If they knew we were here, they would have come down by now."

"But what if they work it out and see how they could use the dark against us?"

Peeling away from the group, Rayne sprinted along a mazy path through the other barriers and pressed her back to the wall beside the stairwell's entrance. Her gun in both hands, she spun in, aiming it one way and then the other before she ascended the stairs. Her feet were all that remained in view, and then even they vanished.

Aggie rocked with her quickened breaths, settling a little when Hawk rested his hand on her back.

Breaking from the pack, Ethan followed Rayne's path, but halted halfway across the dining room when the gaunt woman reappeared. The pair of them returned to the group, Ethan red-faced as he stared at the floor.

Her breathing slightly heavier for the short run, Rayne pointed back at the stairwell. "They're still on the floor above. They seem oblivious."

"For now," Ethan said.

"For now. Are we serious about ending this threat, or should we run? If we want to end it, we have the chance to do it on our terms."

The light glinted off Knives' blade. Always fiddling with

one, she spun it in her right hand. "And seeing as we're here, shouldn't we take it as a chance to attack them?"

"I agree," Rayne said. "We can't run forever, and we're trapped in these blocks for the foreseeable. We'll have to face them eventually. This might be the best chance we get. Even if we're forced back down here, we can retreat to the safety of the shields and take them out when they try to follow us."

They all turned to Aggie. She ran the tip of her tongue across her top lip. "You're right, war with the guards seems inevitable. And right now, we still have surprise on our side. Let's take a vote. Run or fight?"

They said it as one. "Fight."

"Okay." Aggie stood up. "Let's do this."

Ethan and Rayne led them at a quiet jog. From one shield to the next, ducking behind each until they reached the stairwell's entrance.

Following Aggie, Hawk leaned into the wall on the right side of the stairwell's door with William and Ethan. Knives, Rowan, and Ash joined Rayne on the left.

A thumbs up at Ethan, which he returned, Rayne led the way, rolling around the wall like she had before, into the stairwell, and up the stairs.

They ascended one steel step at a time. Step. Pause. Step. Pause.

The scuffling of activity above suggested the guards were at ease. It could be a trick. And even guards at ease could be ready to end them all. If they were well drilled, they should be ready to end them all.

Hawk, like those around him, held his gun in both hands across his front, the target pointing down, visible against some of the deeper shadows.

Rayne and Ethan drew close to the plateau between floors and halted, a one-hundred-and-eighty-degree turn and a flight of stairs away from war. Their chance to end these guards once and for all. To make these blocks theirs.

His heart in his throat, his chest tight, Hawk breathed in through his nose and out through his mouth.

Rayne and Ethan raised their thumbs.

Hawk reached out and rested his hand on the base of Aggie's back. She jumped and turned around.

He forced a smile. Another confession of his love rose and died in his throat. "See you on the other side."

She acknowledged him with a slow blink and a slight dip of her head.

"The stairwell! They're in the stairwell!"

The loud tannoy jammed needles into Hawk's ears.

The slight shuffling of lazy activity above turned into organised mobilisation. Guns being raised. Boots descending the stairs.

Rowan had already pulled Ash back with him, the two of them falling from the final few steps as they ran back into the dining room. To the shelter of the shields.

Moving down a step, Hawk paused. Rayne and Ethan were still waiting by the plateau.

Aggie pulled Ethan back. Knives grabbed Rayne. They turned and stumbled down the stairs. Half-falling, half-running, fully retreating. They ran back into the dining hall as bullets sparked off the stairwell's walls and around the door frame.

Diving for cover, Hawk hit the floor so hard it jarred his body and stung his knees. He gritted his teeth through the pain and leaned around his shield, his gun trained on the stairwell's exit.

Ethan and Aggie were the last to settle, each taking a separate shield. All of them focused on where their enemy would appear. Each of them threw the occasional glance over their shoulders at the darkness on the walkways.

"You can't win this!" The guard's voice filled the stairwell. Pitiful compared to the tannoy's authoritative boom, but he had the backing of whoever was watching them. And how could they hide from unseen surveillance?

"That may be so"—Rayne turned puce with the effort of her shout—"but we'll try, and if we go down, we'll make sure we take you with us."

"If you give up now, we promise we won't torture you. We'll be humane in how we put you down."

Rayne spat on the floor as if the man had left a nasty taste in her mouth. "You don't have a shred of humanity in you, you fuck."

With Aggie just a shield away, Hawk broke from cover to be with her.

"What are you doing?"

Hawk rested his head against hers. "If I'm going to die, I want it to be at your side."

"We're not going to die."

"Fine, if we're going to win, I want it to be at your side."

She squeezed his hand.

"Are you ready for this?"

She nodded. "Always."

They turned away from one another and poked their guns around either side of their shield, waiting for someone to make the first move.

CHAPTER 37

J oni pressed her knife so hard against Andy's throat it turned his voice into a croaky rasp. "But wait!"

"What?" On the monitor to Andy's right, Antonia and Ralph stepped back while firing on another wave of diseased guards charging into the warehouse.

"That button you smashed." A trickle of blood ran down his neck. Joni would turn it into a fucking river before she left that control room. "We have plenty more where that came from."

"I'm sure you do." Antonia and Ralph were now about fifty feet from leaving. Fifty feet away from triggering the implanted chip.

"Plenty of ways to trigger little Antonia's implant."

"I get it. If you're telling the truth. Now make your fucking point!"

He smiled, and Joni pushed harder, the trickle turning to a steady flow. "My people are watching the warehouse's exit. Waiting for me to leave. And if I don't, they'll be coming in here with their buttons. Even if you take them all down, one of them will get within range, I promise you."

"Is there a microphone on the wall?" Matt said. "You can call through to Antonia and Ralph."

"There was."

"That's what the crashing sound was?"

"Yep."

"Shit!"

Andy glanced at Joni's earbud.

Antonia and Ralph stepped closer to the warehouse's exit again.

Matt whined, "You have to believe him, Joni."

"Really?"

"The consequences are too great. Let him go. You need to tell Antonia not to leave. We'll work it out from there."

"Fuck!"

Andy's smile broadened. Joni gripped the knife's handle until her knuckles ached. "Fuck!" She ran out the door, leaned on the railing of the first-floor walkway, and called across the warehouse, "Ralph! Antonia! Don't leave."

Ralph shot another diseased and jumped back from where it fell at his feet. "What? Why?"

Andy ran from the control room, down the ladder, and sprinted for another exit.

When Antonia put her gun's red target on his back, Joni reached out to her. "Leave him!" Her voice echoed in the dark warehouse.

The long-haired sycophant reached the door and leaned outside to check the way. He turned back in and saluted Joni before he ran from sight.

"What's going on, Mum?" Antonia ran to Joni.

"Matt, can you help me fix it?"

"I think so. You need to get back into the control room."

"Mum? What's happening? Why did we just let him go? Why shouldn't we leave?" Ralph joined Antonia, both of them staring up from the ground.

"Does she have a mark on the back of her neck?" Joni lifted her own hair to demonstrate.

Letting his gun's strap take its weight, Ralph lifted Antonia's hair. His gigantic frame sagged. "Shit! She does."

"Fuck!"

"No!" Antonia's voice rang out. "They haven't?"

Ralph shot another diseased guard, the entrances all clear.

"They've put an implant in you. Leaving the warehouse will trigger it."

"What?"

"That's what Andy said. But Matt's telling me we should be able to fix it. Just keep the diseased guards at bay, and I promise we'll work something out."

Tears in her eyes, but Antonia dipped an assertive nod. "Okay." What else could they do but fight? Fight and pray Joni and Matt would find a way to live up to their promise.

CHAPTER 38

"Uh …" Matt said.

The cabin's walls, while as flimsy as card, muted Antonia's and Ralph's gunshots just enough to dull the edges of their sharp cracks. "What?"

"They've turned on a camera in the control hut. We can all see you."

Joni spun one way and then the other. "Where? I'll tear it down."

"Don't. It helps. I can see what you're doing."

"Can you hear me?"

"Of course."

"Can *everyone* hear me?"

"Only the images are being broadcast for now. But assume they have microphones in there too. And at least they can't hear me."

Several more shots fired outside. The screen showed Antonia's and Ralph's red laser targets finding the shambling silhouettes before they dropped them. Antonia and Ralph safe in the centre of the warehouse. For now.

"Am I facing the camera?"

"No. Turn right a bit."

Joni turned right.

"The other right."

She turned left.

"Too far."

She turned back a little.

"That's it."

While biting her bottom lip so hard it hurt, she thrust a forceful middle finger in the air. "See that?"

"Fuck you too."

"Good."

"The control panel Andy smashed. Does it have a port?"

The control panel's indented screen glowed red. The cracks spider-webbing from the point of impact made the display unreadable. But the jack, the same size and shape as all the ports in the prison, remained intact. Joni plugged in her hacking device, wiggling it a little to force it in. The three lights on it glowed as red as the screen.

"You're blocking my line of sight. Is it working?"

The red lights turned green one after the other, and the screen followed suit. Joni stepped aside.

"Good. And you see that?"

A shard of unbroken screen revealed two blinking dots. "I can't see much, but it looks like—"

"A timer?"

"Uh-huh. How long?"

A clacking of Matt's fingers against his keyboard.

"Two minutes. Well, one minute and fifty-four seconds."

"Until the triggers come back on again?"

"I think so."

"You think?"

"You're asking me to be certain when Antonia's life's on the line. If I'm reading this right, you're safe to leave now, but you won't be when that timer hits zero. You have one minute fifty."

"She'll definitely be okay to leave?"

"I hope so."

"I could do with more than hope right now."

"Hope's all you have. One minute forty-five."

"Fuck."

"What about the diseased prisoners? They can be your canaries."

"My what?"

"Canaries. Coal mines. Gas … Are they being triggered as they come in, or do they have a clear run?"

Joni ran out onto the walkway. The warehouse gloomy, each entrance letting in a small amount of silver moonlight. "There aren't any. Can we reset the timer? And keep resetting it until they turn up?"

"That should work. I need you to hack their system again."

Joni plugged in her device. But the red lights didn't come on. "Damn!" She pressed the jack harder. It snapped. "Fuck!"

"What, Joni? What?"

"Don't shout at me."

"Then tell me what's happening."

"My hacking device. It's broken."

"Fuck!"

"How long do we have left?"

"One minute twenty-four."

"Shit." She took off.

Halfway down the ladder, Joni jumped off. Her steps and voice echoed in the vast warehouse. "Where are the diseased?" She picked up her bag of ammo and slipped the straps over her shoulders. She might not have a gun, but she could make sure Antonia and Ralph didn't run out of bullets.

Their guns raised, their red lasers tracing lines from them to the entrances, Ralph's voice boomed. "Dunno."

"One minute fifteen."

"I think I've disabled the triggers on the exit. But only for the next minute or so."

Still teary-eyed and pale, Antonia's mouth fell open. "You think?"

"To be sure, we need to see what happens when a diseased prisoner comes in. Canaries."

"What?"

"If they run in without falling, the triggers are down."

Andy's face burst to life on the far wall. Smug. Glistening with sweat and grease. "You'll regret the day you crossed our leader. He was everything to this place. He led by example. He was too good for you swines."

"One minute ten."

A wild cry at the closest entrance. A diseased charged in. A prisoner. Joni pushed down on the end of Antonia's gun, dragging the target from its face.

It drew closer. It remained on its feet.

The clack of bullet fire. Ralph shot it, driving blood, bone, and brain from the side of its head. The beast fell at their feet.

Joni patted Ralph on the back. "I'm guessing that's us good to go, then."

"Wait!"

Antonia's words twisted through Joni's back.

"One minute five."

She wedged her foot beneath the diseased corpse and flipped it onto its back. "That's Louise."

"You know the prisoner?"

"Guard."

Joni and Ralph said it at the same time. "Shit!"

Still on the screen, his massive head about ten feet tall,

Andy turned puce with his mirth. "Oh dear, what will you do now? Time's-a-ticking, chicken. And herein lies the challenge. The faithless have to have faith. Can you back yourself? Will you leave the warehouse or remain in there forever?"

"Fifty-five seconds."

Andy's massive greasy face gave way to footage outside the warehouse. The guards had blocked off the access from the front of the block, preventing the diseased from getting through. The piss-blonde sycophant returned. "Tick! Tick! Tick!"

"Fifty seconds, Joni."

"Damn!" Her scream echoed around the warehouse.

Antonia and Ralph stared at one another.

"We have less than a minute," Joni said.

"If you get it wrong …" Andy giggled. "Antonia's insides will turn to mush, and she'll drop dead two steps after leaving the warehouse."

"Forty-five seconds."

"Not long now, Joni. Tickety-tick. Lickety-split. Are you prepared to back yourself? To roll the dice on your daughter's life? All based on guesswork from what you saw on an unreadable screen? What kind of mother are you?"

"Mum!" The screen's light glistened off Antonia's moist eyes. "Are you sure the triggers are down?"

"I wish I could say yes." Joni picked up the implant device. "Are you sure they even implanted you?"

"No." Antonia turned to Joni and lifted her hair. Whether they did or not, no one could deny the small horizontal half-inch cut.

Diseased cries at the door. Three guards rushed in. Ralph dropped them all.

As the echoes of his bullet fire settled, Andy's howling

laughter took over. "Round and round and round we go. Will she blow? Nobody knows."

"Thirty seconds."

Again, Andy vanished, and footage from outside dominated the screen. The cult descended on them. Spread out in a line the width of the path, they held their buttons aloft. They either stayed and fought against the odds, or they gambled and risked Antonia's life.

Joni pressed the end of the implant device to the back of her neck.

"Mum!" Antonia reached towards her. "What are you doi—?"

She pressed the button, driving a sharp sting into her flesh.

"Mum!"

Andy laughed again. "Plot twist!"

"Twenty seconds, Joni."

Turning on the spot, Joni shouted, "You want to know what kind of mother I am?" She ran for the door, followed by Antonia and Ralph. She sprinted through without breaking stride.

CHAPTER 39

Twenty feet from the warehouse. Outside and still standing. The cult descending on them scattered when Ralph ran out, stood beside her, and fired.

Despite testing it herself, Joni gasped when Antonia burst from the warehouse. Her heart kicked with every beat, but her daughter remained upright. Her eyes itched with her backed-up tears.

"Joni!" Ralph threw his gun to her.

She caught it and turned on the cult, firing on them, keeping them in hiding while he led Antonia into the maintenance shaft and back into the building.

"Matt, am I facing a camera?"

"Yep."

Joni bit down so hard on her bottom lip it stung. She raised her middle finger again and followed them into the shaft, crawling after her daughter and friend.

As soon as he found a space large enough in the tunnels, Ralph moved aside and held Antonia back to let Joni pass. Her domain, she'd lead them true. Like she'd led them from the warehouse. Trust Mama Bear.

Stopping at another open space, a whirring air-conditioning unit nearby, Joni waited for Antonia and Ralph to catch up. "How does your implant feel?"

With one eyebrow raised and one hand on the back of her neck, Antonia pulled a face. "It doesn't. I still don't know if I have one. You shouldn't have done what you did."

"I needed to be sure the doors were safe."

"Tha …" Antonia cleared her throat and tried again. "Thank you."

"I'd do it again in a heartbeat." Raising her voice to be heard over the air-conditioning unit in the dusty tunnels made her throat itch. "We now need to make sure we keep you away from the guards and those buttons. We can't risk it."

"And you."

"And me. Look, Matt's going to broadcast the collapse of the prison to the south." She pressed her earpiece. "How are you getting on, Matt?"

"Huh?"

Joni shouted louder. "How are you getting on? With the broadcast."

"Oh. I can't really hear you. But fine. Getting there."

She removed her earpiece and placed it closer to the air-con unit. She beckoned for Antonia to follow. Ralph came too. "They're going to see what Louis did. How he turned the prisoners and set them loose. I want you to know, because it might be upsetting."

Antonia's features hardened. She sniffed and shook her head. "Quite the opposite. It's justice for what he's done. But wh—"

"Why are we doing it?"

"Yeah. Not that it matters, I suppose."

"We're doing it to help Olga and the others."

"What? Why?"

The earbud a good ten feet from them, but Joni lowered her voice just in case. "The south has fallen."

"Fallen?"

Joni pressed a finger to her lips. "The diseased got loose. Olga and the others left the prison's south gate open. They couldn't close it. They didn't realise it would matter. As far as they were concerned, the prison hadn't fallen."

The colour returned to Antonia's cheeks, and the force of her words drove Joni back a step. "Why haven't you told the others? Why would you lie to them?"

"Please"—Joni pressed down on the dusty air between them—"keep your voice down."

"Matt doesn't know either?"

"No. He thinks I want to get the footage out to shame Louis, not help Olga. The only people who know are you and Ralph."

"Ralph knows." She shot scorn at the big man, who pulled his neck into his broad shoulders.

"I've only recently told him."

"Shit, Mum!"

"Look, I've not told the others because half of them wanted to join the cult. Half of them thought we could reason with them. And we can't. You've seen that first-hand. Look at what they've done to you. What they did to Carly."

Antonia winced.

"I couldn't risk pushing them towards those nutters. By telling them their loved ones are most likely dead, they might lose their will to fight. Before we do anything, we need to end the cult."

Although Antonia screwed up her face like she might argue, she only managed, "Fuck!"

"I know."

Antonia stamped her foot. "Fuck!"

"But you understand, right?"

Deflating with a hard exhale, she nodded, her voice a weak croak. "Yeah. It's an impossible choice, but you did the right thing."

CHAPTER 40

"I just wanted to say," another guard Joni didn't know clasped her hands before her chest and looked up, blinking away her tears, "what you did for Antonia ... Well, what does Andy know? That was purely selfless. And the act of a *proper* mother." She patted Joni's arm. "I think it was amazing. And thank you for showing me what the cult's like. What Louis' reign was like. It was hard to see when you were a part of it, you know? Anyway. Thank you."

The woman dipped her head, bowing as she pulled back into the crowd before Joni could thank her and help alleviate her guilt by reassuring her she wasn't a monster just because she belonged to and upheld the values of a monstrous regime. For the past hour, the guards had taken it in turns to both compliment Joni on what she did with the chip, and to relieve themselves of their guilt for the life they claimed they'd now put behind them. Pretty much every one of them, save Sarah, had had their turn. Nothing else to do but nod and, when they gave her the chance, end the conversation by accepting the gesture and moving on.

But Joni knew about unburdening herself. She'd done the

same when she'd revealed her secret to both Ralph and Antonia, and she moved with a lighter step because of it. Antonia and Ralph had played their part in confirming she'd made the right choice. So, before they did anything else, she needed to do the same for the guards. Clear their heads and hearts so they could focus solely on annihilating the cult.

Because of Andy's revelations, several guards had taken positions in the shafts, watching for intruders while Theresa and her kill team worked through the rest of the top floor, searching for cult members and diseased alike. Although, as of yet, they'd only found diseased. They'd asked Antonia and Joni to stay back and had made a bubble of protection to ensure no one could sneak up on them and trigger their implants. And when they ended the damn cult, they'd make sure they destroyed every one of those buttons.

Pearl had come back from hunting with the kill team and now sat at Matt's side in front of the bank of screens, the images flicking from one to the next, much quicker since they'd opened up more cameras in the block. She sat in the plastic chair Joni had used. An outcast like Matt. And even now, with her name cleared by Andy's confession, she'd opted to remain by the side of one of the few people who'd held their judgement, whatever the reason. As ostracised allies, they were in good company.

"How are things looking, Matt?"

His face inches from the bank of monitors, his fingers alive like the keyboard was too hot to touch. The tip of his tongue protruded from the side of his mouth. Matt jabbed a key with a definitive poke before leaning back in his chair and grinning.

The relief added an extra weight to Joni's already fatigued body. "It's done?"

"It's done. Every screen and propaganda drone in the south will soon be playing the footage. And for extra effect"

—he winked—"I'll also run it through the prison and this block. Just so the cult can see what the world will soon know about their idol."

"Amazing." Joni grabbed the control desk's headphones and put them on. "Can you put me through to Olga? I want to make sure she knows it's coming and to see if she can get it out through any channels we've missed. This will destroy his memory and the cult." And hopefully keep the others from bringing up the state of the south every time they talk.

Several button taps, Matt twisted some knobs and dials and leaned back in his chair, the old thing groaning with the burden of its years.

"Olga. Calling Olga, come in, Olga."

"Hello?"

"Who's that?"

"Duncan."

"You again."

"You called me, princess."

"You need to wind your neck in."

"What do you want?"

"Where's Olga?"

"Busy."

She couldn't ask Olga to call back. Risk Matt thinking he could help them by getting involved and finding out too much about the south. "Can you help?"

"So you want to be friends now?"

"Don't be a prick."

"As charming as your friends, I see."

"Can you help or not?"

"That depends."

"Have you hurt Olga? I swear, if I find out you've hurt *any* of my friends, I'll—"

"Calm down, dear."

The headphones slipped from Joni's head. She spun

around to catch them, but Matt had pulled them clear and now put them on. He smiled as he spoke. "Hi. Duncan, is it?"

Joni's heart hammered. Antonia and Ralph had come to watch, the pair of them in the doorway between the control room and the observation room. Antonia's brow creased in the middle, and she gripped her bottom lip in a pinch, holding up a mirror to Joni of her own gut-churning anxiety.

A slow and steady tone, his words delivered with an authority, and clearly driven over the top of Duncan on the other end. "My name's Matt. I'm not picking anyone's side here, but I just wanted to let you know what we're doing."

Her hand closed around thin air as Joni rehearsed taking back the headphones. But Matt continued talking, denying Duncan's chance to reply. "You should see some footage coming through shortly. We want the rest of the world to see what Louis' done to the prison, so we've broadcast it throughout the south. We want everyone to know how he's turned many of the prisoners and guards into diseased."

Joni leaned forwards on her toes, her back taut. A coiled spring.

But Matt kept going. "Let me finish. I'm not interested in a conversation. I just want to make sure the footage is coming through. It should be broadcasting through the blocks and propaganda drones."

Matt paused and nodded. "Yep, that's all I need to know."

He nodded again and rolled his eyes at Joni. "Yep. It's working? Good."

This time, Matt frowned and listened like Duncan had something worth saying.

Joni snatched the headphones.

"Ow!" Matt scowled at her and rubbed his ears.

But she slipped the headphones back on again. "Did you get all of that, Duncan?"

"Let me talk to the other man. He seemed nice. Well, he

seemed like a prick, but that's a massive improvement on you."

"The footage is coming through?"

"You want to say anything else first?"

Joni clamped her jaw. "I'm sorry about how I spoke to you. Okay?"

"Okay. The footage is coming through. It'll be playing in the blocks and on the drones shortly. And if it's what you say it is, it's exactly what your friends need right now."

CHAPTER 41

Each of Olga's blinks lasted longer than the one before. Her heavy eyelids dared her to keep them closed, and every time she didn't, the sting gnawing at her eyeballs grew worse. She straightened her back. Rocked from side to side. Stretched her arms up towards the dark ceiling.

Look at her, sat here on the stairs, having the audacity to nearly fall asleep while her friends were in danger somewhere in the other block. Or they weren't. If she trusted Duncan.

"Any more from that oxygen thief?"

"What did she say?"

Olga's fatigue made her less able to cope with Duncan's indignant squawk. It jabbed into her eardrum and ran all the way to the base of her neck. "No, Gracie." Where they'd spoken in whispers, they now talked at a normal volume, their words carrying through the abandoned stairwell. Seemingly abandoned stairwell. Who knew in a place like this? And who cared? Maybe they would have been more cautious if something had happened. But other than the groans of discontent, and the diseased bashing into the other side of the closed stairwell door, nothing had. Nothing at all.

"And we still trust the ruddy-cheeked arse-hat?"

"We trust him, or we do this without him."

"That's right, Olga! You tell her. And I don't have ruddy cheeks!"

"Fuck off, Duncan."

"I don't have to help you, you know?"

"So you keep reminding me."

"Are you trying to call my bluff?"

"What's he saying?" Gracie peered down from the top step. She banged a fist against the door, the creatures on the other side yelling in response.

"Anyway, I'm not trying to call your bluff, Duncan, but we've been here too long."

"You can fucking say that again!"

"Thanks, Gracie."

"She's quite het up, isn't she?"

"We're all antsy and fed up."

"That's not my fault. Your friends are yet to make their move. I'll tell you when something changes."

"Maybe you could guide us over there, and we can see for ourselves?"

"Or maybe you could trust me?"

Olga put her fist in her mouth and bit down on her knuckles. They were back to square one. Did they trust him? Of course they didn't. They were not morons. But the consequences of admitting that could be dire. Like voluntarily blinding themselves. And what would happen to their friends then? "Help us out here, Duncan. This isn't about us not trusting you."

Gracie snorted. "Speak for yourself. I wouldn't trust that prick as far as I could ... hang on, that doesn't work, does it? Seeing as I'm going to throw him from the elevated walkways. That's a few hundred feet to the ground. I wouldn't trust him as far as I could … I wouldn't … I dunno, I just don't trust the prick."

Artan's monotone called through the stairwell. "We get it, Gracie."

"What did she say?"

"She agrees with what I said. This isn't about us not trusting you, but we need something. Help us out here."

"I *am* helping you out. The best course of action is to stay put. Your friends are safe for now. They don't need you blowing their cover."

Olga deflated with her sigh and leaned up along the stairs. The edges dug in at several points, so she sat up again. She pulled her feet onto the stair below the one on which she sat and hugged her knees to her chest. She let go a second later. She rocked from side to side and stretched up towards the dark ceiling. She stood up, and the others all turned her way. Matilda raised her eyebrows. Gracie gasped. The diseased banged and moaned. Olga shrugged and shook her head. "I'm just trying to get comfortable."

"Wait!" The single syllable jabbed Olga's ear.

"What?"

Gracie perked up again. "What's that moron saying?"

"You need to get her to wind her neck in; otherwise I won't tell you."

Olga pressed her finger to her lips. Matilda turned to Gracie and rested a hand on her knee.

"You need to *quietly* go down to the sports hall."

"The sports hall? On the floor beneath us?"

"Yep."

"Why?"

"Just do it."

Waving for the others to follow, all of them now on their

feet like Olga, they descended the stairs with gentle steps. Their friends' lives could depend on their stealth.

The sports hall's bright glow drove away some of Olga's weariness. The projected footage along the massive wall on their left drove away the rest.

Gracie exited the stairs last. "That's the warehouse."

Duncan replied, "The footage you wanted from your friend."

"Joni did it." Olga smiled. "I knew she'd come through." She rocked with the camera, which hovered about ten feet from the ground before it swung into action, encircling Louis and a group of about twenty prisoners.

"And this"—Louis flung his arms out to the sides and turned on the spot like a child in a meadow. His gun swung out on its strap—"is the theatre of dreams." His voice boomed through the warehouse, amplified in the massive building. "This is where the magic happens." He mugged at the camera. A perpetual performer. And not only did he have a button in his hand that would trigger the implant of every prisoner close to him, but he also had the line of twenty prisoners shackled together with chains.

Cupping his mouth, he spoke in a mock whisper. "Now, we all know this isn't how you're treated in this place. We don't keep you in shackles." He laughed. "We're not animals. But let's humour the south, shall we? They love the drama of it all, so let's give the sadistic fucks a show, yeah?" He stepped back, and the prisoners followed his lead.

The camera dive-bombed the line of prisoners and flew along at head height. Many of them stared straight ahead through dead eyes. Some watched the button in Louis' hand.

Louis stepped back until he stood beneath a solitary diseased hanging from the ceiling. Chains wrapped its torso, but its hands were free to slash at the air between them, reaching for Louis and the prisoners.

Swinging, snarling, grunting, growling. Louis pulled another remote device from his pocket and pressed a button. It lowered the diseased. Although he blew the thing a kiss as it got closer, he ducked, avoiding its grasp.

With every passing second, Olga's stomach clamped a little tighter. Her friends all watched on through unblinking eyes, their mouths hanging open. Not even Gracie had anything to say.

The prisoners divided their attention between the diseased, Louis, and the button in his hand that could liquify their insides. "They say it only takes one."

Matilda tutted. "*You* say that, you twisted prick."

Louis laughed. "But we all know that's an urban myth, right? Just one diseased to turn an entire prison?" He threw his head back with his next laugh. "That's preposterous. I mean, the virus is awful and unstoppable in the right conditions, but it takes more than one. Right?"

Dropping to a knee directly beneath the diseased, Louis beckoned the prisoners to come closer.

But the woman at the front shook her head at him and shuffled back with the rattling of chains.

Louis remained on bended knee and rested his gun's red laser target on her face.

"Okay." She raised her hands in the air. "I'm com—"

A spray of bullets ripped into her and blew chunks and a cloud of mist up and away from the back of her head. She fell to her knees before dropping face-first against the hard concrete, her hands at her sides.

The prisoner directly behind her wiped his face while several others cried.

The drone camera pulled back and circled the crowd. It passed so near to the suspended diseased, Olga balked at the close-up of its shredded cheek. Maggots writhing in the deep cuts.

The new lead prisoner finished wiping his face. A tall man with shaggy hair and a thick black beard. Louis beamed a wicked grin and beckoned him forward.

The suggestion of hesitation flickered across the man's face, but when Louis grabbed his gun, he moved, passing the dead woman and then dragging her with him.

When he got close enough, Louis grabbed the dead woman's hair. He shuffled back, dragging the woman with him, her limp arms sliding along the concrete. He only halted when he'd stretched the chain as far as it would go. "We're going to play a little game."

He gripped the woman's jaw in a pinch, the rest of her face shredded by his bullets, and moved her mouth in time with his words, pretending she was speaking. "Oh, I love a game. Please tell me what it is."

"Of course, my dear." Louis grabbed the woman's stretched chain and pulled the line closer to him and the diseased. The creature's fingers were just inches from the top of his head. The man at the front leaned back to stay out of reach. "The triggers on the doors are down, for now. So you have a chance to get away." He beamed up at the lead man. "And who says I'm not fair?"

He slipped a key into the lock on the woman's manacles. "But now you need to back yourselves. I'm the one who says it only takes one. I think we all knew that, didn't we? But you have a chance to prove me wrong. To show the world this diseased threat isn't as dire as we're led to believe."

Duncan snorted in Olga's ear. "He's fucking certified."

The prisoner at the front turned to the man behind him.

"Look at me, you fuck!" Louis turned puce and trembled with the effort of his scream. Crouched like a sprinter in the blocks, he locked with coiled rage. But his anger left him like it had never been there, his delivery even again. "I believe this experiment will prove my

214

theory correct. That because of the diseased, we live on a knife-edge. Just one can turn an entire prison. Can bring thousands to their knees. Can destroy a country. Continents. And now the king has been toppled, I think it's time to fully test my mantra. It only takes one. You'll see. But in the interest of fairness, I'll give you a chance. The second I unlock these, you lot will be able to slip from the chains and run."

Many of the prisoners watched on with blank expressions. Trauma or lack of understanding? In their limited time in the prison, Olga and the others had assumed some prisoners spoke and understood English, but how many? Although, his actions were clear, and the nuance of his rhetoric was much more for the viewers. Much more for himself.

He dropped the diseased a little lower, its fingertips batting his wispy ginger hair. He tugged on the manacles again, pulling against the prisoners' shuffling retreat. "Ah, ah!" He wagged his finger. "You don't get to start until I say. You don't get to run unti—" He turned the key, unlocked the manacles, and stood up.

The diseased clapped both hands to the sides of his face and bit into the top of his head. Blood seeped down his brow into his eyes.

The prisoners at the back of the line fell from where they tried to run too soon. The chain, looped through the manacles, needed to be unthreaded. They had to wait for those ahead of them.

Tripping as he ran, the man at the front burst free, sprinting from the now fallen Louis and the suspended diseased above him.

The next prisoner pulled the chains. But he pulled too hard. They caught on their way through. Those behind him cried out, and his cheeks puffed with his breathing. But he worked it free and followed his friend, towards the door on the farthest side of the warehouse and out of there.

Louis' flaccid form twitched.

Once …

Twice …

His head snapped up. His eyes bled. He snarled and launched himself at the third prisoner, but she slipped from the manacles and got away.

The others turned, ran, and fell. The chains still linking them together.

The third escapee paused at the exit through which the other two had escaped. A gun rested against the wall.

"Just take them down." Gracie's yell made Olga jump. She threw her hand in the footage's direction. "Shoot them. End this."

As Louis jumped on the fallen prisoners, biting the first one he reached, the woman bolted through the exit and ran.

"Shit!" Matilda slumped like she didn't know how this ended.

The prisoners turned, one by one, dragged themselves from the chain and ran out into the prison. Past the guns leaning against the walls. Another part of Louis' twisted little game. Any of the three who'd avoided infection could have ended this before it began. It only takes one. But all three were more concerned with saving themselves than ending the threat that would change the south forever.

Louis left the warehouse last. Stumbling, his arms hanging limp.

Olga flinched when the footage looped back to the beginning. "I thought that was what I wanted to see …"

Matilda put an arm around her. "It's what we all *need* to see."

"How many times do you think it will replay?" Artan said.

Nick stared at the footage through glazed eyes. "And where do you think it's being broadcast?"

Duncan jabbed into her ear. "It'll repeat until those in the prison turn it off. And it's showing everywhere. In every room in every tower block. Every propaganda drone … If there's a means to broadcast footage in the south, it's being broadcast."

"Everywhere." Olga pointed at her earpiece. "Duncan says it's being broadcast everywhere, and on repeat until they turn it off from the prison."

Gracie headed back to the stairwell.

Nick caught her arm. "Where are you going?"

Her eyes bloodshot and swollen, she tugged against his restraint and turned away from him. "Back to the door with the diseased. Joni's done her bit for us; now we need to do our bit for the others and wait until Duncan says they need our help."

Nick followed. Artan next. Matilda walked after them. Olga took up the rear. Joni had done her bit. Mad old Joni. Reliable old Joni. She'd put her life in that woman's hands in a heartbeat. Hopefully, they'd see one another again.

CHAPTER 42

As the footage ended, Hawk exhaled and deflated with the expulsion of his breath. Leaning against a cold hard shield, sat on a cold hard floor, in a cold open room. The table with the water jugs still too far away. To break from cover now would be suicide, the stairwell still filled with soldiers about ten feet away.

The projected footage played on a loop. Louis led the manacled prisoners into the warehouse as if doing it for the first time. It had taken everyone's attention, silencing even Rayne. How were they supposed to fight after that? More death on top of too much already. But only one group would walk away from this dining hall, and they had a simple choice: fight or die.

Knives broke the silence, her voice taking off like a startled bird in a graveyard. "What the fuck was that?"

"The explanation as to how the south fell." Ethan, two shields away, leaned towards Hawk. "I'm sorry I ever gave you a hard time about it. I didn't believe you. I'm sorry."

"S'okay. It's understandable."

"It's really not."

"Why should you trust me? I get it. Honestly, I do."

"Uh …" Aggie pulled back behind her shield and pointed towards the stairwell door.

One guard had tied an empty white pillowcase to the end of their gun and hung it into the room. "We were wrong to blame you two in there for the south's collapse. We can see that now. We want to call a truce."

Aggie raised her eyebrows at Hawk. Not his choice to make, but he shrugged anyway. Why not?

Bullet fire to Hawk's right. Rayne stood with a widened stance and unloaded on the pillowcase, her cheeks shaking with the gun's kick. She left the gesture of peace in shreds, and the guard withdrew.

"What the fuck, Rayne?" Aggie tutted.

Still fixed on the stairwell, her face aglow, the whites of her wide glare stood out like spotlights in the dark hollows of her eye sockets. "They want to call a truce. A fucking truce, Aggie! Like we should just forget everything until this point. After *generations* of oppression, they want to shake hands, pat each other on the backs, and go our separate ways."

A man's voice called from the stairwell, "In case you haven't noticed, you—"

"What?" Rayne stamped her foot. "Vampire trash? Parasite?"

The suggestion of a truce had turned Hawk's body to lead. Finally, he could stop fighting and rest. Quench his thirst. His fatigue had already planted roots.

The man's voice came again. "The world's changed."

"But you clearly haven't. So what, we kiss and make up? Forget what you've done to us? Said to us? What you were just about to say to us then? Forget about everything. Pretend you don't see us as subhuman? Or accept it and live with it like I have for my entire fucking life?"

"Regardless of how we feel about one another, a fight will only result in death."

"Yours!"

"That may be so, but let's not pretend any of us will walk away unaffected."

Although he shared a glance with Aggie, Hawk fought to keep his face neutral. How could he tell any of them to accept the offer? That they didn't have a right to be upset? That they shouldn't be fucking furious about what these people had done to them. Their call to make. And if they decided war, then so be it.

Rayne lifted her gun and ducked out of the strap before she threw it to the side. It clattered against the steel floor. "You know what?" She walked from around her shield. "Me and you. Let's settle this now."

The stairwell barked a single syllable. "Huh?"

"Me and you." She unclipped her knife, discarded it, and raised her fists. "It won't even scratch the surface, but I can't put my friends at risk while I take my pound of flesh. Let's settle this the old way."

Hawk peered around the side of his shield. As Rayne marched towards the stairwell, the hidden guards shoved one of their own out to meet her. Apparently weaponless, save for his boulder-sized fists and six-feet-four-inch frame.

Hawk showed his gun to Aggie, but she shook her head. They needed to let Rayne settle this.

Rayne screamed and ran at the man, who caught her clean on the chin. The *clop* of fist against jaw clapped through the dining hall, and she fell on her arse with a hard jolt. He lowered his guard and stepped back. He didn't want to fight a woman. Especially one as slight as Rayne.

Aggie flapped a hand at Ethan, catching his attention before he joined the fight. Rayne needed to settle this on her own.

Rayne charged at the man and slammed into his midriff, tackling him to the ground.

Hawk and the others got to their feet and emerged from behind their shields. Guards stepped from the stairwell, all of them getting closer to the scuffling pair. His gun hung from his strap, the guards' the same. They eyed one another, both sides waiting for that spark that could tip them over into chaos.

All the while, the footage repeated on the far wall. Louis kneeled beneath the lowered diseased and pulled the prisoners closer.

She might have been smaller and lighter, but Rayne moved like a greased-up rat. She clambered on top of the guard and attacked him with a flurry of punches. Each one landed, cracking against his face, sending his head one way and then the other. Each one slipped through his flailing defences.

But the guard had such power he only needed to land one blow for every twenty of hers to keep the battle in his favour. He caught her clean.

She landed on her back.

His face bloody, he sprang up and smothered her.

Hawk tensed. He should be helping. But Aggie hadn't yet moved. The guards were yet to get involved. It didn't fall to him to escalate this battle.

The man jumped up and wound back his right leg, but before he could kick her, Rayne swung around and swiped away his left. She crawled over him again, swarming him, dripping blood on him from the gash above her right eye. One punch. Two, three. She raised her fist again and paused. The man lay beneath her and covered his head with both hands. She stepped off him and backed away, wiping her deep cut with her sleeve.

Another guard came forward, his hands at his sides, his gun hanging across his front. "Truce?"

Rayne watched on, impassive, while William tore off a strip of his shirt and bandaged her head.

Aggie took the guard's hand. "Truce. We live in a very different world now. We don't like each other, but that doesn't mean we need to kill one another."

The guard dipped his head. "I agree. We have too much else to deal with. With that in mind." He lifted his gun.

Hawk and Ethan stepped forward, both of them laying the red dots of their targets on the man's face. The guards behind him met their aggression in kind, aiming their weapons at the two.

The guard spoke slow and deliberate words. "With that in mind, you'll forgive us if we keep a hold of our weapons."

After flapping her hands at Hawk and Ethan, urging them to stand at ease, Aggie nodded. "Of course. The same goes for us."

Hawk and Ethan relaxed, and the guards followed suit.

Her head wrapped, Rayne pointed at the lead guard. "How do we know we can trust you?"

"You don't. But that works both ways, right?"

Another dry gulp, Hawk crossed the room to the table holding the water jugs. Just feet away, but it might as well have been on the other side of the planet until that moment.

Shaking with fatigue and adrenaline, he spilled some down his front as he drank. The cool liquid eased his stinging throat.

An uneasy truce, but a truce nonetheless. Wiping his mouth with the back of his sleeve, he pulled a tight-lipped smile at Aggie. She raised her eyebrows. They didn't have to like these people, but that didn't mean they had to go to war.

CHAPTER 43

Over the past few days, Joni had claimed a series of victories over her former abuser. Victories, that in her darkest moments, when she sat in her hole in the ground, shivering from where the damp had permeated everything, her clothes, her blankets—she even had to wipe the screens to keep them working—she couldn't have ever believed would happen. From reconnecting with her daughter, to destroying his prison, to his death, and now his exposure. He deserved it all, and while it had to be done, and the world had to know this man and his madness, sadism, and utter disregard for any life other than his own, the emptiness inside her had only grown with each victory. And she'd not only hurt herself, but she'd hurt her daughter. She ran a hand down Antonia's arm, breaking her from her daze. "Are you okay?"

"Huh?" Antonia looked out at the control room and the people in it with the same bloodshot glaze she'd had in the dusty tunnels. Worsened by Carly's murder. Doubled down by yet another revelation about the man she'd once called Dad. Grief and humiliation. Like he'd done with everyone else, he'd duped her into thinking he had something more than his own gratification in mind when he acted. But being so close to him, being a part of him, she should have seen it sooner. Her mind might have told her there was nothing she could have done, but should she have seen it sooner?

And should Joni have acted? She could have ended him a long time ago, but she only did it when she found out about her daughter. How many people had suffered because of her? "About what you just saw. Are you all right?"

"Yeah. No." She threw up her shoulders in a shrug. "I'm just tired is all. Besides, we knew what he did to those prisoners; it's not a surprise."

"But seeing just how he did it was."

"There's a difference?"

"After seeing that, I'd say so, wouldn't you?"

Antonia blew out and blinked repeatedly. "Yeah. They say the reality's never as bad as what you imagine. That's not the case with Da … Louis. Also, I'm not sure I could even imagine half the things I've seen him do. But we've sent out the footage for the right reasons." She looked at Joni for the first time since the footage had played. "Hopefully it helps."

"Hopefully."

Matt's chair squeaked with his sudden jolt. "Oh!"

"What?"

Matt pointed at one of his many screens, Pearl beside him in that shitty plastic chair that should have been destroyed years ago. He'd fixed it so it showed footage from one camera rather than flitting from one view to the next like all the others. "The cult. They're leaving."

"The block?" Joni ran over.

"Yeah. This is outside. Look!"

Several cult members slipped from the maintenance shafts along the side of the block closest to the warehouse and ran across the gap between the two buildings, vanishing into the cover of Louis' temple. "Are we seeing an end to the cult?" They'd not yet disbanded, but how long could such a tenuous doctrine of hate hold them together? Surely the cracks would form under the pressure of trying to stay alive? Joni could finally tell everyone the truth.

"Shouldn't there be more?" Antonia, now at Joni's side, leaned towards the bank of monitors. She blinked like the glare stung her eyes. "Isn't the cult larger than that? Or did we miss the first lot heading in there?"

"Only one way to find out." Joni grabbed her small earpiece, inserted it, crossed the control room to the door leading to the medical bay, and slammed a fist against the door's button. It parted with a *whoosh!*

Antonia ran a few steps to catch up. She rubbed the back of her neck where they'd implanted her chip. "Where are we going?"

"I'd like to know the same," Matt said.

"The roof. It's the best place to watch this play out. If they go much farther, the cameras won't pick them up. And we really need to know if they've all gone."

Through the medical bay, down the left of the central two aisles, Joni reached the door at the end and whacked the button again. She marched down the next corridor to the door that gave access to the stairs leading to the roof. Much more dignified than crawling through the maintenance shafts.

Her daughter a step behind, several more guards followed, some of them dropping from the hatches where they'd been watching for intruders.

The frigid wind stung Joni's face. Her nose and ears tingled as she leaned into the strong breeze. Higher than everything else save for the north and south walls. The sprawling labyrinthine prison stretched away in every direction. A maddening maze of roads and paths. White lines and red lights. Diseased wails. Like a medieval asylum filled with tortured souls. The moon shone down, imbuing the thin and fast-moving clouds with a spectral glow.

"This is all Dad's fault." Antonia's eyes narrowed, her hair blowing across her face. "He set this loose on all these people." She bared her teeth. "I'm glad he's fucking gone."

About twelve guards had joined them, Ralph among their number. Joni led them to the side of the block closest to the warehouse and the clattering clack of firing guns. She rested on the wall, the steel cold against her palms. Her stomach lurched when she leaned over, the drop about one hundred and fifty feet. Members of the cult filled the space between the two buildings. They shot at the onrushing diseased before pulling back into the warehouse, dragging most of the creatures in with them, many of them falling the second they entered. Joni rubbed the thin scabbed line where she'd implanted her chip. A few seconds later, another group burst from a different door to repeat the process. Like they were calling the diseased.

Antonia on her left, Ralph on her right, the guards spread out on either side, all of them leaning over the edge. "You getting this, Matt?"

"Yeah. It's not a bad idea. Those triggers on the warehouse's doors are doing a lot of their work for them."

Joni jumped at the *crack* and then whistle of a fired bullet. Jay, the chef who'd cooked them parsnip soup, fell forwards, leaving a momentary cloud of red mist where his head had been. He buckled over the wall, the guard beside him grabbing thin air, missing his feet as he fell.

"Get down." Joni dropped, and the rest of the guards followed suit as more bullets streaked overhead.

Ralph pointed towards the warehouse. "They're on the fucking roof."

Joni raised her eyebrows.

"Sorry. Bit late to be saying that now."

"Yep!"

Matt came through. "What's happening?"

"They have snipers on the roof. They were waiting for us."

"Are you all right?"

"Jay's dead."

"Damn! Can you fight back?"

"They're using sniper rifles, Matt."

"Shit! Then what?"

"Wait it out?" Some guards, including Ralph and Antonia, nodded at Joni's suggestion. What else could they do. "Hopefully this is a sign of them fucking off and leaving us alone. Why fight that?"

"Do you have anyone watching the front of the block?" Matt said.

"No. Why?"

Antonia frowned at her mum. Only privy to half the conversation.

"Someone's running across the plaza."

Moving on all fours, Joni crawled away from the low wall, away from the snipers' line of sight. Once clear, she ran to the front of the guards' block. She scanned the high points for more snipers, raised her gun, and fired on the running guard.

His arms flew out to either side like he believed he could fly. He stumbled and fell, face-first on the open concrete.

"What did you do that for? He was running away."

"Whatever they were doing, Matt, I don't trust it. Those guards in the warehouse aren't leaving, they're just trying to draw our focus. This is the real reason they're outside the block."

Both Ralph and Matt said it at the same time. "But to do what?"

"I don't know. And I'm not sure I want to find out either."

"Oh, shit!" Matt's words sent a chill through Joni. "The antenna. It has to be."

A twenty-foot-tall rickety tower of poles and dishes sat atop the steel wall running across the front of the block. On the corner where the wall turned into the main road leading all the way to the north gates.

"It's what we're using to broadcast to the south. And how we're talking to each other now."

"Will it stop the broadcast we've already sent?"

"No. That's gone, and there's no bringing it back."

"Good."

"But it will prevent future contact."

"So we need to defend it at all costs?"

"Yep."

Joni jumped at the rattle of gunfire to her left. A guard leaned over the side of the building and shot the ground, but the cult member had learned from her fallen comrade, and took a zigzagging path across the plaza. The cult continued to attract the diseased's attention around the side of the block, but they couldn't get them all. When the zigzagging guard halted to defend herself against one of the vile creatures, she paused that bit too long. The guard who'd tracked her blew her fucking brains out.

Another cult member made a break for it. "How many do they have?"

Matt sighed in her ear. "I'm not sure, but knowing Andy—"

"As many as it takes."

"I'd say so."

Arming a grenade, Antonia launched it from the block.

The explosion's vibration ran through the wall Joni leaned on. It ripped apart fifteen to twenty diseased, but did nothing to the cult members. Speaking for everyone else, Joni turned her palms to the night sky. "What was that for?"

Antonia cupped her ear. The diseased squall provided her explanation.

Wild screams from all over the prison. The massive labyrinth of walkways and roads came alive with the creatures' chorus. They all converged on the block.

Antonia remained deadpan. "That'll make things harder for them."

Half a dozen cult members broke from the block at the same time. They took a mazy route towards the wall with the radio tower.

Joni joined the guards in firing on the runners. Their bullets evidenced by the small dust explosions bursting from the concrete.

One of the cult fell, and two more replaced them.

Clack!

"Fuck!" The guard to Joni's left had run out of bullets.

Clack!

Another one on her right.

Clack! Clack! Clack!

They'd left the ammo in the control room.

Joni eased off her trigger. She had forty-two bullets left. "Any more grenades?"

Antonia shook her head. No one else responded.

A cult member, dodging and weaving, reached the wall on the other side. She clung to a bar of some sort. Several diseased descended on her, cutting off her escape. She threw the bar against the wall, and it stuck. Matt whispered in Joni's ear, "Magnets."

"Like Pocket Rocket and her friends used to break into the prison."

"Why would anyone want to break into here?"

"To head south."

Matt snorted. "At least they achieved their goal."

The cult member stepped up onto the first bar and attached another one higher up just as a diseased caught her and tore her from the wall.

Another cult member shot her turned kin and diseased alike. She reached the wall armed with another magnetic bar and stepped up the first two before attaching hers higher up. Out of reach.

The third member followed up behind, shooting more diseased before he climbed the first two magnets. But when he stepped onto the one occupied by the other member, it slipped because of their combined weight. The new cult member reached down and liberated their step. He held onto the higher bar, but the woman with him slipped and fell. She landed hard and on her back. The diseased swarmed over her while the victorious member climbed higher.

Matt yelped. "My-fucking-god."

"Don't you mean, my-fucking-Louis?"

"Jeez. What's wrong with these lunatics?"

"Everything."

Another member reached the wall, blowing away the diseased who'd feasted on her mate. She aimed her gun at the man already on the wall and shot him before he could defend himself. She jumped aside, dodging his falling body before climbing with her magnetic bars. She made it up the first few, attached her own, and reached the top of the wall and the antenna.

Joni fired, but she had no chance with so few bullets and the distance between them. She pressed her finger to her earpiece. "What can we do?"

Matt sighed. "Not much now. Bu—"

The cult member on the top of the wall kicked the antenna. It swayed. She kicked it again, and it toppled, falling over the edge and plummeting to the ground, breaking into several pieces on impact.

"Matt? Matt?" Joni pressed her earpiece. While he'd been an irritant, his sudden absence left a hole. Maybe he'd been a better guide than she'd given him credit for.

Ralph raised his eyebrows, and she shook her head. "He's gone. Cut off."

"Fuck! That's our comms with the south done."

The cult member thrust their middle finger in the air at Joni and the others. She turned backwards to climb from the wall, missed the first magnetised bar, slipped, and fell.

Her scream ended when she hit the ground. The diseased in the vicinity paid her no mind.

Leaning on the wall beside her, Antonia shook her head. "Caitlyn. I used to quite like her. What a fucking waste."

CHAPTER 44

Cut off from Matt, cut off from the south, unable to broadcast any more damning evidence of that vile man. But at least they'd gotten out the most important footage. Helped Pocket Rocket and her friends and shown the south the depths to which Louis would plunge to serve his own agenda. A vile and soulless man. A narcissist of the highest order. And at least they could walk through the block rather than crawling in the shafts like intruders. Slowly, room by room, they were taking control of this place. And soon enough, the entire building would be theirs.

Joni led the guards from the stairwell, down the bright corridor, the brushed-steel walls and floors soaking up the shine from the strip lights' glare. They were one less, Jay fallen to a sniper on the roof. Hopefully Theresa and her kill team were faring better.

She led them through the medical bay, down an aisle between clinic rooms that had only recently played host to diseased. The tables, beds, and chairs had been scattered, many upturned by their clumsy occupants. Blood glistened on every surface from their violently haemorrhaging orifices.

Back through the corridor towards the control room, she hit the next button, and the door opened with a *whoosh!*

Sarah had remained in the room. Alone. Protecting herself. She cowered in the corner and turned her back on them while peering over her shoulder, snarling. If she had to die, she'd go down fighting.

But she didn't deserve the attention. Fuck her. She'd get hers soon enough. People like her always did, even if it took twenty years.

Matt swivelled in his chair when Joni entered. "Andy and the cult have left the warehouse."

She reloaded her gun from the ammo stack. She slipped two more magazines into her trouser pockets. "Where have they gone?" She removed her earpiece and laid it on the side, the screens flicking from one camera to the next.

"They're back in the block."

"Fuck."

"And it wasn't all of them."

"So some have remained in the warehouse?"

Matt shrugged. "Or they never left."

The end of the cult would have given Joni the chance to tell everyone the truth. Matt, the other guards, the parents pinning their hopes on meeting their children for the first time … While she'd never wanted to be cut off from the south, at least now she could choose when to reveal what had happened. No chance of Olga, or more likely that tool Duncan, dropping her in it.

A wild scream called to them from several rooms away. Human. Yet to be turned. Fucking furious.

Antonia spun towards the sound. "Have more diseased broken through?"

Matt scanned the screens. "I don't se—"

Distant gunfire.

"Fuck!" Matt dedicated one of his screens to a specific camera. About ten cult members had engaged Theresa and her kill team in battle. They chased them down a corridor, firing as they ran.

Ralph caught up to Joni in the control room. "You and Antonia have to stay here."

"What? No way!"

"All it'll take is the press of a button and you're both gone. You *can't* let them get that close."

Antonia threw up her arms. "What, so we stay here like cowards?" She pointed across the room. "Like Sarah."

"Fuck you, Antonia."

"Am I wrong? You spineless fuckwit."

Sarah recoiled again, returning to the shadows where she belonged.

Gunshots called through the building. The guards from the roof left to join Theresa and the others. Joni rocked from side to side, adrenaline flooding her system, daring her to run. She squeezed her gun. "Antonia's right. We can't just wait here."

"We might need you. Last line of defence. Maybe Matt can let you know if they're coming at us from another direction."

"We know they're not coming from the roof, Ralph. There *is* only one direction."

"Joni!" Ralph's large hands smothered hers. "Don't make this battle harder by forcing us to worry about you and Antonia. We don't need that distraction."

"You're saying I'll hinder more than I'll help?"

"I wouldn't put it that way."

"But that's what you're saying?"

"That's what I'm saying. Yes."

Ralph loaded his gun, stashed more magazines about his

person, and followed the line of guards, leaving Joni, Antonia, and Sarah in the control room.

Hanging back in the shadows, Sarah watched on with narrowed eyes. A laser-sharp focus. A coward and a snitch. Gathering information. Always gathering information. Ammunition. Fuck her. She'd get hers soon enough. Joni spoke so only Antonia heard. "I don't want you to do this with me, but I have a plan."

"Ralph wanted us to stay here."

"He wanted to not have to worry about us. And because he thinks we're back here, he won't. But again, while I can't tell you what to do, I'd rather you stayed here. I just want to tell you my plan."

"Which is?"

Guns went off in the building. Call and response.

"The shafts."

Antonia tilted her head to one side.

"While they're fighting on the ground, they'll have their hands busy. We should be able to move through the shafts unnoticed."

"And if they notice us?"

"We're screwed. One of them will have a button."

Antonia gulped.

"But there's a chance we can control them from above. Set our traps and get the hell away from there. Get out of range. Again, I'd rather you st—"

"I'm coming, Mum. You know I'm coming. Your plan, even as you said it, was *we* not *I*. Did you really expect any other response?"

Matt could have helped them see more of the block. Help them plan what they were heading into, but he always had opinions. Opinions they didn't need to hear. The chair Antonia had used to access the hatch earlier remained. Joni stepped onto it, threw her gun around so it rested against her back, and climbed into the shaft. Antonia followed.

Dusty, cold, cramped. The shafts had never bothered her when she'd been a loner. When she had no place in this block. But she now had some control here. She and the others were reclaiming this building, and she'd walk its corridors like she belonged. Something she'd longed for since she'd left, but never truly admitted to herself. Belonging. Part of a community. One of the gang. But also a betrayer. She'd deceived them. Encouraged them to fight in a war they might not have otherwise chosen. Not when the prize of seeing their loved ones didn't exist.

The deafening cries of war raged below them. Fired bullets and screams. Ralph and the other guards had joined Theresa and her kill team. They might have had the numbers on their side, but the tight corridor handicapped their advantage.

Each side occupied one end of the hallway. Each of them behind an opening and closing door. An operable shield. Theresa led the fight on their side. She whacked the door's button, attacked with three other guards, and withdrew as the doors closed. The rest queued up for their turn. Locked. Loaded. And ready to go.

The cult fired back. They mimicked Theresa's tactics. A stalemate with few casualties. So far.

Several columns of light shone from below. Wayward bullets having pierced through the steel shaft's bottom. A gauntlet to be run. Joni's plan was dependent on them reaching the other side unnoticed.

Her heart in her throat, she turned back to Antonia and raised her thumb. She mouthed, *Ready?*

Antonia raised her thumb in return.

Joni crawled along the shaft towards the cult. The button carriers. The lunatics who'd not only turn their insides to liquid, but they'd turn the shaft into a cheese grater if they got wind of their presence. She froze as another bullet punched a small hole up ahead. It tinged off the ceiling and fell with a gentle thud. How something so small could cause such devastation …

The battle below made Joni's ears ring. Unrelenting. Eight to ten cult members holding their own against Theresa's small army.

Joni held her breath while she passed over them. A section of the shaft popped beneath her pressure, and she froze. Every muscle in her body locked tight. Powerless. Waiting for bullets to tear her to shreds. Or for someone to liquidise her with the press of a button.

But the war raged on beneath them. They had too much else going on. Joni crossed the rest of the way, over the heads of the cult, Antonia behind her. They headed for the stairwell at the end of the hall about one to two hundred feet away. And a couple of closed doors from the cult.

"That was close."

Antonia raised her eyebrows.

"I want you to stay here while I go downstairs and get the diseased."

"Why do you get to go down there and I stay up here?"

"Because it's my plan. Besides, I know the maintenance shafts better than anyone."

Antonia's lips tightened. If she could have argued, she would. "So, what's the plan?"

"The kill team has already cleared many of the rooms down there. And I imagine this racket has attracted the diseased's attention. I'm hoping I'll go down and find an army of the fuckers gathered behind a locked door."

"So you're going to unlock that door?"

"And lead them back up here."

"*Lead* them?"

"Yeah. I'll be the rabbit. Give them something to chase. Make sure they find their target."

"That's suicide."

"Not if you're waiting here to pull me back in."

"And then what?"

"We lock the doors, trapping the cult in with the diseased."

Antonia lay on her front and lifted with her inhalation. She opened her mouth and closed it again. She inhaled for a second time. "Okay."

"Okay?"

"Yeah. Okay. I'll be here, ready to pull you back up into the shafts."

Joni leaned forwards, and they touched heads.

"I've lost too many people already. Please make sure I don't lose my mum before I've gotten to know her."

With that motivation, Joni would crawl through fire and survive. She kissed her daughter's forehead. "Don't worry. I'm coming back."

CHAPTER 45

B ack in the stairwell, the diseased still gathered on the
  other side of the locked door. Louis' broadcast had
replayed so many times, Olga could recite every fucking
word of the sadistic encounter. The light from the massive
projection on the sports hall's wall below countered some of
the red emergency glow. The recording masked Olga's and
her friend's sounds, their shuffling, their coughs … but it also
masked the sounds of their enemies. Guards and diseased
alike. If they were close, they had no fucking idea.

Gracie banged against the other side of the door, and
Olga jumped. Again. The diseased roared and shouted in
response, but they soon quietened down to their low-level
snarling. Took a back seat to Louis' torture of the prisoners.

The footage had weighed heavily on them all. It was what
they'd needed, and what they had to show to the south if they
were ever to rid themselves of the blame put upon them, but
that didn't dilute the broadcast's potency. Heartbreaking.
Disturbing. Vile.

Sniffs and the occasional broken sob from above. Nick
comforted Artan, his arm around him as the pair huddled on

the same step between Gracie and Matilda. And maybe they needed to be grateful for that. The footage had triggered something in Artan. Something he'd needed to release. The boy carried his grief like an overfilled water balloon. He needed to let a little out lest he burst. How would she deal with such a burden? She'd fucked up with Max, but she hadn't been the one to end it. Artan had murdered his father. Not even a slither of ambiguity in which he could hide. A crevice of comfort.

"I wasn't liked very much as a child."

Olga pressed her finger to her ear. "Huh?"

Matilda and the others perked up behind her.

"I wasn't liked very much as a child."

Olga patted the air. They could relax. No news worth sharing. Duncan wasn't liked much as a kid. No shit?

He dragged a wet sniff. "I was always really needy."

Was? She gritted her teeth. The only way she could hold onto her reply. When you had nothing nice to say …

"And that pushed people away. I didn't get the love from my parents that I so craved. I sought it in my school friends, but they were a ruthless bunch of little shits. Most kids are, right?"

"Right."

"Well, they wholeheartedly rejected me. Hell, they made a fucking game of it. They'd say they were coming over to play, and I'd wait for them. But they'd never show up, and the next day, they'd tell me they came and someone sent them away. Some adult I'd never heard of. We had radios between rooms so we could talk at night, but when I'd call, they'd make up an excuse to go away for a moment. They'd pretend they were going to the toilet, or to get something from the other room. They'd put their radio down and never come back. I'd wait for hours, desperate to believe they wanted to talk to me as much as I'd wanted to talk to them. And then I'd catch them sniggering to one another in class. Making a joke about how long they left me hanging. It was hard, but I suppose I'm the one laughing now, eh? Where are they? Bleeding through their fucking eyes and driven by the single desire to infect anyone and everyone."

There weren't many times where Olga had nothing to say, but a reply utterly evaded her.

"Not so funny, right?"

"Right."

"I suppose what I want to say is, I can see I was annoying. I *am* annoying."

Again, Olga bit her tongue.

"I'm not stupid. I get it. But it …"

"What?" Olga pressed her finger harder into her ear, and her friends perked up again. "What is it, Duncan?"

"Oh shit! I wasn't paying attention. Shit! I'm sorry."

"What is it?"

"I wasn't watching the screen."

Not for the first time. He insisted they trusted him, got offended when they didn't. But he'd already failed to notice when an army of diseased came towards them, and now this. "What is it, Duncan? What's happened? Is it William and the others?"

"Yeah. They're in danger."

"Get to the point, man."

"They're under attack. The guards have found them. They're flooding the stairs."

"*Flooding* the stairs?"

"Not literally. They have them outnumbered." His breaths grew short.

"Calm down, Duncan. We need to deal with this logically. They're still in the next block?"

"Yeah."

"In the dining room?"

"Yeah."

"And the guards are coming down from above to attack them?"

"Yeah."

Nick stood up with Matilda.

"So, what's the best course of action?"

"You want my advice?"

"I'm asking for it, aren't I?"

"No, it's stupid."

"Just tell me!"

He spoke fast, one word running into the next so she couldn't interrupt. "Lead the diseased back to the other block. Along the top walkway, through the meeting room. Unlock the door you locked earlier and rain hell down on the guards. You can get down, back into the cinema room and away. There are only a few guards on that floor now. You'll be able to fight them and probably bring the others up as the diseased are running down."

"But won't that send the diseased down on William and the others?"

"It will, but they'll go for the guards first. It'll give William's lot a chance to run while they're distracted. Otherwise, I don't see them getting away."

"Shit. Really?" Gracie said when Olga had relayed Duncan's plan. On her feet like the rest of them and still closest to the door and the diseased on the other side. She peered back through the tall and thin window. Clumsy fists hammered against the glass. Some dragged their hands down the other side of the pane, fingerpainting with the muck left behind from where they'd peered through. Pressed their bleeding eyes against the reinforced glass. Their puss-filled wounds. Their vomit- and claret-coated lips.

"Really." Olga bounced where she stood. "So, what do you all think?"

"I'll go." Matilda stepped down towards Olga.

Artan wiped his nose with the back of his sleeve and rubbed his swollen eyes. "I'll go with her."

Olga glanced at Nick and shook her head. "No. I will."

"But you can't climb like I can."

"Rate yourself, don't ya?"

"I'm just saying." Nick pulled Artan closer to him. They couldn't let him go. Not in his current state.

"I appreciate your concern, Artan. I really do. But I can do it. You need the rest right now."

"I'm fi—"

Nick grabbed Artan's hands. "Stay back, Art. Please."

"Nick's right." Matilda reached up to her brother and stroked his arm. "Just this once." She took a fresh magazine from Nick and reloaded her gun.

The glowing digits on Olga's read one hundred and seventy-four bullets. She waved away Nick's gesture of both a refill and his ammo bag.

"You're sure you have enough?"

"Hopefully. We need to travel light, and if we get to the point where we need more than four hundred bullets between us, I doubt we'll have time to reload anyway."

Olga led Matilda towards the sports hall. Gracie remained on the other side of the locked door, keeping the diseased distracted until they needed them. Their steps called down to the lower floors, but Louis' broadcast buried them. If there were diseased or guards in the building, they'd have to be close to hear them.

The projected footage showed a close-up of Louis'

porcine face as the diseased bit into his head. Olga focused on the elevated walkway on the other side of the sports hall.

The second she stepped out into the cool night, Duncan said, "You need to get up to the next floor from this side. Get too close to the other end and the guards might see you from the cinema room. Blow your cover too early and this won't work."

The walkway above and over to the right. "Duncan's saying we need to go up from this side. There are guards in the cinema room."

Unlike the rest of the block's exterior, where the steel shutters covered the windows and gave them something they could climb, just, the windows on these floors were larger, each shutter too big to use as a ladder rung to the next level. Olga clicked her tongue. "Any ideas?"

The squirrel of the group. The cat. The lizard. Matilda could scale glass if needed. She always had an idea. But how long would it take to come? And how long would be too long?

CHAPTER 46

J oni reached the floor below, sliding down the vertical shafts running alongside the stairwell. She shook with her haste, her movements clumsy. But the longer she took, the greater the risk to Antonia's life. Alone in the shafts, the cult and their buttons beneath her. She might be invisible to them now, but what if they got wind of her movements? What if the dust made her sneeze? Or the shaft popped beneath her pressure? What if she got caught by a wayward bullet?

The hallway on this floor stretched twice as wide as the one above. Mostly guards' rooms on either side, broken by the occasional storage-cum-cleaning cupboard. The rooms were all of a similar size. They'd made the quarters for one. The monastic life of a guard. Like every celibate organisa-tion, they expected and aggressively encouraged abstinence except by those at the top. The rule makers didn't need guid-ance and restrictions. It forced the guards into secret liaisons where the children, who were now probably a part of the vast diseased horde in the south, were conceived. In secret. In the shadows. Although, more than likely, observed. Every interaction. Every personal moment. Observed. Noted. Cards marked. And probably broadcast to the south as part of Louis' entertainment empire.

The flat steel of the shaft popped beneath Joni's pressure. The hallways and layout might be different from the floor above, but the tunnels were the same. Dusty. Gloomy. Cold. Splashes of light shone up through every grate.

The first hatch in Joni's path hung open. It could have been where the cult emerged. It landed them as close as they could get to the stairs leading to the floor above. Stairs clear of diseased, thanks to Joni locking all the access points on every floor when they'd barricaded themselves in earlier.

Joni hung from the hatch, the blood rushing to her head. Diseased corpses lay scattered through the hallway, guards and prisoners alike. Utterly still, they lay like a hellish diorama. The air reeked of their spilled rotten blood. Sweat, shit, vinegar, and rot. Theresa and her team had done a fine job. One clear-out of many. But when they were done, they'd be facing a mammoth clean-up. And would they ever rid this place of their stink?

The rattle of gunshots called through the shafts. The battle raged on the floor above. But what if one of the cult had already pressed their buttons? What if, instead of having Antonia waiting to pull her to safety when she returned to the top floor, Antonia lay in a shaft, limp and haemorrhaging her liquified insides? She slammed the heel of her right palm against her temple. "No point in thinking like that, Joni. Optimism until you have no choice, girl."

The snuffling, snarling, and snorting of diseased called to her from farther along the corridor. Joni crawled away from the stairwell to the hallway's first door. It had been locked from the top, keeping the diseased out. She slotted her knife into the screw's groove. But if she unlocked it now, did she really have the time to get back to the open hatch and ahead of them up the stairs? A few she could outrun or fight, but what if she flooded the section of hallway and couldn't drop ahead of them? She had to get the bulk of this mob farther away to stand any chance of their plan working.

Joni passed over the locked door, the stench of living diseased riper than that of their immobile kin. So thick it hung like high humidity and mixed with the stale taste in her dry mouth. She crawled over a grate, the hallway packed, and continued to the next door leading to the third hallway, this one unlocked, as it needed to be if she were to encourage the mob to come deeper into the block.

A woman's scream rang through the tunnels. Joni gasped. "Antonia?" She should be able to recognise her own daughter's voice. But voices didn't have a fingerprint. They were subjected to too many externalities. The acoustics of where they were. How far away. The state of the screamer. She held her breath and lifted her ear. But the next scream never came. It could have been one of many women. And until she knew otherwise, she needed to continue with the plan.

Joni drove both palms against the grate, the hatch swinging away from her on squeaking hinges. The blood rushed to her head when she leaned down. She scrunched up her nose. The same stench hung in the air. The aftermath of playing host to many diseased. But the hallway was clear. The scream could have belonged to anyone. Driven by her galloping pulse, she turned in the tunnel, threw her gun across her back, and slipped from the shaft.

The section of hallway stretched about one hundred feet from end to end. A slug trail of waste ran down its centre, evidencing the diseased's pilgrimage. She swallowed against her heave.

"Shit!" The single syllable ran through the empty section of hallway. She'd come down here to alert the diseased. To drag them back so she could get above them, open the first locked door, and get to the stairs ahead of the mob. But she needed something to stand on to boost back into the shaft. A chair. A stool. A chest of drawers. All of which were easy enough to find, but she should have checked which rooms were clear. And now she couldn't get back into the shafts without one.

Most of the doors running down either side led to guards' rooms, but one in every section accessed a storeroom. They were usually packed with crap no one needed. Spare chairs. Brooms. Mops and buckets. Cables. Always cables. Mostly for outdated tech, but stored all the same in case, one day, they slipped into some sort of technical regression.

Diseased roars and cries a corridor away. A button press away. Antonia lying in the shaft, ready to be blended from the inside. Joni crossed the hallway, drew her knife, and hit the button by the storeroom door. *Whoosh!*

Two diseased on the other side. Joni drove her knife into the first one's head, killing its scream before it left its mouth. She pulled out her blade as the creature fell, toppling a stack of chairs. She attacked the second with a wild swing and sliced open its throat, cutting its cry short, blood streaming down its pallid neck in a neat waterfall. But the beast stumbled towards her, its mouth flapping, desperate to sink its yellowed teeth into her face. It grabbed her wrist and clung on. Strong. Newly turned.

Joni spun around, pulled the creature towards her, and flung it into the other stack of chairs in the small room. It hit them back-first, let go of her wrist, and fell to the ground. She ended it like she had its friend, stabbing the side of its face, burying her knife to the hilt. Turning it off.

Wriggling a chair free from the fallen stack, Joni reached for the button to reopen the door, but froze. Heavy, slamming footsteps descended on the small room.

Pulling against the wall, her back to the cold steel, Joni

placed the chair down and raised her knife.

Crack! The wall shook with the clumsy button press.

Whoosh! The door opened.

A low snarl. A phlegmy rattle. The diseased leaned into the room, three feet from Joni. It stared at the far wall through unblinking eyes pregnant with blood. She turned her knife around, angling the blade up, ready to drive it into the diseased fuckers' chin. Turn it off like she had its friends. More diseased steps approached from outside. They were queuing up to be slaughtered.

But the first one pulled back, and the door closed. Joni fell against the wall and exhaled hard.

Squalls and growls accompanied the heavy steps outside, the hallway filling up. Antonia waited for her above. She sheathed her knife, lifted her chair, and pressed her ear to the cold steel door.

The diseased in the hallway padded back and forth. Aimless. Nothing to chase. No reason to move on. How many waited out there? Could she get to the hatch in time? And if not, how long before she could?

"Fuck this!" Joni whacked the button, screamed as she left the room, and made a beeline for the open hatch. The eight diseased in the hallway gave chase, and the doors leading to the packed corridor opened, more bursting through. A mob of concentrated fury. She fought the urge to drop the chair and grab her gun. Firing shots down here would attract the wrong attention. Give the cult a heads-up. More diseased burst from the guards' rooms.

"Come on, you fuckers!" Joni threw the chair ahead of her. It slid across the floor, its legs lifting and slamming down again as it teetered on the edge of its balance.

She stepped up, gripped the edge of the shaft, and pulled herself in, a stampede clearing the chair away as the diseased missed her and filled the space she'd just occupied.

The echoes of her own breaths for company. Diseased faces stared up at her. Snapping jaws. Outstretched arms. Twisted fingers. Fifty to sixty of them. Now she needed to introduce them to the cult.

Joni quickened her pace through the shafts, the steel sheets popping beneath her. A few diseased below, but most remained at the open hatch she'd climbed into like she might reappear.

Drawing her knife as she crawled, she reached the locked door, drew a deep breath and slipped the edge of the blade into the screw's groove.

A diseased hit the door's button.

Crack!

Whoosh!

Nothing to chase. They remained in the doorway.

Joni reached the open hatch the cult had used, and dropped into the hallway feet-first.

The diseased in the open doorway gave chase. The pack considerably thinned for her dragging many of them back. She ran into the stairwell.

Her superior co-ordination giving her a lead, Joni reached the plateau between floors and the large crimson light on the wall. She turned one hundred and eighty degrees and left the diseased behind.

She opened the door to the top floor and froze. "Shit!" The cult were in this section. They had their backs to her, but the hatch in the shaft remained closed. Probably a good thing. If she'd have gone into the shaft, they would have followed. But where was Antonia?

Diseased raced up behind her.

One of the cult members turned and pointed. "You!" She lifted a button.

Joni countered with all she had in that moment. "Oh, fuck!"

CHAPTER 47

His thirst quenched, Hawk returned to the group, all of them stepping away from the shelter of their shields. The footage played on repeat, one wall aglow with Louis' sadism.

Rayne's opponent stood with the help of a colleague, his face bloody and bruised. But the man smiled at her all the same and stepped forward to shake her hand. Her hiss halted his advance.

One side of Hawk's mouth twisted with a smirk, and he raised an eyebrow at Aggie, who pressed her lips tight and dropped her focus to the floor. Their uneasy truce had a long way to go before they could openly mock them, and maybe they'd never get to where Rayne had anything to say to these people.

William pointed at the stairwell. "Who was that man?"

The man who stepped forward, the leader, self-appointed or otherwise, leaned towards William. "What man?"

"The voice. The one who said *dining hall* when we were on the stairs."

"Oh, him." The lead guard swiped his hand through the

air, batting away the comment. He lowered his voice. "He's a prick. He was leading us to you. I think he wanted us to fight more than your friend does."

Rayne stepped forwards, but Knives thrust out her arm to block her.

"He led us up to the cinema room when you were heading there, so we could cut you off. He then went quiet until he finally said *dining room*."

Hawk turned on the spot. They had two small cameras in the room. One in the corner between the two exits leading to the elevated walkways, and one above the stairwell door. The one above the stairwell had a cracked lens and hung from wires.

The guard clearly fought against his need to gesticulate. "Don't look back now because it'll make it too obvious, but he's watching through the cameras. As you can probably tell, the one above the stairwell door is broken, so, while he can see us from that one over there, he won't be able to hear what we're saying. I suggest we keep it that way. Keep him guessing."

"But he's one of you."

The man scoffed and shook his head. "He looks after number one. He's a fucking snake. We don't trust him and wouldn't ever let him join us. In fact, when I finally see him, I'll take great pleasure in launching him from an elevated walkway. The heavens know I've wanted to do it for years."

"So what now?" Aggie flinched as the diseased bit into Louis' head again. She turned her back on the footage. "It seems like we have a choice. We either hunt down that prick who's watching us, or we try to find Matilda and the others?"

CHAPTER 48

A second to react.
   A second to decide.
It would take a second for a zealot to produce a button.

A second to press it.

A second to save her and her daughter's lives.

Her daughter's at the very least. She'd gladly give her own in sacrifice.

Joni darted back into the stairwell as the door closed, turning sideways through the tightening gap. Chased by bullets, they tinged against the steel barrier. A temporary shield, but nothing could shield her from the trigger. Nothing other than distance from the vile cretins who devoted their lives to the teachings of her abuser.

The ascending diseased packed the stairwell from wall to wall. They slipped and tripped in their haste.

Joni ran down two stairs and kicked out. She caught a diseased in the stomach. It bent over, its mouth stretched wide as it released a heavy gasp and foetid stink.

But the creature stumbled back. Away from Joni into its

brethren behind. They toppled like dominoes. A test of their balance. Those that hadn't already tripped, fell. Weak. Pathetic. They landed in a pile on the plateau between floors. A pit of stinking hatred. Writhing bodies highlighted by the weak glow from the crimson bulb.

Snapping the butt of her gun into her shoulder, Joni stood on the stairs and laid the red target on the glass dome covering the light. She pulled the trigger. The crack of fired bullets. The splash of shattering glass. And then darkness. It stoked the crazy. Added fuel to the wildfire of madness. The diseased filled the stairwell with their screams. Wild. Unhinged. Shrill. Fucking furious. They'd had her in their sights, and she'd hidden like a coward. Turned them all to silhouettes in the shadows. Become one of their stinking number.

Her red target danced in the darkness. Lay on the writhing mass of pandemonium. She flitted from one head to the next. Not enough bullets for them all. Wait for one to break away and then blow its fucking brains out.

Crack!

Someone hit the button to open the door behind.

Whoosh!

Joni swivelled, drew her target around, and aimed it up at the empty doorway. She froze in the light cast from the top floor. The light revealing her to the diseased.

Joni jumped. Like a kid launching themselves at a sandpit, she sailed towards the diseased mass.

Crimson eyeballs. Bared teeth. Grasping hands. She fell into the writhing churn of sweat- and shit-slick bodies. They coated her in their perfume of foetid waste. Their slimy excretions like amniotic fluid in an infected womb. The light from the floor above shone down on her as if in divine judgement. A silhouette filled the doorway. Watched over what they'd caused.

But the unfocussed chaos now had a clearer target than her. Backlit and stood on the top step. Served up on a platter. Those closest to the door fought and twisted. Snarled and snapped. Their teeth clacked, and their hands stretched ahead of them as they broke away and ascended the stairs on all fours. It gave them greater balance, propelling them like wild hounds.

Joni stayed down, the diseased more concerned with the cultist above. She crawled away on all fours. A diseased stood on the back of her head, slamming her brow against the ground. Another one kicked her in the side of the face, leaving behind a wet stamp of excrement from its clotted trousers. One walked over her back. She held in her cry.

The cult member hit the button like repeated attacks would make it close quicker.

Crack! Crack! Crack!

Theresa's kill team on one side, an army of diseased on the other. The cult opened fire just as Joni rounded the bend, heading back down. The thick coating of diseased slime combined with poor light shielded her from the diseased. It made her one of the mindless mob.

Her ears rang, her face throbbed from where she'd been kicked and trampled, and she reeked. But they cared more about the cult than her. A prize they could see.

Her head throbbed, and her right knee burned from where she must have whacked it. She headed towards the bulb at the plateau a storey below. A replica of the one she'd shot to throw the stairwell into darkness, a glass dome covering the weak glow. She shot it like she had the first, turning the next floor dark as she stumbled down, the diseased all rushing up.

Joni slumped in the shadows on the dark plateau, the cold steel against her back, fire in her knee and guts. Her face throbbed, and she stank like a week-old corpse pulled from a river of sewage. Keeping a hold of her gun, her eyes stung from where she refused to blink.

All the while, the light from the floor above guided the diseased to the cult.

CHAPTER 49

L ike Sarah had in the control room, Joni stood in the stairwell's shadows. Waiting. Watching. Calculating. Thinking of the ways she could get the better of her targets. She'd yet to come up with an answer. Maybe she didn't have Sarah's level of scheming. Sarah probably saw angles on top of angles. After years of being a snide little snake, she played her moves like a chess grandmaster.

The battle cries subsided. The top floor door closed with a *whoosh!* The diseased stumbled back to the floor she'd released them from. But they moved with less zeal. Stumbled. Shambled. How long before they fell into their resting mode of disinterest and a dazed lack of focus? Waiting for something to attack. Something to make a noise. Something to shift in the shadows.

And if they didn't find her, how long could she wait? How could she let anyone know where she'd hidden? There were no cameras in the stairwell. No maintenance shafts. And the doors to access every floor were locked, apart from the two above. Maybe someone else had unlocked the doors lower down, but she could waste a lot of time and find nothing.

Armed with a gun and two fresh magazines, she didn't have enough ammo to fight them all.

Surely one of the diseased would find her eventually. Sniff her out. With many still on the top floor, would she get a better opportunity than this to make a break for it? Waiting would only give them time to come back down. To pack her path more thoroughly. An awful time to run, but that didn't mean it couldn't get a lot fucking worse.

Pushing through the searing agony in her right knee, Joni took off, ascending the stairs two at a time. She slammed several diseased aside and hit the door's button, her contact exploding through the stairwell like a detonated grenade.

Crack!

The air lit up with diseased cries.

Her back to the door, Joni shot those she'd shoved, and attacked the ones drawn to her noise. They rolled onto the plateau above like a landslide. She dropped those at the front, the ones behind tripping over their fallen kin. They reached out as they stumbled. She fired on those who got too close, saving as many bullets as she could. The door opened wider, and she fell backwards, landing on her arse.

Firing as she got to her feet, the stairs laden with fallen diseased, she let her gun fall to its strap, got up, and ran, the open hatch in this section of corridor too high to reach.

Crack!

Whoosh!

She opened the next door, kicked several diseased back, and shot several more, creating an opening. She darted through. Hands reached for her and slid off, her shirt her only protection against their long and filthy nails.

Clumsy steps chased her down the hallway. Many slipped and fell on the slug trail of filth that ran from one door to the other like a brown oil slick.

Crack!

Whoosh!

Joni ran through to the next section. The hatch she'd accessed earlier remained open. Fifteen to twenty diseased to her right, gathered around the chair she'd used to boost herself into the shafts. They turned her way as one. Her slimy coating might have confused those in the dark, but under the strip light glare in the hallways, she stood loud and proud as bait.

Joni fired. She dropped three or four. Take down a few more and she could grab th—

Clack!

Her gun bucked. The two numbers on the top of her weapon highlighted her predicament in duplicate. A pair of zeros. Double fucked.

With shaking hands, Joni tore the magazine free and launched it. It bounced off a diseased's face. Cut a gouge in its waxy skin. It only served to invigorate its charge.

Joni ran for the closest guard's room, reloading on the move.

Like she'd done in the stairwell, she whacked the button, pressed her back to the opening door, and bought precious seconds by spraying bullets.

Stumbling back into the room, the door opening wider, inviting in her attackers, Joni continued firing. She dropped another pair. Two old men. Chaz and Dave. But more streamed in from the other hallway.

Joni ripped the flimsy mattress from the guard's bed and blocked the door. She leaned against it as it bucked and shook. Every contact had the potential to send her flying. Leaning at an angle, she used her bodyweight against their attack. She stumbled when the diseased pulled the mattress through from the other side and nearly went with it.

Firing on the diseased again as the room's door closed, Joni tore a wild woman's face to shreds. Put a hole through the forehead of another. Her next line of bullets tore open the throat of what used to be a guard, and his head fell back, but remained attached to his body. She attacked the door's button, blowing it to pieces.

The door halted. Half-closed. "Fuck!" If she'd known it would have worked, she'd have waited. The diseased still had a way through. "Fuck!"

Trembling with fatigue. The slimy layer from the stairwell pulled her skin taut as it turned into a dry crust. Several diseased hit the gap in the door as one. Three faces. Six arms. They all wanted to be the first. Collectively, they prevented each other from achieving that goal.

Her gun levelled on the fuckers, Joni paused. Their single-minded drive had given her the seconds she needed. She dropped her gun to its strap and grabbed a bedside table. The lamp, still plugged into the wall, smashed against the steel floor when she dragged it away.

Standing on the wooden drawers, she reached up to the maintenance shaft hatch, wedged her knife beneath the grate, and pried it free. It swung down and smashed into her forehead, knocking her to the ground. The diseased now upside down behind her. Upside down and breaking through.

Joni jumped up, fired, killed three, stepped back on the bedside table, and pulled herself into the open hatch just as another stampede cleared out her makeshift step.

Stinking. Panting. Her throat tacky with thirst and ready to turn inside out with her next heave. Her hair matted with shit, blood, and vomit. Joni lay on her front, rested her face against the cold shaft, and gave herself the moment she so desperately needed. A moment of calm, feet away from pandemonium.

She'd gotten free. The cult members who'd attacked the

top floor must be down. But she had to get back to the control room and check on Antonia. The small cut on the back of her neck rough with a line of scabbing. What if they'd already pressed the button? What if, on her way back through the tunnels, she found her daughter's corpse?

CHAPTER 50

"You need to hurry."

"Fuck off, Duncan."

"What have I done?"

His whine cut to the base of Olga's neck like fingernails on a chalkboard. She rubbed the spot where the skin had clenched. The strong wind in her ears, she pressed her earpiece. "Do you have anything more useful than hurry?"

Matilda rolled her eyes.

"Because, in case you haven't noticed, neither of us can fly, and I'm not sure there's any other method that'll get us to that walkway."

"No need to be like that."

"Well, try to be helpful, then. Or say nothing at all."

"Fine."

"You have something helpful?"

The wind filled the silence.

"Fine."

Nick ran from the sports hall, wrapped in ropes. He carried a pink plastic bar, which had lumps on each end. He tied a rope around it.

"What's that thing?"

"It's a rope."

"I can see it's a rope. That stupid pink thing."

Tying off the knot, Nick frowned. "I think it's a weight of some sort. A paperweight. A door stopper. Dunno, but it works."

"For what?"

Artan followed Nick out. He took the other end of the rope and tied it to another length. When he gave Nick a nod, Nick spun the rope with the weighted end in large circles like a slingshot. He turned it quicker and quicker until it became a blur. He launched it towards the walkway above, the rope slipping through his hands.

It hit the underside with a clang and dropped, falling past them.

Catching the rope, Nick reeled it in and tried again. He grunted with the effort and launched it for a second time. It sailed over the walkway and came around the far side with a pendulous swing. Artan grabbed the back of Nick's shirt as he leaned out and caught the weight, pulling it back and tying it to the handrail.

Pressing his foot against the railing, Nick pulled the knot until the rope was guitar-string taut. He stepped back, hands on his hips. It ran dead straight in a diagonal line from them to the walkway above.

Olga leaned on the railing and peered down. Her stomach lurched, and the backs of her knees tingled. The blinking plaza over one hundred feet below. Filled with diseased and the dead and broken body of the fallen woman. Did she think she'd fare better? "Will the rope hold?"

"Dunno." Nick shrugged.

"Helpful."

"I wouldn't bet my life on it."

"But you'd bet mine?"

"No. That's up to you to decide."

"You need to hurry, Olga."

"Fuck off, Duncan."

Nick rolled his eyes and shook his head.

"Can you even see what we're about to do? Would you climb across here?"

"No. But are you prepared to let your friends die?"

While Olga argued with Duncan, Matilda leaned away from the bridge and pulled on the rope.

Olga pressed her finger against her earpiece. "Surely there's an easier way to get up there?"

"There's not. You have to pull the knife from the handle on the stairwell door by the meeting room; otherwise you can't open it to let the diseased down on the guards. And I don't see those diseased on the other side of Gracie's door letting you through."

"What about going around the blocks and coming at it from the other side?"

Matilda pulled back from the rope and watched Olga's conversation.

"Nope. Won't work."

"Why won't it work?"

"It'll take too long. And there are diseased in the other blocks too."

"There are diseased there too?"

"Is there an echo?"

"I'm trying to help Matilda understand what you're saying. How many diseased?"

"Small crowds dotted through all of them. They'll slow you down too much."

"Shit. There must be anoth—"

Olga yipped when Matilda vaulted over the railing. She wrapped her legs around the rope and crossed her feet over so when she swung beneath, she remained locked on. She hung down and skittered up. A squirrel. A monkey. A koala … She climbed like she'd been born to do it, reached the walkway above, and dragged herself over, vanishing from sight.

A jack-in-the-box, Matilda popped back up from the other side of the railing and pointed at the neighbouring building with their friends in. "I can do this on my own."

"There you go, Olga. You don't have to climb now."

That was the option he'd choose. Every fucking time. "I'm coming, Matilda."

Nick grabbed Olga's arm. "You're sure?"

"I'm not a coward, Nick."

"That's not what I asked."

"I won't make Matilda do this alone. Never again!"

Nick backed away with his hands raised.

"Never again!" No more obstructions. No more excuses. Olga pulled on the taut rope. Thin, but strong enough to take Matilda's weight, so she'd be fine. She jumped over the side and latched on like Matilda had. She hung in the wind like a beehive on a thin branch. Her gun hung lower. One hundred and seventy-two bullets would do little here.

As she edged closer to the higher walkway, Olga's body trembled and her muscles weakened. She paused, the wind swinging her and the rope.

"What are you doing?"

"Fuck off, Duncan."

"You need to get moving."

"You think I don't know that?" Her entire world flipped upside down when she dropped her heavy head to peer at the plaza again. Her stomach hit her chin, and her heart beat like it wanted out. Easier to go back than keep going. If she returned to the middle floor, she had gravity on her side. Gravity and shame. Maybe Matilda would be okay. The strong wind turned her tears cold against her cheeks. But she couldn't leave her on her own. They didn't do that. No matter what. Never again. And they'd done harder things before. They'd climbed the wall to get into the prison. She could do this.

"Come on, Olga."

Her words tore her throat when she let it all out. "Fuck off, Duncan."

"Olga!"

Olga dropped her head back to look up at Matilda.

"You need to hurry."

"What?"

Matilda pointed into the ballroom with the mirrored floor. "They're coming!"

"Go back, Olga. Let Matilda do it alone."

"Fuck off, Duncan."

An inch at a time. Hand over hand. The wind played with her. Toyed with her. Swung her from side to side. Threatened to rip her from the rope. But Olga climbed. Her knuckles sore, her body trembling, the left side of her face numb from the stiff wind.

Olga nearly let go when Matilda grabbed her. Nearly put the burden of her safety on her friend.

With Matilda's help, she reached the railing above, lay across it, teetered on the edge, and fell onto the walkway, hitting the steel floor like a sack of rocks.

Jumping to her feet, ready to run, Olga paused. "What the fuck?" The ballroom with the mirrored floor stood empty. "Where are the diseased?"

"I figured you needed some motivation to help you push through the fear."

"Shit, Matilda."

Twang!

The rope snapped. It whipped past them as it slid across the top of the walkway. Olga and Matilda leaned over the side. It hung from the railing below like an old vine from a derelict building. Nick and Artan watched them, Nick's cheeks puffing as he blew out.

Olga laughed. "Fuck."

Matilda joined in. "That was close."

"Too close."

"Are you two ladies going to stand up there giggling all night?"

"Fuck—"

"—off, Duncan," Matilda said.

They laughed harder than before and hugged one another. Olga pulled back and held Matilda by the tops of her arms. "That was close. But the hard part's over."

"You're sure?"

"Let's at least pretend it is."

"Fair enough. Now to bait the diseased."

"You ready?" Olga said.

"As I'll ever be."

Hand in hand, they walked into the ballroom with the mirrored floor. Olga whistled like she would to call a dog.

But these dogs were furious and out for blood. Their cry burst from the hallway, and Duncan dropped his voice so low it tickled her ear. "Let the chase begin."

CHAPTER 51

T he door they would have needed to lock to contain the cult had already been locked, and Joni had passed the point where she'd left Antonia. That had to be a good thing, right? She must have gotten away, trapped the cult with the diseased, and crawled to safety. Unless someone else locked the door? They might have found Antonia and dragged her corpse back to the control room. But if someone had pressed the button, surely there would be some evidence of Antonia's death. A pool of blood. A slick trail from where they'd moved her?

Joni's breaths quickened with her progress. But what if she'd fallen through one of the hatches? Or what if the cult had climbed up, pulled her into the hallway with them, and then pressed the button? What if she lay in the corridors below as a sacrifice? An example. They loved a grand gesture.

About ten feet from the hatch leading into the control room, Joni paused. Voices below. Many she didn't recognise. She'd not known any of them long enough. They were subdued. Sombre. In mourning? For Antonia?

Joni sniffed herself. They say you can get used to any

THIS WORLD OF CORPSES · BOOK FIFTEEN OF BEYOND T...

stench, but had anyone smelled this bad? The acrid tang of sick added a vicious kick to the excrement and vinegar rot. The slime had dried on her eyelids, in her ears, under her chin, and in her nostrils. Every time she breathed in, she inhaled their reek. She fought the urge to blow her nose. To alert the others to her presence. What if she didn't want to go back? What if she decided to leave? If Antonia hadn't made it, then she should go. At least she'd never have to admit to the lie. She'd helped liberate Pocket Rocket. She'd broadcast the truth to the south. And those who wanted to join the cult could do what they pleased. Become one of their number. Pray at the altar of Louis.

The diseased crust clotted her hair. She gripped a chunk and bent it until it cracked.

She should leave now. Come back when she'd cleaned up. There were plenty of guards' rooms. Plenty of clean clothes and running water. And she had access to them all.

"Where do you think Mum is?"

Joni lifted her head. Her whisper snaked away from her. "Antonia?"

Running on instinct, she boosted towards the hatch, spun around, and slid into the control room, feet first. She landed two-footed, and a guard jumped aside.

"Mum!" Antonia ran to her, her arms wide. But she stopped as quickly as she'd started. Halted a few feet away and turned up her nose. "My god, you stink."

The room's attention on her, Joni shrugged. "It got messy back there."

"Matt told us what happened." Breathless in her delivery, Antonia reached towards Joni like she wanted to hug her, but her instincts kept her away. "How you ran into the cult on the top floor and vanished back into the stairwell. But then the diseased came out. Then he saw you on the floor below. Saw you fighting your way back into the maintenance shafts.

Mattresses. Diseased. The lot!" Her eyes wide, her mouth agape. "What … how … I don't get it."

Joni laughed. "For someone who doesn't get it, you've done a good job of summarising."

"Wow." Antonia stepped back while shaking her head.

"But you're okay? I was worried the cult might have pressed a button when you were close."

Antonia batted the comment away and rubbed the back of her neck. "Theresa and her kill team kept them occupied. I waited until they'd driven them back into the final room; then I locked them off from above and got the hell out of there."

"Well, this is nice, isn't it?" Sarah appeared from the shadows and folded her arms as she looked from Joni to Antonia. "Happy, are you, Joni?"

"Well"—Joni shifted her weight from one foot to the other —"my daughter made it, and the cult's down, so yeah. Of course. Are you saying I shouldn't be?"

"I'd expect nothing less. Considering."

"You're toxic, you know that?"

Sarah looked Joni up and down and sneered. "You're a fine one to talk. You're a walking disease. Look at you? And you're a selfish arsehole."

"Selfish? Do you know what I've do—"

"Coming down here stinking the place out." Sarah's ruddy cheeks turned a deeper shade of crimson. "Playing happy fucking families with a daughter you barely fucking know. Cut the act, Joni."

"Excuse me?"

"How can you be so happy and connected? So pleased to see someone you abandoned?"

Joni stepped forward, but Antonia blocked her path.

"And that's not the worst of it." Sarah pointed at Joni. "Did you even stop to think, for just a second, about those who didn't make it?"

Since landing in the control room, Joni had fixed solely on Antonia. Many of the guards stood around, heads bowed. Some with bloodshot eyes and damp cheeks. Some were still in the throes of grief.

"Try thinking about someone other than yourself for a change, yeah?"

"Fuck off, Sarah." Ralph appeared from Antonia's right and shoulder-barged the vicious woman. He sent her stumbling into a wall, and she fell, although from the way she went down, she'd certainly added a flourish for effect. But if she sought sympathy, she'd picked the wrong crowd.

Mary stepped forwards carrying a guard's uniform. "I found these in the comms room."

Joni kept her hands by her sides.

Sarah lay crumpled on the floor. "Too good for a guard's uniform?"

"Fuck off, Sarah."

"I've got your number, Joni. You're no good for this group."

Had Joni's secret gotten out?

Joni took the uniform and dipped a nod at Mary. "Thank you."

"And there are showers in some of the medical bays. You want us to come and watch your back while you wash?"

"Thank you. That'd be nice."

ALTHOUGH JONI RETURNED to the control room shower fresh, the diseased stink remained with her. It would take more than soap and hot water to remove their reek. The guard's uniform was a good fit. Too good. She'd change at the first opportunity.

Mary dragged a chair from the side of the room and sat Joni down next to the blue control console. She produced a hairbrush and stood behind her. The steady strokes settled Joni's heart. Eased some of her tension. Antonia smiled as she left them to it.

"How man—" Joni coughed to clear her throat. No one had ever looked after her like this before. "How many—"

"Fell?"

Joni nodded.

"Five. Alfie, Rachel, Jackie, Karen, and Joe."

"To the diseased?"

"No. The cult shot them. The diseased were never a threat because Antonia had already locked the door."

"I'm sorry."

"It's not your fault."

But would they be fighting if they knew the truth? Maybe they had a better way to settle things? They could have talked it out. Found a harmonious resolution like many of them had wanted. But how could they find harmony with a group that imprisoned and sacrificed them? In a life where she'd questioned everything, she'd never been more certain. The cult needed to be stopped. Whatever else happened, their reign had to end.

"Thank you, Mary."

The woman behind her paused. "For what?" She started brushing her hair again.

"For looking after Antonia when I couldn't. I can see how much you love her and she you. And, as hard as I find that, you're not the one to blame. I shouldn't have taken it out on you."

"It's okay. I understand."

"Having gotten to know you a little, I'm grateful. Pleased

you were in her life when she needed it most. It's a comfort to know she was loved and nurtured when growing up. That someone gave her what Louis wouldn't."

"Honestly, you don't have to thank me. I always wanted kids, but it's not an option when you're a guard." She tied Joni's hair in a ponytail and ran her finger along the cut at the back of her neck before squeezing her shoulder. "It was my pleasure to have her. Always."

Joni covered the back of Mary's hand with her own.

CHAPTER 52

Clean from head to toe and dressed in fresh clothes, even if it was a guard's uniform, and even if she'd sworn she'd never wear one again. Her hair tied in a ponytail. So exhausted, her entire body buzzed like a faulty appliance. But for the first time in years, maybe even in her life, full. Filled with love and nurturing from another person. And closer to the woman who knew an Antonia she never would. A woman who'd helped guide her on her way to being the fine adult she'd become.

"Happy, are you?"

Joni broke from her daze. "Huh?"

Even the way Sarah walked suggested her bitter twist wound through her spine. A tree planted in toxic soil had no chance of growing straight. "You look happy with yourself."

"Wha—"

"Sitting there smiling. Thinking about all the dead guards, are you? Of those lost to the cult?"

Joni pushed against the sides of her chair, but Mary's gentle hand on her shoulder kept her seated. And she had a point. Sure, she could beat Sarah black and blue. To within an inch of her miserable life. She could permanently wipe that sneer from her vicious face, but where would it get her? Other than making her look like the arsehole. They didn't have time for infighting and backstabbing. They had a cult that needed to be toppled.

A large rectangle of light burst to life on the far wall. Projected from a cube on the ceiling, it blinked and flickered before presenting a close-up of Andy's greasy face. She squirmed where she sat like she could wriggle free of the discomfort generated by his image.

Hidden speakers projected his heavy, snorting breaths around the otherwise silent room. The skin at the back of her neck clenched. She rubbed the small cut from the implant.

The man stepped away from the camera, bringing more of his body into shot. He held up a button. Joni pulled her hand away while Antonia reached up to her own scar.

"You might have gotten away once, but it's just a matter of time before I get close enough to set you both off." He held up his left index finger. "But first, I have something to show you. This is from my personal collection."

Recorded footage replaced Andy. So murky, Joni leaned forwards. They were viewing something through a dirty lens. She clapped a hand to her mouth. Not dirty. Steamed up. A naked body in a hot shower. She called through to the observation room. "Turn it off, Matt."

"Don't!" Antonia said. "Let this sick fuck show us what he's got. His need for attention might be his undoing. He might show us something that will help us end him once and for all."

"You're sure?"

Watching the footage through squinting eyes, she nodded. "It's only me naked. What's the big deal?" She snorted. "And it's hardly exclusive. Millions have already seen it thanks to Dad."

Andy's heavy breathing grew heavier. His voice wavered. "I've watched this footage many, many times." He laughed, his shrill tones pulling Joni's back tight. "And that was just yesterday. It's what got me so excited to have her watching me for once. I thought I'd return the favour. Put on the same show."

Sarah tutted. "You knew you were being watched when you showered?"

"Of course she didn't fucking know." Joni ignored Antonia's glare. Someone had to stick up for her if she didn't have the energy to do it herself.

Sarah threw a hand towards the screen. "Look at her. That's someone who knows they're being watched."

"That's someone who's showering."

"The filthy whore has it all on display. She's performing."

A gentle squeeze from Mary on her right shoulder kept Joni in her seat. "How do you shower, then, Sarah? While wearing a chastity belt and with your hands over your tits?"

"Wouldn't you like to know?"

"Leave it, Mum."

Andy's puce face returned, commanding the room's attention. His skin glistened with a fresh sheen. "I'll bet this has aroused some of you, right?"

Antonia winced.

"And some of you feel sorry for her? But this might change your minds. Help you see how much pain and suffering she's caused. How she's not the victim here."

The footage changed to a close-up of a woman in her forties. Her face contorted, wrinkles on her dark skin. Her black hair, cut in a bob, had streaks of grey.

Antonia stepped towards the footage. "Rose?"

Joni frowned. "Who's Rose?"

Mary leaned closer to Joni as the footage pulled away. Andy tied Rose to a wooden cross in the shape of an X. She kept her voice low. "She taught her art. Every week for years. They were close, and Antonia had a genuine talent for it. But Rose's leaving caused her too much pain, so she gave up."

The camera spun so quickly it made Joni dizzy. But the nausea in her stomach came from somewhere else. Louis, entering through the same warehouse door they'd exited via earlier. His mouth flapping, but his words muted, replaced by Andy's running commentary.

"Little Antonia told Daddy this woman wasn't giving her enough attention."

"What?" Antonia stamped her foot. "I said no such thing."

His mouth wide in a muted scream, his veins standing out on his neck, Louis swung for the restrained Rose and caught her with a clean punch to the chin. The woman's head snapped to one side, her bob flying out like a whirling dervish.

Andy spoke with a mock childish whine. "Rose isn't very interested in me, Daddy. It's like I'm invisible." The life left his voice. "But I suppose that's the problem when you've been raised like a princess. When you think you're the most important person in the world. All Louis did was love you. You turned that good intention into poison."

The on-screen Andy stood to the side while Louis went to work. He might have thought he hid it, but the glint in his eyes and smirk tickling his mouth spoke of his enjoyment.

Blood ran from Rose's nostrils, over her lips, and dripped from her chin. She cried, her pleas muted like the rest of the recording.

Antonia turned to the room. "I didn't say *any* of that. Andy's lying. I loved Rose. She was the highlight of my week." She watched more of the footage. "I asked Dad if I could have more art lessons, and Rose left soon after th—"

She pulled into herself, pressing her elbows into her stomach like she'd received the next blow.

A quick left and right. One, two. Louis sent her head one way and then the other. The Andy in the warehouse threw his head back with muted laughter.

Louis walked away and waved a hand through the air. Andy skipped a couple of running steps to catch up with him. The camera pulled back to show more of the warehouse, their path to the control room, and finally, the chained diseased hanging from the ceiling. It lowered towards Rose, reaching out. Desperate to grab her.

"Now, I love Louis and everything about the man, even his failings. And his habit of listening to his daughter every time she had even the most minor of complaints was a massive failing. The only one I could see in an otherwise perfect man. It meant no one was safe from Antonia's condemnation. But we have new leaders in this place now. We're more considered. We'll treat you fairly and with open minds. We won't run things on the whims of a spoiled brat."

"We don't need to watch any more of this," Joni said.

"Oh, I think we do." Sarah took in the rest of the room. "I think we all need to see who else has been punished because of Antonia. Just how much suffering she's caused."

"How do you know there's more of this?"

"Come on, Joni. Everyone knew the consequences of crossing Louis' little princess." She turned to Antonia. "You wonder why people didn't like you? Why the others are still afraid to speak their mind? You have blood on your hands, girl. Gallons of blood."

Joni ran at Sarah and caught her clean with a right hook. Sarah's legs weakened, and she stumbled back into the wall, bathed in the glow of the projected footage of a twisting and twitching diseased.

"Stop!"

Antonia's scream lit up the room and halted Joni before she attacked again.

The footage changed to a young woman. Younger than Antonia. Restrained like Rose had been. "What did I do to her? I don't even know her name."

"It's Georgie." The youngest of the three men who'd talked about the woman he'd gotten pregnant, the boy in his twenties, Darren, stepped forward, like getting closer to the footage would somehow pull him closer to his estranged and ill-fated lover. "She was carrying my child at that point." Although he stood close to Antonia, he fixed on the screen. He couldn't look at her.

"I don't even know her." Antonia reached out to the boy, but he pulled away.

"All the worse, isn't it?" Sarah wiped the blood from her nose and got to her feet on uneasy legs. "She doesn't even remember sentencing this woman to death."

Antonia's words broke. "What did I do?"

Andy cut the chat dead. "Antonia didn't like the way this girl looked at her. But I've seen the footage. A sideways glance in the cafeteria. That's all, and that was enough for her to go running back to Daddy, making up lies, knowing full well what would happen."

Georgie's lover bared his gritted teeth.

Joni gripped her knife's handle.

He dropped his gaze to the ground between them. "Why would you do that?"

"You believe that toxic piece of shit?"

"Mum! Let him speak. Let him grieve."

"But this *isn't* your fault."

"We're all watching the evidence, Joni." Sarah spoke with a mischievous glint in her eyes. Narrowed cunning. Moving the pieces. Turning the mood of the room to her advantage. "And it would suggest otherwise."

"Is this really a woman you want to …" Andy's voice grew quieter.

Matt called through from the other room. "I've found the audio controls. I'm muting Andy and pulling up the original sound from the footage."

A voice Joni hoped she'd never hear again. She shuddered. Gooseflesh crawled on her arms. "You fucking slut!"

Andy giggled in the background. A cackling hyena, parroting the words of his idol. "Fucking slut! Dirty whore!"

"What are you doing getting pregnant out of wedlock?" Louis punched her in the stomach with all his weight.

Georgie fought for breath. She gasped between words. "Even if we wanted to … we couldn't get married here. Not that … we should have to. What we do is our … own business."

"Not on our time, you dirty bitch. And what, we have to deal with the consequences? We have to raise the kid? Provide support? Or abort it? You think we'd do that?" Louis pointed at his own temple. "You think we're that fucking cruel? We value life in this prison too much to end it." He threw his hand in the air and walked away. "We will not murder babies."

A carbon copy of Rose's footage. A diseased wrapped in thick chains lowered from the ceiling. Slow. Inevitable. The winch clacking in the background. The diseased snarling and growling. It slashed at the air. Bit at the space between them. Reached and grabbed for her until it got close enough to grip either side of her head, pull itself down, and sink its teeth into her skull.

The footage played a close-up of Georgie's face. Her sclera turned crimson, and she cried blood. Her grief twisted into rage. Her snarls grew quieter from where Matt lowered the volume.

"Leave it!" Antonia called through to Matt. "Let them hear what this cult's about. Let them have the unfiltered truth."

Matt turned the volume back up. Over the next twenty minutes, it filled the control room with women's screams. Shrill. Ear-piercing. Heartbreaking. Every guard in that room cried. Everyone knew at least one, and most knew several, if not all the victims.

"Warren?" Ralph's broad frame slumped, and he fell to his knees. The footage now showed a man. "No, please."

Joni lost the air in her lungs, and Winston appeared at Ralph's side. He kneeled next to him and put his arm around his shoulders.

Tied up like the others. In the centre of the warehouse. A man with blond hair and piercing blue eyes. Striking. Beautiful. Proud. Tied to Andy and Louis' cross, he stared straight at the camera. Unflinching in the face of their abuse.

"You're not natural, you know that? You go against the very will of our creator."

Warren's words were calm and measured. "You know our creator, do you? How's she doing?"

"Him!" Louis stamped his foot. "*King Louis* speaks to me."

Warren smirked. "So this all-seeing entity's a man, is he? Would you listen if it were a woman?"

"It's not a woman. But I bet you would, wouldn't you?"

"I'm not sure I'd be convinced the voices in my head were coming from anywhere other than myself. From a poisoned well deep in my soul. I can't believe you think I'm the one with issues. Your head ain't right, you insignificant little man."

Louis' finger shook at the end of his outstretched arm. "Who you are and what you want is unnatural. And you had the audacity to ask if you could live that life here! Under *my* nose. In *my* block! Who is it? Who's the man you love?"

Ralph's glazed eyes stretched wide, and his mouth hung open.

"The creator." Warren winked. "And he loves me too. Halle-fucking-lujah."

"You blasphemous wretch!" Louis' voice wavered. His face glowed red. "You *will* tell me. What you do is inhumane and needs to be stopped. Both of you need to be culled before this disease spreads."

"It's not catching, you moron." Warren laughed. "You're fucking simple, you know that?"

"I won't fall for it."

"For what?"

"Your distraction tactics. Make me so angry I don't torture you. So I don't force you to tell me who the other man is."

"And what if I told you the man who'd caught my eye is you? That I felt like the feeling was mutual, but you're too afraid to admit it?"

Ralph spoke through his clamped jaw. "Just tell him, Warren."

Louis let go, wild in his attack. Punch after punch after punch. He beat Warren bloody and then beat him limp. He continued attacking him, turning his face to a swollen and featureless mush.

Andy came into shot and dragged Louis back. He put himself between him and Warren and ushered him away, leading him to the control room.

Unlike on all the other bits of footage, when the diseased came down from the ceiling this time, they hung limp. They had nothing beneath them to infect.

Ralph remained on his knees, his head in his hands. But at least this time, Sarah had had the good sense to keep her opinions to herself. It would seem even she had lim ...

"Where is she?"

Mary came to Joni's side. "Who?"

"Sarah."

Mary turned on the spot and shrugged. "I don't know. But if she understands what's good for her, she won't come back."

CHAPTER 53

"Well, I suppose this is what we wanted." Olga and Matilda stood on the walkway while the mob crossed the mirrored dance floor. Laser-like focus, they pinned their hateful sights on the pair. But she held her ground, chewing the inside of her cheek, bouncing on the spot. They needed to get them all.

The reflective floor doubled the number of diseased, turning a century of the bastards into two. Several took the turn too wide as they appeared from the hallway, clattered into the far wall, and slid to the floor, twisting and turning, locked in a furious battle with their lack of co-ordination as they scrambled back to their feet.

Matilda took off first.

A second or two longer. A few more charged around the bend. Olga ran after her along the elevated walkway.

The thunderous and clumsy chorus of the diseased pursuit joined their own steps, the walkway shaking with the weight of so many bodies. How often did these bridges between towers fall?

Having opened up a lead, Matilda slowed a little.

"Don't you fucking dare!" Olga shooed her away. "Run. Now. I'll catch up."

The buzz in her ear. The annoying fly. "They're getting closer, Olga."

"Fuck off, Duncan."

"Will you stop saying that?"

Every reply stole more of her breath. "Well, stop stating the obvious. Prick."

A third of the long walkway to go. The bridge shook like it could come loose and drop at any moment. The diseased grew louder. They could taste her. They'd already won. Matilda vanished into the meeting room.

"You're on your own now."

"Fu—"

"Fuck off, Duncan. Yeah, yeah. I get it. But that doesn't change your situation."

Her head wobbling with the effort of her run, Olga ducked into the meeting room.

She reached the other side as the first of the vile creatures entered with the same clumsiness they'd carried across the walkway. Several failed to take the slight turn to follow the clear path along the back wall, and went flying over the chairs and long table. Olga's legs weakened at the gut-wrenching *crack* of breaking bones where momentum met resistance. But broken legs or not, they wouldn't give up the chase.

The knife they'd used to block the doorway discarded on the floor, the only evidence of Matilda's presence. Olga reached the door, ripped it open, and darted into the stairs.

"You need to be faster."

Her escape thrown back at her in the gloomy stairwell, Olga's stomach lurched with her descent. So poorly lit, it would only take one misstep … The crack of breaking bones echoed through her mind.

MICHAEL ROBERTSON

"You need to be careful."

"Which one is it?" She jumped to the plateau between floors, pushed off the back wall to help her turn, and ran down the next flight towards the cinema room.

"Both. Fast and careful."

"Who's up there?"

"Fuck!" Olga reached for her swinging gun, missed, and grabbed it with her second try.

"Guards, Olga."

"All right, Captain Obvious." Olga reached the entrance to the cinema room. Matilda would be dealing with the guards in there. The ones from beneath rounded the bend, reaching the plateau between floors. She opened fire, sparks where bullets hit the steel walls. It drove the guards back.

The diseased appeared from the floor above. Falling over one another. Tripping and stumbling. Fighting to get back to their feet.

The guards below aimed their guns at Olga. Several bullets whistled past.

Pulling back, Olga grabbed a chair from the cinema room and launched it at the doorway. It hit the steel wall and fell across the threshold. She threw several more, a couple sailing straight through the gap and clattering down the stairs.

"What the fuck are you doing?" A guard's voice drew closer.

More chairs, Olga lifted and threw, lifted and threw. She added to the pile blocking the door.

Several more bullets cut whistling paths across the room and sparked against the wall.

"Fuck you!" Olga fired back. She'd given the guards and diseased the best chance of meeting one another. The best chance of the chaos dropping to the floor below. But, as she turned to run, a familiar voice halted her mid-step. It came from the floor below.

"Olga?"

"William?"

"He can't hear you."

"Fuck of—"

"I'm being serious, Olga. William can't hear you."

Diseased descended the stairs. The guards came back up. Olga shot two, and the rest retreated. The first of the creatures bashed into her chair pile. It held.

Olga stepped closer to the stairs. "William?"

"What are you doing up there?"

"Run, William. Now!"

"Why?"

"Diseased. Run! Now!" She shot another guard, turned, and ran across the back of the cinema room to the clatter of more diseased hitting her makeshift barrier. The crack of gunfire met their wild cries. She paused before leaving the room. The pile enough of a deterrent, the diseased ran past and down to the next floor.

Back out onto the walkway. The middle walkway of the three, Matilda about halfway across, Olga quickened her pace.

Matilda, her gun raised, her brow creased, kept her aim on the cinema room, but she touched Olga's arm when she reached her. "Are you okay?"

After several deep breaths, Olga nodded, swallowed a dry gulp, and finally managed, "Yes. Thank you."

Both hands on her gun, Matilda stepped past Olga, closer to the threat. "For what?"

"For not patronising me by waiting. For letting me get myself out of there."

"I wasn't happy about it."

"I know."

"Oi, oi!"

Olga laughed at the grinning Gracie. She hung over the

barrier on the walkway above. She'd just come from the meeting room.

"I've locked the stairwell door from this side, so those bastards can't get back up here." She pointed towards the block with the mirrored dance floor. "I'm heading back now."

Olga saluted their friend as she departed and then grabbed Matilda's arm. "I spoke to William."

Matilda lowered her gun. "You did?"

"I told them to run. You think they'll be okay, Duncan?"

"You've given them the best chance at survival."

Matilda turned her head to one side.

"He just said we've given them the best chance at survival."

"Artan and Nick are unblocking the door below to call them across."

Olga's breaths settled, and her heart rate slowed. "Then we've done all we can. Now we need to make their escape as safe as possible." She raised her gun, rested the butt in her shoulder, and stood beside Matilda, the pair of them fixed on the cinema room. "We need to make sure nothing leaves that room. Do that, and everything else will work itself out."

Matilda shifted her stance and stared down the barrel of her gun. "I hope you're right."

CHAPTER 54

R alph's booming cry damn near shook the room. Primal. Birthed rather than screamed. Involuntary and untethered. "What a fucking fool!" He hammered the steel floor with his massive fists. The shock of his contact vibrated through the soles of Joni's boots. "What an idiot. Why did he do that?" He attacked the floor a second time like an enraged primate. "Why?"

Every one of Ralph's blows twisted through Joni's heart. The very pulse of this group. The compassion and support. Empathy in abundance. But that empathy worked both ways, and right now it cut to his core. It made the consoler inconsolable.

And then there were the others. Now fewer than forty guards because of their losses. Every one of them stood dejected. Broken.

Winston remained at Ralph's side, rubbing the big man's broad back as he sat with his head drooped.

"But we were doing all right." Ralph sat hunched, breathless, and febrile. "Why did he feel the need to say anything?"

"Maybe he wanted more? Was fed up with having to hide

his feelings. He wanted to live life with you to the fullest. He aimed for the stars, Ralph."

"And drowned in the fucking ocean when he crashed back down to earth. Oh, Winston. All the things I've thought and said about him since he left. I *hated* him for abandoning me. I've blamed him for years of unhappiness. I believed what Louis told me. I trusted that cretin rather than giving Warren the benefit of the doubt. I blamed him for leaving. How selfish am I? I made it all about me. I thought he'd wanted a way out of our relationship."

"Quite the opposite."

Ralph frowned. "What do you mean?"

"When I was his apprentice, he always talked about you."

"He mentioned me by name?"

"No, he couldn't. But he talked about his love. And how this life prevented him from living. How he just wanted to be happy."

Her throat tight, Joni gulped. How much different Ralph's life would have been had he known the truth. It wouldn't bring back Warren, or dull the pain of losing him, but he sure as hell would have resented him less. Would have seen the nobility in the man's act rather than assuming he ran off like a coward. It would have at least taken the poison from his grief. And he deserved the truth. They all did. Especially as the blame for their loved ones' demise rested squarely on Louis' shoulders and had nothing to do with the diseased in the south. She had to tell them. And now they had no reason to head south, maybe it would be easier for them to hear.

"This ends here!" Mary stepped from the crowd and pointed at the floor. "Today. We have to finish the cult now. How many guards have we lost because of Louis' twisted world view? How many more will go if Louis two-point-o gets his way? Like rot, the longer we allow them to settle in, the more they'll poison this place, and the harder they'll be to remove."

Theresa appeared at Mary's side. "I think what we just saw was Andy's panic. He's been playing a game the entire time, and he's acted like someone who believes they're in control. But I think we now have him on the back foot. He failed when he tried to kill Antonia. He couldn't stop us from telling the world what Louis did. And they attacked us up here and paid the fucking price. Their numbers are dwindling, and maybe their faith too. In a final desperate act, he's just played the ace up his sleeve. That was his last roll of the dice. What can he do to hurt us now? I think he's close to blowing his own brain out in his bunker. He knows he's done for, and we need to make sure we reinforce that belief. We've got our foot to his throat. All we need to do now is press harder."

Joni chewed the inside of her mouth, her head spinning from Theresa's metaphorical barrage. Antonia rubbed the back of her neck.

After a slight pause, her gaze lingering on the pair, Theresa pointed at the open hatch. "We need five of you up in the shafts now. You need to make sure you don't let anyone get close to Joni or Antonia with those buttons."

Joni should tell them about the south before they went. Give them all the information and then let them decide if they want to protect her and Antonia.

"I don't deserve protecting." Antonia gave a weary shake of her head. "Were it not for me, all those people would still be alive."

"That's bullshit." Darren's eyes were puffy and swollen. "None of that was your fault. How were you to know what your dad was doing? He killed Georgie and the others because they were pregnant. And Warren went to him. He died because of Louis' prejudices, not because of anything you said." He turned to Theresa. "I'll go into the shafts. Or I'll go to war. Whatever you need from me. I'm with you. We need to end this today."

Mary took Antonia's hand. "And what happened to Rose …"

Antonia winced.

"That was Louis' jealousy. Rose meant the world to you. He couldn't cope with that."

Theresa took over again. "Joni and Antonia, I want you to promise me you'll stay here. I know you'd both fight if you could. You have already. But you're too vulnerable. Please let us get on with it this time. Don't go crawling through the shafts after we've gone, okay?"

Of course Joni would return to the shafts. Do what she could to affect this war. But how could she expect Antonia to stay if she left? She dipped a nod. "Okay."

While biting her quivering bottom lip, Antonia copied her mum. "Fine."

Pearl came through from the observation room and joined the others. They armed themselves from the pile of ammo, checking and double-checking their supplies.

Joni skirted around the crowd's edge and joined Matt at the bank of screens in the observation room.

He acknowledged her approach with a flick of his head. "Looks like you're one of them now."

"Come on, Matt, they've accepted you too."

He sighed. "Not yet they haven't. They might not be giving me grief, but I'm still a loner out here. Pearl's the only one who'll talk to me through anything other than necessity."

"They'll come around. People have a great capacity for forgiveness and understanding." Did she believe what she said to him or simply wished it were true so it would be easier to reveal her lie? "I'm sure most of them already understand your choice. Join the cult or die. Those were the only two options, and you've more than proven you're not on the cult's side."

"Thank you."

Joni pulled a tight-lipped smile. She nodded at the microphone on the desk. "Nothing from the south?"

"No. And there won't be. They cut us off when they dropped that antenna. You know that. We have no comms. Nothing at all. Nada." He rested his hand near a red button. "All we have left is the tannoy. And …" He tilted his head. "You look relieved."

"What? No."

"What's going on, Joni? You've been hiding something."

A glance over her shoulder. The guards finished taking the ammo. "You can keep it to yourself?"

"It's hard to make that promise when I don't know what it is."

"There are only two other people who know this."

"Ralph and Antonia?"

"I told them recently. For the most part, I've kept it to myself. That was my choice, not theirs."

"You're talking in riddles."

She stepped closer and lowered her voice. "The south has fallen."

"Fallen?"

"Shh!" Another glance behind. The group was too preoccupied with the impending war. "Yes. Fallen. The diseased have gotten out and are running wild. Because they came from the prison, the people in the south have blamed Olga and the others for bringing it with them …"

"Which is why you wanted to get that footage out? To prove the diseased came from Louis."

"Exactly."

"Why haven't you told everyone?"

"We need to take down the cult."

"And you think telling them would make them not want to do that? That doesn't make sense."

"Half of them were considering negotiating with them to avoid the fight. What would have happened if they'd realised they had nothing to fight for? That their loved ones in the south were probably already dead? I couldn't take away their motivation. We wouldn't have stood a chance without that."

"But they know that now. Do they look unmotivated?"

"No. And they also hate Louis and his ideals much more than they did. They now truly understand why the cult needs to be taken down. Nothing will steer them away from that. Had I told them before now, it might have jeopardised everything."

"But how did the diseased get south?"

"The gate jammed, and Olga and the others left it that way. They didn't see it as a problem because they didn't know the prison was overrun with diseased."

The guards in the control room lined up by the chair beneath the open hatch. Matt leaned back in his chair. "And you're still not going to tell them?"

"I will. But after the cult's been taken down. Surely you understand why?"

"Yeah."

"But I wanted to be honest with you. I've had to hide the truth from you for so long, and keeping this secret is tearing me apart. Thanks for understanding."

"Sure." Matt rocked back in his chair again. "No problem."

CHAPTER 55

E very time Joni revealed her secret to someone, the weight pressing down on her eased a little. She even stood slightly straighter. Soon, she'd tell all the guards, and everyone would understand why she'd held onto her secret. Some of them had needed the time to see sense. She'd carried this burden for them. Lived with the turmoil. When she finally told them, they'd probably even thank her.

Since telling Matt, he'd stared at his bank of constantly changing screens, his right elbow resting on his desk, supporting his chin with his hand. He scanned the flickering images of the corridors and rooms. Some abandoned. Some filled with diseased. Some of the shambling freaks were on the move while others stood aimlessly. The occasional cult member flashed through a shot and vanished. How many spots did they have that were free of surveillance? How many of them had gone straight to Louis' quarters?

She'd said it several times in her mind, the silence growing with each passing second. If she held onto it much longer, she wouldn't get it out. "A-are you okay?"

"Huh?"

Pretending he hadn't heard her. Stalling for time. Avoiding the question. "I said, are you okay?"

His eyes wide and unblinking. Moving from one screen to the next. "It's a lot to take in."

"The footage?"

He frowned at her.

"Ralph and Antonia also found it hard."

"So why did you tell me? You could have kept on lying."

"I'm sorry."

"The others hate me as it is. And now"—he held out his hands, making a bowl with them like he wanted to catch water from a tap—"I've got to carry this. I've got to keep it from them. More deceit. Another thing to keep me on this group's periphery."

"I'm sorry. I didn't think."

Matt raised his eyebrows. "No shit."

"Joni's so selfish. Thinking about herself. Unburdening herself, but that weight has to go somewhere, doesn't it? Pass it on. Make someone else carry the deceit. She's already burdened Ralph and Antonia, and now you. Selfish, horrible Joni. No good."

"Are you … okay?"

"No." Joni stamped her foot, the room's acoustics taking her raised tone and throwing it back at her. "Joni's not okay." Several guards peered through from the circular control room. She knocked her head with her fist. "She's absolutely not okay. At all. She's been unkind to you. You've been nothing but a support, and now she's shackled you with this. She's not okay." She turned her back on Matt and strode from the room.

"Joni! Wait! Don—"

"I have something to tell you."

Over thirty guards turned towards her. Many of the faces

296

were now familiar enough for her to call them friends. At least, until that moment. But she had to tell them the truth. She couldn't drag anyone else down with her. "The south's fallen."

Theresa stepped forwards, hands on her wide hips. "What are you talking about?"

"Joni's been keeping secrets from you. The south, it's fallen. When Pocket Rocket and the others left, they couldn't close the south gate. But they didn't realise it would be a problem. When they left, there were no diseased in the prison. Other than the one in the warehouse. But it only takes one. The twisted fuck was right. One, gone, the beat of a drum."

Antonia elbowed her way through the crowd, but Joni showed her a halting hand and stepped away. "Pocket Rocket and her friends weren't to know. They couldn't close the gate, so they left it open. So what if a few prisoners got out, right? What had they done wrong, anyway? No harm, no foul."

"Except there was harm." Oscar. Or Oswald. Joni couldn't remember. "You're saying the south has fallen? So the people we were fighting to see aren't there?"

"They're not there, anyway. Louis—"

"Killed them all?"

"Andy just showed us the footage."

"Oh, that's all right then. So you being a deceitful arsehole doesn't matter?"

Theresa swept her arm across the man, easing him back. He batted it down, and she turned on him, chest and chin raised. But he remained focused on Joni. "What about all the *other* people?"

"Other people?" Joni shook her head. "What other people?"

"Family. Friends. Those we left behind when we became

guards? What if this was our chance to leave this life for good and go back to our old lives? What now?"

"It's not Mum's fault the south has fallen."

Oscar turned on Antonia. "You knew, too?"

"Not for long. Joni found out first and kept it to herself. Joni's only just told her."

He stared at Antonia. "And you also kept it to yourself?"

"I agree with Mum's motivation for keeping the secret."

"Which is?"

A booming authority. The voice of reason. Still broken from what Andy had shown them, but Ralph came to Joni's side. His shoulders and broad back hunched. His booming rasp and grizzly bear's growl. "We need to end the cult. In the beginning, some of you wanted to join them. I believe you were one of them, weren't you, Oswald?"

The man pointed at Ralph. "Don't put this on me."

"But it's a valid reason. Do you have a different perspective on the cult now? Do you still want to talk to them like you did? Negotiate with them? Make friends with the fucks who k—" Ralph lost his words. His rasp deepened as he pointed at the wall where they'd projected Warren's death. "Killed those we love?"

The rest of the room watched on as Oswald lost some of his tension. His tight features softened. He turned one way and then the other. "This isn't about me. This is about the lie. That she took away our agency because she thought she knew best."

"Turns out she did." Mary shrugged.

"Of course you'd stick up for her. Anything to protect Antonia, eh?"

"First, she needed protecting from that man. I will not feel guilty for loving a lost child. Second, I'm sticking up for Joni because I believe she made the right choice. There's no agenda here."

"And you knew about this too?"

"I only …" Joni lost her voice. She cleared her throat. "I only told Ralph, Antonia, and Matt."

Several guards scowled through to the observation room.

"I've only *just* told Matt."

"You said that about Antonia."

"I told Antonia a few hours ago. Matt's the reason I'm telling you now. He helped me see I shouldn't be keeping it from you anymore. And he didn't want to hold on to the secret. He didn't want you to have more of a reason not to trust him."

"How noble of him." Oswald pointed at the open hatch, the chair beneath it. "We were about to go up there to protect you. To go to war for you."

"You were about to go to war to end the cult." Mary sneered. "You can't blame Joni for everything. I get you're pissed, and you have every right to be—"

"How gracious of you to give us permission to be angry."

"*But*," Mary said, "you need to pull your head from your arse and stop being such a self-righteous prick. I believe what Joni did was right. She saved half of you from yourselves."

Many of the guards watched on with tight lips on puce faces. Narrowed eyes. Shaking heads.

And Mary seemed to pick up on it too, addressing the rest of the room. "What would have happened had you known earlier? Half of you would have gone to the cult. Andy would have kept the footage to himself, and you never would have known the truth."

"So we should thank her for helping us see that?"

"You'd rather join forces with someone who did those heinous things?"

"Well …"

Ralph cut in. "It was hard to watch. For all of us. But

necessary to help you see what the cult's about. Or Andy and his agenda at the very least. Even with all the sacrifices. With them locking you up. With the abuse and zealous rhetoric, some of you still considered joining them. You needed to see them murder Carly. Andy pleasuring himself when being watched by a girl he'd known since she was a child. You needed to see you couldn't reason with the unreasonable, no matter how much easier your life would be if you could. If only in the short term."

"And we needed to see we can't trust a shaft-rat."

Antonia charged. "Are you fucking mad?"

Mary caught her arm and pulled her back.

Tugging against her restraint, Antonia wailed, "Did you see what Mum just did to end that attack from the cult? She ran into a stairwell filled with diseased to stop this war. She got close to the cult, even though they could have turned her off like a light. She implanted herself to test the exit from the warehouse before letting me leave."

"But she also killed Malcolm."

The words slammed into Joni's stomach, and she stumbled back a step.

Theresa had been relatively quiet until that point. "No, Oswald, she didn't. That monster she killed wasn't Malcolm. She did what no one else had the courage to do. She made the tough choice for the sake of us all."

"Like hiding the truth?"

"I think she made the right choice."

"You too?"

Theresa folded her arms.

"Okay, fine." Oswald shrugged. "Let's say we decide we still need to fight the cult."

"You think we don't?" Theresa said.

"Let's say we do. Should we still limit our chances of

survival by leaving five people back here to protect Joni and Antonia? Or shall we bring them with us?"

"Let me end this," Joni said.

"What?" Antonia threw up her arms. "What are you talking about?"

"Let me find Andy. Alone. Let me end this cult once and for all."

"Are you mad, Mum?"

"It might be better anyway. Quieter. I can move through this place like carbon monoxide. Kill them before they know they're dead. Send an army down there, and they'll hear them coming from a mile away. They'll shoot you like fish in a barrel. I should have thought of it sooner. Let me go alone. I can end this war."

"No." Antonia shook her head. "You can't. It's too risky."

"I agree," Ralph said.

Mary nodded. "Me too."

Theresa stepped forwards. "And me."

"Me too," Matt called through from the other room.

"See, it's too dangerous, Mum."

But she couldn't have Antonia going down there with her implant. "I've done this a thousand times. I know this place like the back of my hand. I'm the quietest and quickest through the shafts. You all stay here. Let me make up for holding onto my secret for so long."

"No!" Tears filled Antonia's eyes. "I won't let you."

"Take a vote." Joni turned to the others.

Antonia stamped. "I won't le—"

"Who thinks I should go down there on my own? Do what I do best." She raised her eyebrows at Oswald. "Use my skills as a shaft-rat. End Andy and the cult before they can do any more damage?"

Three-quarters of the guards raised their hands.

"No!" Antonia's cry whipped around the circular room. "You're not going alone."

Mary said, "She wants to do this. And it might work. I don't like the idea of her risking herself, but it's the best plan I've heard. She's right. If we all go down there, they'll hear us coming from a mile away."

"But what about her implant? What about your implant, Mum?"

Joni filled her backpack with ammo. "I'll be fine. You need to let me do this." She picked up a gun and slipped her head through the strap. One hundred and thirty-eight bullets in the loaded magazine.

"This is bullshit." Antonia walked away while shaking her head. "This is fucking bullshit. Fuck the lot of you." She entered the abandoned comms room and closed the door behind her.

Matt had remained in front of the screens the entire time, and he didn't look up when she entered the room. "I'm sorry."

"No, I'm sorry." Joni rested a hand on his shoulder. "I shouldn't have put that on you. You're right. No more secrets."

"We're good?"

"Yeah. Now, I know the earpiece is useless, but I need you watching my back, okay?"

"Always."

"I trust you to judge if it's right to use the tannoy. You've led us true so far."

"Sure thing."

"Thank you."

Joni patted his shoulder and returned to the control room. She met Mary on the way through and leaned close. "Antonia's been through a lot in a short space of time."

"She has. She'll simmer down soon enough."

"Will you do me a favour? I can't do this if I think Antonia might follow me."

"Make sure she doesn't?"

"Yeah."

"I can. But only if you do me a favour in return?"

"Go on."

"Make sure you come back."

"You're a good woman, Mary."

"So are you. And what about your implant?"

"I'll be fine. I'll be on them before they have time to press their buttons." Joni flung her gun so it rested against the base of her back and stepped onto the chair leading into the shafts, now higher than anyone else in the room. "I'm sorry. Please believe me when I tell you all I thought I was doing the right thing. That my decision was with you all in mind. And this isn't on anyone else but me. I made the choice alone."

Matt appeared beside her and held up a small camera on a strap. He hung it around her neck like a medallion. "I might not be able to talk to you, but with this, I will be able to see how you're getting on."

Darren stepped from the crowd. "I'll still protect a shaft. We need to make sure no one gets in while you're away. Antonia has an implant too. Good luck, Joni."

"Thank you."

Seven more guards stepped forwards. They'd keep this place and Antonia protected.

Joni pulled herself into the dusty shaft. Her rucksack heavy on her back, the edges of the magazines sharp against her body. She might be crawling towards her own death, but at least the guards understood. And at least Antonia would be safe. And she still had Mary. With that peace of mind, she could face this next challenge alone. Do what she did best. Move through the tunnels like carbon monoxide. End Andy, no matter what. And if she died, then it would be a worthwhile sacrifice.

CHAPTER 56

F our or five guards fell over as William burst from the stairwell, flapping his arms and shooing them away. "Diseased! Run!"

"What?" Hawk froze, Aggie beside him. "What's he—"

"Diseased, Hawk. Fucking diseased. Run!"

Rowan didn't need to be told twice. He grabbed Ash and ran for shelter behind the farthest of the guards' shields. Knives joined them a second later.

Hawk pulled Aggie back with him, and they copied their friends.

The clack of bullet fire met with the wild roar of diseased, their hammering steps a landslide in the confined stairwell.

They ducked behind the last line of shields closest to the doors out of there, but still a few hundred feet from an exit. William joined them. "Olga." He pointed at the ceiling. "Was up there. She shouted about diseased coming down. She got away, but they're attacking the guards. They'll be on us soon."

"Shit!"

Flashes of bullet fire lit the dim stairwell, and the

diseased's calls swelled in the confined space. It would take more than a small army with guns to stop that lot.

"So what do we—"

Ting!

A bullet struck Hawk's shield.

"What the fuck?" Rayne bared her teeth and gripped her gun.

"Wait!" Aggie reached out to her. She shouted at the guards, "Why are you shooting *us?*"

A man's voice came back. "This is on you." More bullets cracked against their shields. "Your friends brought those fuckers down here. And now you're running and leaving us to die. Some truce. It smells like a fucking set-up." His gun barked with shots.

Aggie's eyes widened. "So what do we do n—"

"Call me a coward again, I dare ya!"

"Rayne!" Aggie reached towards the gaunt woman, but she'd already gotten to her feet, her slight frame jolting with the kick of her weapon as she stepped from cover and closed in on the guards.

Ethan followed her, screamed, and unloaded.

The chaos of war filled the dining hall. The chaos of a diseased horde about to appear. And underneath it all, the sadistic tones of Louis as he infected himself and the prisoners again.

Hawk leaned around his shield as one guard convulsed while eating Rayne's attack. He fell to the floor to be replaced by another man whom Rayne dropped even quicker.

Several guards spread out behind their shields and fixed on Rayne and Ethan. One poked her head up, and Hawk shot her in the face. All the while, war raged on in the stairwell behind them.

The guards had to divide their focus between two threats. It rendered their numerical advantage useless.

306

The bodies piled up. The guards who found temporary shelter remained behind their shields. The first of the diseased ran into the dining hall.

"Rayne!" Aggie's scream cut through the madness. Rayne halted, and Aggie hooked a thumb toward the doors leading to the walkways. "Kill 'em all and the diseased will come for us."

As more diseased appeared, Rayne lowered her gun. The guards were now fully focused on their foetid foe.

Rowan and Knives pulled Ash to her feet and led their escape.

Some of the diseased gave chase, but the mazy path through the shields proved too much of a challenge for their poor coordination. They crashed into them, tripped, and fell, some landing face-first on the corners of the steel barriers, their skulls giving way to the unyielding angles.

Still in the lead, Knives turned back to Aggie and pointed at both exits. She shrugged.

"We blocked the door back there." Aggie pointed. "We have to go the other way."

Rowan, Ash, and Knives led them onto the elevated walkway. Aggie and Hawk halted at the exit and covered William, Ethan, and Rayne so they could get free. The diseased remained predominantly focused on the guards. They took them down quicker than the guards could defend themselves. A few made it through the shields.

Hawk shot four, and Aggie seven before they followed the rest of them onto the bridge.

Waiting for them on the walkway, William handed them both fresh magazines. "I don't know what's going on with Olga. I don't know how or why this happened."

Ejecting her old magazine and tossing it over the side of the walkway, Aggie loaded her new one and slapped it in place. "Hopefully we'll survive long enough to find out."

Rayne spat after Aggie's empty magazine. "I never liked the idea of a truce with those fuckers, anyway."

CHAPTER 57

One eye closed, her cheek resting against the butt of her gun, her feet planted shoulder-width apart to deal with the recoil, Olga remained fixed on the cinema room's exit, waiting for that first furious face. Those bleeding eyes. Torn skin. Clumsy gait. "But what about the guards?"

Matilda stood beside her. "Huh?"

"The guards that Duncan told us were in the cinema room."

"They left as you were on your way down," Duncan said.

"They left when we were on our way down?"

"Is there an echo?"

"Matilda needs to know what you're saying."

"Looks like you got lucky."

"Lucky?"

"It could have been worse."

Olga leaned over the walkway, the scraping of steel down and behind them from where Artan and Nick worked the tabletop free. From where they were about to offer William and the others an escape.

"Where are they?" Matilda leaned over beside her and

309

aimed her gun down at the dining room entrance. Chaos called out into the night, but, as with the cinema room, it remained inside for now.

Back at the cinema room's exit, holding her gun with her right hand, her index finger hooked over the trigger, Olga pressed her finger to her earpiece. "Can you see what's happening down there?"

"Nope."

"You can't see *anything?*"

"Nothing of any use."

"Can you contact them on the tannoy?"

"It's not suddenly working, you know?"

"A simple no would have done, you facetious prick."

Artan and Nick appeared beneath them.

"Shit!" Matilda pointed down.

Olga traced the line with her eyes. "Shit!"

"Look at what they're running towards." Ash, Rowan, and Knives ran along the walkway leading to the other neighbouring block. William, Hawk, and the others appeared a few seconds later. Matilda leaned over the railing. One slip and she'd be a silhouette on the pulsing solar panels.

Olga pressed her finger to her ear again. "Duncan, what the fuck? Why didn't you warn us about the diseased in the next block? We knew they were on the middle floor, but not the lowest of the three. William and the others are heading straight for them."

"I didn't see them."

"How did you miss them? Again. You useless fuc—"

"You need to hold your tongue. I've helped you out enough already, and all I get is flack."

"You think you've helped us? You've landed us in more shit than you've helped us avoid."

"Fuck off, Olga."

"You fuck off. I swear, when we get back to that control

room, I'm going to help Gracie throw you from that walk-way, you useless piece of shit."

"William!" Matilda leaned out farther and cupped her mouth.

But the wind and diseased insanity bursting from the doorways buried her calls. William and the others continued towards their death at a sprint.

Artan cupped his mouth with his hands and shouted up at them, "Don't worry." He pointed at William and the others. "We'll go after them and bring them back."

"No! It's too dangerous."

Artan shrugged. "We don't have time to discuss it!"

Olga returned her attention to the cinema room. Still no diseased and no guards. They must have all gone downstairs. At least that part of the plan had gone as intended.

Artan and Nick crossed their walkway at a flat-out sprint. Matilda rested on the railing and dropped her head. "Damn! I feel so useless up here!"

Olga put her arm around her friend. Her brother and Nick heading into diseased insanity in one room, her boyfriend heading for the same in another. And the only power they had was to aim their guns at where the diseased weren't.

"They'll be okay, won't they, Olga?"

The blood-curdling call of the diseased welcomed Artan and Nick to the dining room. Olga gulped. When you couldn't say anything nice …

CHAPTER 58

Carbon monoxide. The silent killer. Joni can move through this block like a ghost. Like she doesn't exist. And by the time Andy realises she's there, it'll be too late. His regrets will flash through his mind faster than her blade into his temple. Where's trusty rusty when she needs him?

Sweaty from the crawl, but at least the uniform fitted her perfectly. Like a second skin. Although she'd take discomfort over this oppressive symbol of compliance any day. And the second she found an alternative, she'd take it. For now, she'd dress like them. Play the game. One of Louis' army. Focus on the task at hand. Reject conformity later. And conformity to whom, anyway? With Louis gone, maybe, in the future, the uniform would stand for hope? But for now, it stood for comfort. Nothing more. A distraction she didn't need while she made sure those damn buttons didn't get anywhere near her daughter.

Even with a motivation as strong as saving her daughter's life, reluctance tugged on her momentum as she drew close to Louis' quarters. Somewhere she'd planned on never revisiting, yet here she was. Again! She'd spent enough time here already. Locked away. Denied contact with anyone else. But she had to do it. For Antonia.

A diseased crowd gathered outside the room, their motivation to move enervated. Joni counted three freshly turned guards with guns slung across their fronts. Were they the ones who'd dragged her from the hatch? The creatures bumped and shoved into one another. Some were so ripe, their acrid funk hung in the shaft like mist and clung to her like vaporised grease. Other than the three guards, the crimson glisten in the others' eyes had dulled, the blood congealed. Their wounds were dark, almost black, and some of the deep gashes were glazed with the milky white of a cut turning bad. She swallowed back her heave and pushed on.

Louis' quarters sat empty. As empty as when he'd locked her in there. Alone. Waiting for him to return. To feed her. To quench the thirst that swelled her throat until it nearly closed. To ease her pounding headache and her febrile rasp. She'd spent days staring up at the hatch. At a freedom she could comprehend, but had been too scared to take. Like an elephant that had been restrained with chains and now only needed a piece of string to keep it in place, she sat on the floor, a few feet from escape. But until she freed herself in her mind, it might as well have been on the other side of the galaxy.

She turned around. Turned her back on her old life. On a Joni who'd accepted his control. Turned her back on her first guess at where she might find Andy. She needed to look elsewhere.

AT THE TOP of the vertical shaft, her breathing heavier for the climb, Joni crawled to the first grate overlooking the hall. Twenty feet from the ground. From the rows of chairs. From the small stage. From the banners decorating the back wall, capital *L*s in circles at their pointed tips. From the corpse in the corner, her face twisted with the horror of her final moments. Her mouth stretched wide with the scream stolen from her. Her head on her shoulder, her snapped neck unable to support its weight.

Only memories occupied this space. Memories and a motivation that stoked the fire in Joni's belly. Whatever happened, she needed to put an end to the cult. For Antonia's sake. For the sake of the twisted corpse. No more. Never again.

But where now? Even if she were in contact with Matt, how much use would he be? He watched through the camera slung around her neck. If he saw the need to use the tannoy, he would. Other than that, she was on her own.

THE KITCHEN like they'd left it. The table in the middle of the room scratched and covered in dirt from the soles of their boots. The fridges hung open and empty like the wide mouth of a corpse. The ovens stained black from where Joni and Pocket Rocket had needed a diversion. Evidence of activity, but only theirs, and now empty. Where else could they have gone? The warehouse? The basement? The—

Joni jumped and lifted her head. It snaked through the tunnels. Calling to her. A siren song. It both drew her closer and repelled her. Her target, but possibly her demise. The haunting tones of their hymn. Just a few rooms away.

Crossing over another hallway, this one clear of diseased, she headed for the dining room, the door locked from above.

"We will avenge him and all he stood for. We'll rebuild this block as he desired." Andy accentuated his points with the slap of his fist against his open palm. He paced back and

314

forth, the only one on his feet. The rest of the cult sat around a long table. Each had a plate containing meat and bread. They each had a cup of water. About thirty in total, the cult watched on, some of them with open mouths. Exhaustion? Shock? Horror at what they'd become? Every one wore a gun attached to a strap. "We'll be tougher. Stricter on those who disregard his rules. We'll entertain the masses on a global scale. We'll go bigger and better. Take things to the next level. All in his honour."

Andy took the closest cult member's gun and slid a plastic tray onto the table in front of her. Joni's heart kicked when she placed a button inside. "We lay down our weapons when we eat. This is a holy ceremony. Out of respect for Louis, we don't bring war to the dinner table. And we show our faith by acknowledging he will protect us while we dine in his honour. We bathe in the glory of his protective light."

Each member, after handing over their weapons, and when Andy had turned their back on them, pulled a face at their colleagues. Why did he need to disarm them? Why did they need to show their faith in that way? Why not let their guns *and* Louis' light protect them?

"Louis protect us. Watch over us. Bathe us in the light of your love." Andy worked his way down one side of the table, taking gun after gun as the tray slid down the centre, filling with buttons. It passed beneath Joni, and her chest tightened. She quelled the rising panic with deep breaths.

"Forgive us for not being there for you when you needed us most, but know we will make this prison yours again. We will show the prisoners what it is to live under your regime. We will rule with an iron fist." He clenched his own, tears shimmering in his eyes.

At the end of the table, one side relieved of their guns, Andy moved the tray filled with buttons to a small side table and made his way back down the room, disarming the rest of the guards as he went.

"No!"

Andy held one member's gun, but the man clung on. He inhaled, looked up at the ceiling, and exhaled hard before looking back at the man. "No?"

"I won't hand it over."

The air thickened. The hairs on Joni's arms stood on end. A charge hung in the room. A thunderstorm about to break. "What's wrong, brother? You don't trust in Louis and his guiding light?"

"I trust in it."

"Him!" Andy stamped his foot. "You trust in *him!*"

"Fine. I trust in him. Whatever."

The skin beneath Andy's right eye twitched.

"But I don't see why we need to lay down our weapons."

His teeth clenched; his red face turned a deeper crimson. The light glistened off the tears in his eyes and the grease on his skin. He tucked his hair behind his ears, brushed down his shirt, and straightened his collar. But no amount of order could realign him.

"Fine!" The man tutted and slipped off his weapon. "Take it. What—"

Andy shot him dead. Unloaded into his face. Tore his features to shreds. Blew his fucking brains across the table and over half the cult's meals. He caught the man before he slumped forwards and dragged him off his seat so he landed on the floor on his back.

The rest of the guards had their guns ready. Andy moved along the table quicker than before. He stacked the weapons in the corner, keeping his own, switched off the hymn, and took his seat at the end of the table. His meal splattered with blood and brain matter, he lifted his roll. A fleshy chunk fell back onto his plate. "To Louis!" He took a large bite from the bloodiest spot and chewed. The man's essence mixed with his saliva at the edges of his mouth, turning it a foamy pink. He spoke while he ate. "Forever in your honour and your name."

The cult watched on, aghast. Several lifted their bloody rolls, and the side of the table who'd avoided the human condiment ate with their leader. But the room's attention rested on those yet to take a bite. Not a single guard watched the tray filled with buttons.

CHAPTER 59

Hawk, and Aggie beside him, froze when Rowan stopped before entering the block they were heading for. He turned around and shooed them back.

William, Rayne, and Ethan paused a second later.

A solitary diseased stumbled into view. So quick, her hand a blur, Knives launched a blade. A glint from where it caught the flashing red lights around them before it sank into the vile beast's face and buried to the hilt. An elegant solution to their problem.

Holding his finger up on his right hand, Rowan spun it in the air and pointed back the way they'd come.

Ethan took off, charging towards the room Rowan had just told them to avoid. Rowan blocked his way by slamming his forearm across his chest. "There are too many that way."

Ethan pointed at the room they'd just left. "More than back there?"

Rowan nodded. "Twice as many."

Hawk said it at the same time as Ethan. "Fuck!"

Ethan threw up his shoulders. "So either way we're screwed?"

"There are degrees of screwed." Rowan had a hold of Ash's hand. "Back the way we came is a safer option."

As much as Ash had said she didn't want to be protected, her compliance suggested otherwise. And they were all happy to help. More than that, they had a duty to look after her and Rowan's unborn child. Every choice should be about the safest predicted outcome, now more than ever. And where there might have been room for discussion in the past, Ash and Rowan now carried the trump card. They swayed the argument. They needed to look after her. And to do that, while they'd have to face what remained of the guards and the diseased in the room they'd left behind, they needed to head back.

Hawk grabbed William and pointed to the middle walkway linking the building they'd just left with the block in the other direction. "Look!" Matilda and Olga waved their arms. If only it were in greeting. They, like Rowan, knew what waited for them at the end of their current path.

"And look." Aggie pointed lower down. The tabletop they'd used to block the doorway had been pulled clear. They had a way out.

William nodded and raised his gun. "I'll buy you some time." He charged back to the dining room they'd just left.

Hawk stepped after him, but Aggie grabbed his arm. "Let him do this for us."

"But he might die in there."

"I think he knows that."

Ethan stepped forwards. "I'm going with him."

"No you're not," Aggie said.

"So you're happy for William to die, but not me?"

Tightened lips and narrowed eyes. A shimmer of tears flickered in her glare. Aggie turned her back on him.

"He needs my help." Ethan dragged Hawk a step closer to the block and a step farther away from Aggie. "I love her."

"Huh?" Hawk shook his head. "What?"

"I love her."

"That's what I thought I heard. Shit. I—"

"You don't have to say anything. There's nothing you can say. I just wanted you to know before I go in there. My dad and family left the camp we were living in, and I stayed because of her. I pretended I'd been orphaned, and they took me in. But that was well before you turned up." William fired shots in the dining room. "I'd already made my peace with her not loving me. Not like that, anyway. You and her have a chance at happiness. I want to give you that. So make sure this isn't for nothing."

"I—"

"Just make sure you survive, okay? Make sure you both get through this and Ash has her baby. Be ready to run when we say."

Ethan's words scrambled Hawk's mind. And from the swirling emotional malaise, he could only manage, "Uhhh ..." But by then, Ethan had already vanished into the dining room.

Seconds later, Artan appeared in the doorway. Nick behind him.

"Art? Nick?"

Artan waved them through. "It's clear. Come on!"

Rowan led Ash first. Knives and Rayne behind them. Hawk waited for Aggie, grabbed her hand, and led her back the way they'd come. "It's going to be okay. We're all getting out of here. *All* of us."

CHAPTER 60

The dining room had two doors. The one she'd already passed over had been locked from above. Joni crawled to the other door, towards the table holding the tray filled with buttons and the grate closer to that end of the room. They'd locked the second door too. The cult was trapped in there with that lunatic.

Biting down on her bottom lip, Joni laid the edge of her knife into the screw's groove, missed it because of her shaking hand, got it in on her second attempt, and turned it with a gentle *click!*

Back at the grate close to the side table. The clean end, free of blood and brain matter. She laid her face against the cold steel shaft and peered along the room. The cult members with the bloody rolls held them like they had before. Andy took another bite, but while he might have been trying to lead by example, he clearly set an example none wanted to follow.

One member, a short woman in her forties, stood up from the table and threw her roll at her plate. "I'm not eating it."

Andy snarled. "What?"

"I'm not eating it. You can't make me."

Another member stepped away from the table. His gaze flitted between Andy and the short woman. "I-I w-won't eat it either. This is a step too far."

"How dare you challenge Louis' authority?"

A third member threw down their roll and slapped their hands against the table as they stood up. "But it's not the word of Louis. It's the word of Andy."

"He speaks to me."

"Convenient."

"What is?"

"How you *claim* he speaks to you." The man made air quotes with his fingers. "And how no one can ever prove you wrong in that assertion."

"You doubt Louis?"

"I doubt *you*!"

A fourth member stepped away from the table. She pointed at Andy. "You're taking it too far. You're using it to control us."

Andy held his gun across his front. "Do we have a problem?"

Six more cult members got to their feet. He might have disarmed them, but he couldn't fight them all. Although, from the hatred on his twisted features, maybe he'd not yet done the maths.

Just two members at the bloody end of the table remained seated. Looking around, they too stood up, as did the six remaining members at Joni's end. They stood strong. A unanimous mutiny.

They closed in on Andy, who matched their steps with his retreat. Still the only one with a weapon, he'd do more damage than any of them, but he couldn't take them all.

The highly charged atmosphere turned Joni's throat dry.

It might be a shit-show down there, but what better chance would she get? She opened the grate with a hard whack.

Slipping from the hatch, she landed on the table, shattering several plates. She jumped towards the tray filled with buttons.

"Intruder!" Andy's cry rang out.

Joni reached the plastic tray as the cult ran for their weapons. She upended it, the buttons spilling across the floor, and she stamped on them, shattering each and every one.

The first bullet whistled past her and sparked against the wall.

Another burst hit the floor in front of her.

She kicked over the small steel table and crouched behind it.

The vibrations from where it soaked up bullet fire ran through its frame and stung her hands gripping its legs.

An inch at a time, she backed towards the unlocked door, dragging the table with her. The cult had taken cover at the other end of the room. Like their mathematically challenged leader, they were yet to see their clear advantage. If they charged, they'd overwhelm her in seconds. But she only needed seconds.

Andy jumped onto the main table.

The cult ceased their attack. Let their leader do what leaders did. Let him finish the intruder. Show them they could rely on him. Spearhead the attack.

Joni took aim. One hundred and thirty-eight bullets, she'd unload every single one of them into him.

But Andy's gun hung loose. He reached the first hatch in the maintenance shaft, tore it open, and climbed in. His feet vanished from sight as he slithered away, crawling on his belly like the snake he was.

Joni reached the far wall, bashed the door's button, and ran out, darting right as bullets followed her through.

Panting, she raised her gun and took aim. She had the ammo and the advantage. The doorway would funnel them through, and she'd drop them in ones and twos. End this fucking cult once and for all.

"Joni?"

"Whoa!" Joni jumped at the echoing intrusion from the hallway's hidden speakers.

"It's Matt."

"No shit!"

"I can see you're talking, but I can't hear you."

"That's a shame, fuck-nut. Now, do you have anything use—"

"Diseased are heading your way. A shitload of diseased."

"Fuck!"

"There's only one other door in that hallway, and they're on the other side."

"Shit!" Trapped between a flock of angry guards and a horde of vile diseased. "Shit!"

Like in most rooms in the block, this one had a maintenance shaft running along the ceiling down the centre of the hallway. It had three grates, each one ten to fifteen feet apart. It could have had ten and it wouldn't have mattered. She couldn't access any of them. Not without …

One hundred and thirty-eight bullets in her gun. It should be enough. She slammed her fist against the dining room door's button.

"They're getting closer, Joni."

Her gun kicking with her depressed trigger, Joni ran into the room and shot the ceiling.

The cult ducked and scattered.

The tannoy echoed through the block. "They're about to open the door. They'll be on you in seconds."

Her arm aching from holding her gun with one hand, her bullets spraying everywhere, she grabbed the small table with the other and dragged it with her, backing out of the room.

"Don't go back out there! You'll die."

And who didn't need a good vote of confidence to keep them motivated?

Crack!

Whoosh!

The door at the other end of the hallway opened.

"Oh, fuck!"

Diseased. Snarling, snapping. Bloody eyes. Gashes on faces. Ripped clothes. They charged.

"Hurry, Joni!"

She dropped her gun so the strap took its weight and turned the table upright.

The diseased's steps vibrated through the steel floor.

"They're close!"

"You think I don't fucking know that?"

"Shoot them, Joni. Shoot them!"

Twenty feet away.

Joni stood on the table.

Fifteen feet away.

She pulled on the hatch, but her sweat-slick fingers slipped.

Ten feet.

She drew her knife, wedged it between the hatch and the shaft, and popped it away, the hatch swinging down. She ducked at the last second, a waft of air from where it narrowly missed her head.

Five feet.

Joni pulled herself into the shaft as the diseased clattered into the table, sending both them and it sprawling.

Scooting along on her front, Joni reached the door to the dining hall, slipped her knife into the screw, and turned it.

Crack!

A diseased hand slammed against the button on the other side.

Crack! Crack! Crack!

But the door remained closed.

"She's locked it," a woman from the dining hall said. "She's stopped the diseased getting to us."

"I'm not here for you." Joni jumped at the sound of her own voice in the small space. "This is about Andy."

"Then thank you." The same voice as before. "And if you cross over the top of us, we promise we won't fire on you."

It gave her the best chance of catching up with Andy. But she had to trust the guards wouldn't pull the trigger. Only twenty feet of maintenance shaft to cross. But in times like this, twenty feet could feel like miles.

CHAPTER 61

B ack into the dining room with the guards' shields, Louis' footage played on the wall, lining up prisoners to be slaughtered all over again. Hawk and Aggie ran across the back of the room, cutting from one walkway to the other while Artan and Nick joined William and Ethan, the four of them forming a line against the diseased, firing as the clumsy creatures negotiated the sprawl of shields with their uncoordinated charge. Some slammed into them and fell to the side. Some dived over the top, coming down on the steel floor head-first. Some never got back up. Knocked unconscious, or having had bullets driven into their fallen forms.

Of the four of them, Ethan stood the farthest forwards and edged closer to the shield maze. He'd committed to dying today, and now he'd told Hawk about Aggie, how could he possibly take that back?

Ash, Rowan, and Knives were already halfway across the walkway towards the reopened tower block.

Hawk, Aggie, and Rayne walked backwards along the bridge, guns raised, ready to take over when William and the others needed cover.

Halting first, Aggie leaned on the barrier and aimed past the retreating quad. William dragged Ethan with him. She shot a diseased on their tail. It stumbled and fell face-first, tripping the next two behind.

Hawk leaned on the other side of the walkway, rested his target on a diseased face, and pulled the trigger.

Rayne joined in as Ethan, the last of the four, passed her. They walked backwards, firing at the emerging diseased. Olga and Matilda helped from above.

The beasts fell, but more filled the spaces. A maul of the vile creatures. They packed the walkway and drove those at the front forwards, even after they'd died. Flesh shields, their dead kin ate bullets that could no longer hurt them before they fell away to be replaced by a fresh layer of corpses. All the while, the diseased gained ground.

Thirty bullets remained in Hawk's gun. "Aggie, we need to swap around."

William and the others had all reloaded and stood in waiting.

They swapped, Hawk taking three magazines from Nick as he passed. He handed one to Aggie and one to Rayne, ejected his own, launched it from the walkway to the creatures on the plaza, and slapped the fresh one in place.

Four guns made little difference compared to three, other than to waste more bullets.

The diseased drew closer. Matilda had stopped shooting and turned her gun towards Hawk like he could see the digits. Too far away, but he didn't need to read it. She'd run out of ammo.

A ten-foot gap of walkway separated those shooting and the diseased.

They passed the bridge's halfway point, now closer to their destination than the hall the diseased emerged from.

The gap between them and the flesh shield was now down to eight feet.

Three-quarters of the way across, the front diseased were now six feet away.

Artan raised his gun above his head. Out of ammo. Nick and William pulled back. William grabbed Ethan again.

Hawk, Aggie, and Rayne took over. Twenty feet from the entrance to the dining room. About five feet between them and the diseased.

Rowan peered from the darkness, through the narrowed doorway from where he'd partly pulled the tabletop across.

William shoved Ethan in and followed. Artan and Nick vanished next.

Ten feet from the entrance, the diseased so close their vinegar rot caught in the back of Hawk's throat. Rayne turned to him. He nodded back. She ducked into the room behind.

Hawk shouted over the bullet fire and the diseased wails, "You first, Aggie." They were five feet from the door. He kicked out at the obliterated corpse shield, blood spraying from the holes they'd shot in the bodies. The diseased continued forwards with an unstoppable press.

The tabletop ready to fall across the doorway. Ready to defend against the creatures. But they were too close. They'd follow them through.

Hawk kicked out again. "Aggie! Go!"

She remained fixed on the diseased. Her jaw tight, her gun kicking as she unloaded into them. Their hands reached around their dead shield, inches from grabbing her.

A foot from the entrance. His hands buzzing with his bucking weapon. Hawk held his ground. "Aggie. You first!"

Someone reached out and grabbed a handful of Hawk's shirt. They pulled him into the room, and he whacked his elbow on the way through. He tripped over his own feet and fell, reaching out to Aggie as she got farther away from him.

He landed on his arse on the hard steel. The tabletop fell across in front of him. Rowan wedged a table leg between the top and floor, blocking the door. Shutting Aggie out. Leaving her on the walkway.

"No!" Hawk jumped up, but Knives knocked him back. "No!"

CHAPTER 62

A binary choice. Trust the cult or don't. Die while crossing or survive. Right now, she had a chance of catching Andy. Take another route to find him and he might slip away forever.

She rapped her knuckles against the side of her head. "If you're going to go, then go, Joni. Take too long and the question's irrelevant. Andy will be long gone. So long. Too strong. Too fast. Too smart. And that can't happen. Not smarter than Joni. No smarter than a rock. A smarmy, greasy rock."

Little point in masking her progress. A dozen or more cultists below. One of them would track her, no matter how quietly she crawled. She passed the first open hatch, the table and smashed plates from her landing. Several cult members stared up at her. Their faces blank. Unreadable. Were they playing a game? Just doing this to fuck with her? Give her hope and then rip into her with the combined force of a small army. Her abs tensed in anticipation. Like a six-pack would repel bullets ...

Driven by adrenaline, she reached the second hatch. More members down this end. The table splattered with blood and brain matter. While they were all armed, she couldn't see a member gripping their gun. They all hung from their straps across their fronts.

Crossing the next door, Joni exhaled hard. "T-thank you." Her voice echoed in the tight space. "Do you want me to leave this door open or closed?"

A few seconds of hushed conversation before a woman replied, "Open, please."

Still shaking, Joni wiped her sweating palms on her trousers, drew her knife, and slipped it into the screw. She turned it with a gentle *click!*

"Thank you." The same female voice. "And good luck."

Years of crawling through the shafts had made Joni more adept at the task, strengthening muscles that suited this particular skill. Someone like Andy didn't stand a chance. She turned her ear, lifting it towards the ceiling. The distant pop and bang of someone making progress called back to her. It had to be him. Even weighed down by her backpack, she had the beating of the man. She took off, following his sounds like a hound on a scent.

Left, right, up to the next floor, right, and right again, Joni closed in on him. His thuds and pops gave way to the crash of a grate followed by the squeaking of rusty hinges. He'd gone to ground. Harder to track, but she had him. Over a febrile, pathetic creature like him, she had the advantage in every way.

Dust in her throat, sweat burning her eyes, Joni turned the next left, the light shining up through the open hatch. A beacon. A marker. A checkpoint before they began their final battle.

In one fluid movement, Joni slipped from the hatch. But she caught the shaft as she dropped. Snarls and cries descended on her. Heavy steps. Slathering rasps.

Dragging her legs up, Joni pulled herself against the underside of the maintenance shaft.

One diseased stood taller than the others. Over six feet, he reached up and grabbed her backpack. He tugged, testing her strength.

Lying horizontally, supporting her bodyweight with her trembling arms, Joni's feet scraped against the underside of the steel shaft, desperate for some kind of purchase on the flat surface. Some way to relieve the pressure on her upper body. The booms of her kicking toes making contact called out. A trapped and panicked animal. Cornered. Fucked.

Her knuckles burned, and her arms shook. The diseased tugged harder. She let go with her left hand and swung towards the mob. Several threw air-bites at her fingers. She slipped from one of the bag's shoulder straps, yelled out, and grabbed the hatch again.

Joni let the other strap slide as three more diseased grabbed the bag now it hung lower. All four fell with the effort of their tug. With the force it would have taken to remove her from the shaft.

Still clinging horizontally to the underside of the shaft, her entire body shaking, Joni swung her legs down, kicked out, and pulled herself back in. Her head. Her shoulders. Her upper bod—

The tall diseased man grabbed her gun and tugged, pulling her back out again.

Joni kicked the tall beast in the face with a wet *clop!* She dragged herself back into the shaft and lay on her front, panting.

The diseased screamed. A catch that should have been theirs. Now lost forever.

Her entire upper body ached. She'd definitely pulled muscles, but she pushed on. She reached across the open hatch, the diseased a carpet of furious faces. Bloody eyes.

Deep and infected wounds. One clutched her bag like a trophy.

A distant pop of someone progressing through the tunnels. Joni's whisper ran away from her. "Motherfucker. Fool me once …" She chased after it.

Right, left, up another floor, right, left, left. But with every third or fourth turn, Andy seemed to be farther away than before. The echoes through the tunnels messed with her tracking. The pops and booms suggested he was in two different spots at once. Like there were two of him. Imagine!

Joni halted. Waited. The sounds of his escape were impossible to track.

Her heart pounded like it wanted out.

Always go with your heart. Antonia had said it makes the best decisions.

But her heart had sunk into a quagmire of dread. It drowned in anxiety. It could only mean one thing. The message couldn't be any clearer. He was heading to Louis' quarters.

Why hadn't she thought of it sooner? Where else would the little sycophant go?

But was it too obvious? Would he bank on her going there and head somewhere else?

Or maybe a double bluff? Head there because it was so obvious. She'd overthink it. Talk herself out of the best choice. She'd tie herself in knots. End up paralysed by the permutations.

Although resting, her heart rate quickened. It had the message. Loud and fucking clear. He'd gone to Louis' quarters. And if he hadn't, she couldn't track him through these tunnels, anyway. From here, she could get there first. She knew these shafts better than anyone. Use that to her advantage. And it wasn't like she had a better choice.

Joni turned on the spot and crawled back to the closest

vertical shaft. Her sweaty palms against the cold steel on either side, her boots pressed against the shaft's walls, her shoulders and arms sore. She trembled as she climbed to the next floor. Towards Louis' quarters. She'd get there before him. She'd be waiting for him to drop. Waiting to cut his throat. The silent killer. Carbon-fucking-monoxide.

Right, left, left, right. Over the hallway still packed with diseased from earlier. Waiting in case something showed up. The door still locked.

Joni reached the hatch and rested the side of her face against the shaft. The cold steel cooled her hot left cheek. She leaned on the other side, on the other cheek. A fresh angle into the empty room. She'd beaten him to it. She slammed her palm against the grate, dropped into the room, closed it behind her, backed into a corner, adjusted the camera around her neck, and drew her gun. A knife would be fun. Especially if she'd still had trusty rusty. But she couldn't risk it. She had forty-two bullets. Enough. Andy would turn up soon, and when he did, she'd put an end to the toxic fuck-nut.

CHAPTER 63

The railing pressed against Olga's ribcage as she leaned over and aimed down at the diseased on the walkway below, the blinking plaza even more dazzling for it being night. Her laser target wobbled because of her shaking hands. It ran from one creature's head to the next like it couldn't decide which one to end first. It found bald scalps and deep gouges from bites. Exposed skulls and matted hair. But they were all too close to Aggie. One tremble too far and she'd kill Hawk's girlfriend.

Aggie had remained outside to save the others. Her back pressed up against the tabletop blocking the door, she stretched out her leg, the sole of her boot resting against the corpse shield. Arms reached towards her. Slashed at the air between them. She shot what she could, adding to the dead bodies between her and the active diseased. But how long could she keep the creatures' press at bay?

The walkway shook behind Olga. William, Ethan, Nick, Artan, and Rayne ran past her and leaned over the same side overlooking Aggie's bridge. They unloaded on the diseased farther back. Bursts of bullet fire, explosions of red mist from where their shots sank into heads, shoulders, and arms. The corpses piled up, creating a foetid blockage, a barrier between those diseased still coming from the dining hall, and the ones doing their best to crush Aggie.

"Aggie!" Hawk burst from the sports hall and knocked Olga aside when he leaned on the railing. "What are you doing? Can't you see she needs help?"

"What do you think we're trying to do?"

"Dunno, but you're not doing it well enough."

"Hawk!" Matilda showed him her hand. "Calm the fuck down and let us deal with this. Aggie's in control."

"You call that in control? You must be looking at something very different to me."

"She's holding them back."

"For now."

Olga hit three diseased in a row, starting close to Aggie and then running back. If nothing else, it would ease the weight of the press. "Hawk?"

He spun on her, his shoulders pulled back and teeth bared.

"We've got this, but do you really want us to stop what we're doing to talk you down? Aggie needs us, and the more you argue, the more you take away what help we can give her."

His balled fists unfurled.

"Now go down there with the others and kill as many diseased as you can. Stopping the flow will help."

"I swear!" He pointed at Olga.

"Fuck off, Hawk!" Next time she'd fucking swing for him.

Hawk ran to be with the others. He leaned over and shot into the tens of diseased crammed onto the walkway. Half the group moved closer to Aggie, thinning the diseased press, while the other half worked back towards the dining hall.

There were now more diseased down than standing.

Aggie continued to send short bursts into those who got too close. Those who slipped through. She continued to lean against the blocked door and continued to keep them at leg's length.

Another diseased found a gap in the corpse wall. It slipped through several of the fallen. An eel through mud.

Aggie aimed at the beast while Olga rested her target on the top of its head. Just in case.

Aggie paused and looked up. She showed Olga her gun. Out of bullets.

"Fuck!" She'd not shot one this close, and Matilda had no ammo left. Olga's target drew erratically widening circles on the diseased's head, her aim growing increasingly unsteady. She pulled her trigger and winced. Her bullets landed true. "Aggie's out of ammo."

Gracie had been in the sports hall the entire time. She ran out with several ropes, like the ones Olga and Matilda had used to climb to the walkway above. She'd plaited them, making them stronger and thicker.

The diseased pressed in on Aggie. Her straight leg wobbled, trembling with the weight of their press. She jabbed the barrel of her gun into the face of the closest diseased, straight into its eye, driving it back. But it returned with renewed vigour.

"Aggie!" Gracie, one end of the rope wrapped around her waist, threw the other end over the side.

Aggie reached for it and missed. She grimaced with the effort of holding back the creatures' collective desire. The rope stopped swinging, the end about three feet away.

"Shall I go down?" Olga pointed at the rope.

Gracie shrugged. "How will that help?"

"I dunno."

Aggie's straight leg had now bent. How long before it completely failed?

In one fluid movement, Aggie snapped her leg away, hopped onto the railing, and jumped. The diseased fell towards the blocked door. One slapped her feet, spinning her to the left, mid-flight.

Olga's heart beat in her throat, and her stomach turned somersaults. The blinking plaza and hundreds of diseased below. Aggie would shatter on impact.

But she caught the rope and hung on. The jolt dragged Gracie into the railing.

Catching her friend around the waist, Olga hung onto Gracie and leaned back, anchoring her against Aggie's swinging weight.

Hawk ran over and hung onto Olga, pulling Gracie back a little.

All three of them rocked with Aggie's climb.

Hawk gasped when she poked her head over the top, and for a second, he loosened his grip on Olga like he might let go, clearly thought better of it, and clung on tighter than before.

With Matilda's help, Aggie pulled herself over the handrail and fell onto the steel walkway.

Hawk pulled her to her feet and threw his arms around her. "Thank the heavens. You're all right. I was so worried. So, so worried."

Bullet fire to their left. Ethan and Artan shot the diseased breaking from the cinema room. They fell, more crashing over the top of them.

Gracie cupped her mouth with one hand and pointed back at the block they'd just left with the other. "Let's get the fuck out of here."

Their collective retreat echoed through the sports hall. Artan and Ethan continued to shoot the diseased on their tail. Louis' footage played on the back wall.

Olga followed Gracie, who passed Rowan, Ash, and Knives on the stairs. They all beat a thunderous ascent.

Holding the door open for them, Gracie waited until Artan and Ethan came through before she slammed it shut and wedged a knife through the handle like they'd done in the building with the meeting room.

About twenty seconds later, the first of the diseased clattered against the other side of the door. They pressed their faces to the glass. Bit at the pane. Turned it slick with their blood and pus.

"And the other door's locked?"

Gracie nodded at Olga. "Yep. Like this one. The diseased can't get up either side of the stairs. We're safe. For now."

"For now." Safe didn't exist in this world. The blocks were all connected to one another. Nevertheless, Olga threw her arms around her friend. She moved on to every one of the group, even those with Hawk's party. And finally, to Hawk. He held on tight and leaned close to her ear. "I'm sorry. I lost my head a little back there."

"I think we all did. Aggie's a warrior, eh?"

"Tell me about it. Thank you, Olga. I don't know what I would have done if I'd have lost her."

"I get it." She swallowed against the permanent lump in her throat. The lump that had been with her since Max's death. "I really get it."

CHAPTER 64

Time moved at a different speed when you were standing in the corner of the room of your night-mares, waiting with a loaded gun aimed at a hatch through which you expected to meet your enemy, forty-two bullets, each one with their name on. But Joni had spent plenty of time here before. Time where she had no agency, let alone the upper hand. She leaned back against the wall and focused on her breaths. She had this. She could wait. Rest, so she had that final burst of energy needed to bring this mess to an end.

Crash!

The grate swung into the room, squeaking with its momentum.

Joni rested the butt of her gun in her shoulder, peered down the barrel, and closed one eye.

A pair of boots appeared.

She laid the red dot of her laser target on the black leather and applied a little pressure to the trigger.

Andy landed on the chair, and his already slack jaw damn near hit his chest. "Oh, fuck!" He raised his hands in the air.

"Your time has come, motherfucker." Her pulse accelerated. Her sore upper body tightened, lighting up the stinging pain from earlier. She had but one purpose: to drive white-hot fury into his pasty, grease-slicked body.

Andy kept his hands raised and stepped down from the chair and closer to her. "Calm down, love."

"*Love*? You fucking *prick*." She coughed, dust in her throat from the hatch. "Get against the wall now, you fuck!"

"Okay, okay." Slow and steady steps away from her. Towards the corner of the room farthest away.

"Stop! Go over there." Joni flicked the end of her gun to show where she wanted him. She matched his retreat by stepping forwards until she stood close to the chair beneath the hatch.

But Andy continued towards his intended destination. She'd had too many power battles in this room. "I said, go ov—"

Joni shot backwards from where someone grabbed a handful of her shirt and pulled her away from him.

Knocking the gun from Joni's grip so it hung from its strap, Sarah spun her around and raised her own. She aimed it straight at her face. "Surprise, motherfucker!" A door hung open behind her. A small room no larger than a closet.

"What ... where ...?"

"Did I come from? Where did you get that uniform? You have no right dressing like us."

"Fuck off."

She smiled. "Now come on, mad old Joni, don't be like that. And don't tell me you're surprised to see me."

"No. I suppose not. It's obvious you were a snake from the start. You think we didn't have your number from the beginning? Although, how did you get the cult to attack us?"

"I have a panic button. When you went to the roof, I pressed it, and they came running. I had it from the second they put me in with you lot. If heads needed to be smashed, I pressed it. If a revolutionary spirit grew too strong, I pressed it." She flashed a facetious smile. "Nothing like a sacrifice to dampen the mood. Isn't that right, honey?" She reached out to Andy, who stepped closer and took her hand.

Joni's stomach clenched, and she tasted bile. "None of this is a revelation, Sarah. Apart from how you got them to attack. You wear the fact that you're a weapons-grade arse-hole like a badge of honour. But where did that room come from?" She rested one hand on her gun. Outnumbered, but not defeated, despite their clear confidence.

"The panic room's always been there." Andy flashed her a yellow-toothed grin. "I used to hide in there for days. Watching you when Louis locked you up. Waiting for you to get to the brink of death before I used the same button Sarah had to call Louis so he could come in and save you."

"That prick never saved me."

Andy continued, "I got good at it too. At first, I pressed the button too early. You still had some fight in you. Some hope. But with each button press, I learned to push it a bit later. By the end, I had the timing so you passed out as Louis arrived." He looked at the backs of his nails. "It's quite an art, you know."

"How do I know you're not making all this up?"

"Huh?"

"I've forgotten a lot of things from my time here, including you. Are you sure this isn't some fantasy you've had so many times you now believe it to be real?"

Andy's top lip twitched. "Wh—"

"He's going to watch *me* now." Sarah pushed her breasts up from the bottom, accentuating her cleavage as she winked at Andy. "I'll be his little project. He'll watch over me. Protect me. Fantasise about me while he's in his little box."

Joni scoffed. "Hiding like a rat in his little secret bunker."

But the comment fell dead. Andy watched Sarah with the green-eyed glare of a psychopath. The only lust in his dead stare yearned for control. Poor Sarah might believe she had agency, but he'd modelled himself on a vicious narcissist. If only she knew how much of a favour Joni was about to do her. Andy needed to be taken down. Cut the head off the snake. End this cult now.

Joni snapped her gun into her shoulder, aimed at Andy, and pulled the trigger. The burst crashed into the wall where he'd been a millisecond earlier.

In one fluid movement, Andy slipped behind Sarah, shoved her towards Joni, and jumped into Louis' panic room. He slapped a button, and the panel slid across.

Sarah ran after him, but as she reached the closing gap, Andy shot her, blowing her brains out of the back of her head. A light sheen of bloody mist pinpricked Joni's face. The door closed like the room had never been there.

Sarah's corpse lay on its side and watched Joni through the one eye she had left, a hole where the other had been. Watched her with the glazed and absent stare of the dead.

CHAPTER 65

Hawk stepped away from the door, the diseased attacking it from the other side again, testing the improvised lock. The knife rattled, but remained through the handle. It would fall out eventually, but it held for now, which was all they needed. The glare from the ceiling's strip lights glinted off the ballroom's mirrored floor. The two walkways leading from the block were clear. Ethan had vanished around the bend leading towards the control room. Since their last proper conversation where he'd confessed his love for Aggie, it made it easier to have him away for now. Easier for Hawk to do what he'd wanted to do for ages. What he'd wanted to do every second in her company. He held Aggie's hands and leaned close. She met him halfway, and they kissed. Properly kissed.

Grinning, Hawk breathed heavily as they pulled apart. "I've wanted to do that since the second we met."

Aggie's gaze flicked from one of his eyes to the other. "Me too."

William and Matilda also held one another before William broke away. "I owe you an apology." He turned to the others. "All of you. What I did back there. Walking off like a petulant child. I can see now I was wrong, and I'm truly sorry. It was selfish." He nodded at Aggie. "And misogynistic. I felt sidelined, and I dealt with that by sulking like a baby. I hope you can all forgive me."

Pulling him close, Matilda kissed his face. "I'm just glad we're all back together."

"And we have a future. Something to work towards."

"Huh?"

William pointed at Ash and Rowan. "They're pregnant."

Olga snorted a humourless laugh. "No way? Well, shit."

Hawk stepped forwards. "Like William said, it's a future. A reason to try to change this world for the better. A responsibility to look after the next generation."

The attention clearly bothered Ash, who stepped back from the others, away from the mirrored floor and towards the bathroom door. A *click* stopped her in her tracks. She glanced down at her foot. Some kind of trigger.

Aggie knocked Hawk aside as she charged at Ash. Her steps joined another's coming from inside the bathroom. A small red light turned green on the door. She shoved Ash away just as the door burst open and diseased flooded out. She raised her gun and pulled the trigger. She tilted her weapon. The digits on the top showed two zeros. She'd not reloaded since being trapped on the walkway.

"Aggie!" Hawk reached out as a diseased woman lunged at her and bit into her shoulder.

"No!" He joined the others in shooting the emerging diseased.

Knives blocked Hawk's path and shoved him back. The others stood over Aggie and the fallen diseased. All of them levelled their guns at Hawk's love.

Aggie sat on the floor, slumped, holding her shoulder. Blood leaked through her fingers.

Ethan had returned. He dragged Hawk away. But Hawk twisted and fought against him. His voice broke. "Aggie!"

She lifted her head. Crimson tears cut tracks down her cheeks. Her lip rose in a snarl, her face set with hatred. Her head snapped back, and blood sprayed the wall from where Rayne shot her. She fell to the side.

Rayne fixed on Aggie and cried.

Ethan let go of Hawk, who dropped to his knees. His love stared at him through the dead, bloody glaze of her kin. His body turned limp where he sat. Devoid of strength and will.

CHAPTER 66

Joni wedged her foot beneath Sarah's shoulder and flipped her over. Easier to look at the matted and bloody mess of an exit wound on the back of her head than her dead eyes and still smug face.

She banged against the false wall. "I'll wait out here as long as it takes for you to crawl from your bunker. We'll do it in shifts. We have supplies and all the time in the world, and after your little display down in the dining hall, I wouldn't bank on any of your followers coming up to rescue you. You've pissed on your chips there, sunshine. And you've just killed your only ally."

His voice was muffled. "I want to negotiate my release."

If she heard him so clearly now, how had she not heard him when he'd been in there years ago? A sneeze. A fart. The grunting of what had probably been his furious and non-stop masturbation. "You have no leverage."

"Give me a chance to get out of here."

"Why? What makes you think you've earned it? You wouldn't do that for me."

"You're better than I am."

"You could say that of every living thing on the planet."

"Come on!"

Thirty-five bullets left in her gun. Joni aimed it at the wall. "Throw your weapons out first."

"You'll negotiate with me?"

She shook her head as she said it. "Yes."

Crack! The door opened, and he slid out a handgun and rifle. He sent a knife after them and held his hands in the air, his fists clenched like he'd swing for her given half a chance. But she wouldn't give him half a chance.

"I'd spend days in that room, you know? Pissing and shitting in a bag. Eating where I shat." He grinned. "Watching you pace and moan like a restless dog."

"I think you're imagining things. I don't believe any of the nonsense you're spouting happened. Or are you so forgettable that you made zero impression on me?"

"How's this for an impression?" Andy opened his right hand to reveal an implant chip trigger. "It didn't work through the closed door. I had to convince you to let me out."

"Fuck!" Joni lowered her gun. "I figured you would have revealed a button earlier if you'd had one."

Andy laughed. "And me trying to negotiate didn't give it away? You think I'd trust you to be true to your word? That the vicious little slut who broke Louis' heart would show me mercy?"

"Broke his heart? He didn't fucking have one."

"Throw down your gun."

Joni lowered her weapon and placed it on the floor.

"But I'm not going to kill you. I'm going to keep you like Louis did. And I'll do one better. I'll keep Antonia too. I'll have the pair of you locked up. Utterly reliant on me. Desperate to be with me. To touch me. To consume me. I'm going to become your god."

Bile lifted onto the back of Joni's tongue again. "You fucking won't!"

"Shall I turn you off? You and little Antonia?"

She'd rather die than be at someone's mercy again. Joni lunged at Andy.

He jumped aside, leaping backwards over Sarah's corpse. He wagged his finger. "Don't say I didn't give you a chance." He held his button towards her, and she yelped when he pressed it.

Who knew what would happen next? Searing pain. White-hot agony hijacking her central-nervous system. Haemorrhaging from every orifice. Or simply being turned off like a light.

Andy held the button towards her and pressed it again. And again. "What? It doesn't work."

Joni laughed.

"What's so fucking funny?" He dashed the button against the steel floor, shattering its plastic case, a spring and several green circuit boards spilling out. He picked up his knife.

Joni drew hers. "Do you know how much time I spent deactivating those buttons?"

His jaw looser than usual. His hair had untucked from his ears and now framed his docile and greasy face.

"For over twenty years, I deactivated every one I could. And in all that time, I still didn't see you."

"I was here!"

"I saw a lot of Louis, and you were never that close. Did he keep his distance?"

"He trusted me to act on my own!"

"So not even your idol could stand being around you?"

His voice rose in pitch. He waved his blade at her. "This is a stalemate! Let me go."

Joni's smile broadened.

"What?"

"It's the only mate you've ever had, isn't it? Also, I have the advantage, you just haven't realised it yet. I don't care if I walk out of here. I simply need to make sure you don't."

"You still have to beat me."

The wall to their left lit up. The small cube on the ceiling projected footage, and Matt's voice boomed through the tannoy. Omnipotent. "Hello, Andy."

The long-haired pissant snapped alert.

"I hope you're watching this. This is what your idol thinks of you ..."

Joni stumbled back from the enlarged image of Louis' face. The camera pulled out, revealing him and Sarah. The footage paused.

"This is from Louis' private collection, which Joni got from the warehouse. Thanks for leading us there, by the way. This video wasn't that hard to find. I started with his most watched, and this was second only to his daughter in the shower."

Joni shuddered as the footage resumed.

"*I* know he's a little grease-rat, and *you* know he's a little grease-rat."

Sarah shrugged. "So why not cut him loose?"

"He's like a stray dog. Feed him once and you're stuck with him for life."

"Stray dogs can be put down."

Louis giggled. "He is a sad little man."

"I think you find his existence flattering."

"How so?"

"He idolises you. Wants to be you. He spends every second he can watching you. Mimicking you. He's so far up your arse, he's like your own personal butt plug."

Despite herself, Joni laughed.

Louis' enlarged face twisted. "Ew!"

"Too much?"

"Far too much. Look, I'll get rid of him one day. When he's served his purpose. I'll take him out to the woods and set him free. But he'll do anything I ask. For a laugh, I used to leave him in my panic room for days and set him tasks that didn't need doing. He obliged. Fuck, he was happy to help."

His head bowed, his hair hanging across his face, Andy glanced into the small space he'd just vacated.

"He's willing to end whoever needs to be ended," Louis said. "When dirty work needs to be done, he gets into it up to his elbows."

Sarah scoffed. "He smells like he's in it up to his neck."

Both Louis and Sarah broke into laughter. Louis bent over at the waist, howling at her comment. Red-faced and tears in his eyes, it took him a full minute to recover.

"But what about the cost of his company?" Sarah said.

"Cost?"

"You have to put up with him. That takes its toll, right?"

"I avoid him as much as I can, but that's the kicker, isn't it? Is it worth i—"

Bang!

Joni screamed as blood sprayed the projected footage on the wall.

Andy fell to the floor, back through the open door of his bunker. His handgun still in his grip. He'd picked it back up without her noticing. She should have been more alert.

The projection faded with their laughter before starting back at the beginning.

The greasy Andy lay on his side, blood pooling beneath his face. Tears ran from his dead eyes.

CHAPTER 67

D espite there being twice the number of them in the control room compared to when Olga had been in there last, the large space felt emptier than ever. Sobs and sniffs cut through the muted atmosphere. Hawk and Ethan huddled together in a corner, consoling one another. The rest of Aggie's crew wandered around puffy-eyed and in a daze like diseased with nothing to chase. Her own stomach in knots, she rested on the main control console and closed her eyes. So many people lost, and how many more would fall before they finally found somewhere safe? Somewhere they could call home.

Gracie shifted from one console to the next. A frantic bee collecting pollen from flowers, she gathered information from the screens, scanning the monitors before moving on. She came close to Olga.

"Nothing?"

"Not yet. But I promise you, I'll find him." Her raised voice pulled the room's attention to the pair. And maybe that was why she did it. There had to be consequences. "Duncan won't get away with this. I'll slowly remove every one of his fingers and toes and throw him from the highest elevated walkway."

"What if he's already gone?"

"Where? How could someone like him get away from these blocks?" She sneered and shook her head. "No chance."

"What if he's been bitten?"

Gracie slumped. "Maybe you're right. Maybe I'm giving him far more credit than he deserves. And if he is one of them, he—"

"He'll blend in with the others? Stupid clothes. Stupid hair."

Gracie's eyes narrowed. "Stupid fucking self-satisfied grin. They even have it when they've turned." She leaned closer, pointed at the radio mic next to the tannoy, and spoke so only Olga heard. "And he tried to call the neighbouring blocks." She pointed at the wall. "The ones out there in the distance."

"How do you know?"

"The transmission logs. When we were in here earlier, I rigged it so he could only call Joni, but it would show if he tried anyone else."

"What's happened with our connection to Joni?"

"It's dead. I think it's at her end, not ours."

Rayne stood as dazed and bloodshot as everyone else. Her sallow cheeks streaked with glistening tracks. The room's bright lights caught her angular features, like she'd been made from the same steel as most of their surroundings. She pointed at the control desk. "He used that to fuck us over."

Olga laid a soft hand on Rayne's shoulder and kept her tone even. "Used what?"

Rayne stared into the middle distance through unfocused eyes. "When we were running across the walkways to the cinema room, he used the tannoy to tell the guards we were heading that way. That's how they blocked us off before we reached them. And why we had to jump to the lower level. Then, when we were on our way up the stairs, to see what was going on with the guards above, maybe get a little look at what they were doing so we could plan our next move, he called through again and told the guards we were there. We heard it that time, ringing through the stairwell."

"You didn't hear it the first time?" Gracie flicked a glance in Olga's direction. Did Rayne know what she was talking about?

"No."

"So, how did you know what he told the guards?"

"They told us."

"What?" Olga this time.

"We called a truce when the footage came through." She snorted a laugh and refocused. "For what that was worth. They lost their anger towards us when they realised Hawk and William had nothing to do with freeing the diseased. But they hadn't really thought long term. About how hard it would have been for us to get along. They represent oppression and exploitation"—her voice deepened—"and I'm not sure I could have been trusted not to cut their throats the second I got a chance. So I suppose it was handy when the diseased came down on us. It forced the inevitable."

Olga rested on the main console. "So you'd called a truce when the diseased came down on you?"

"For what it was worth."

"Duncan told me to lead the diseased down on top of you. Told me you were in trouble and the diseased would help swing the fight in your favour."

"There was no fight at that point."

"Fucking prick." Gracie spat the words. "If he's still alive, I *will* find him."

"I wouldn't be so pissed off. It took down a small army of the fuckers who used to live here, and we all got away. By turning them into diseased, maybe he did us a favour? Saved us from killing them later. Why do you hate Duncan so much?"

"It's not obvious?"

"Well, I hate them all, so I get it. But Duncan in particular. What's he done to you?"

"Kids!"

Gracie's word sent the image of the baby in the bathtub crashing through Olga's mind. The squirming worm sloshing about in blood and shit. The soft little head through which she'd buried the tip of her knife.

"I'm sorry"—Rayne cocked an eyebrow—"but you're going to have to give me more than that."

"We ran into kids in the block. And we tried to help them get free. Get them away from here. And we nearly did, right, Olga?"

It snapped her from her daze. Pulled her back into the large and brightly lit room. Banished the violent images of a baby being turned off like a fucking appliance. "Huh?"

"We nearly saved the kids …"

"Yeah. And we would have were it not for that fucking cretin. He was so scared, he attracted the diseased's attention with his whimpering. It was a slaughter."

"Uh, you might want to look at this." Nick hunched over a console for the fifth tower block, leaning closer to the screens.

Olga's stomach sank. "What now?" She crossed the room with Gracie and Rayne, the others, even Hawk and Ethan, gathering around. Half the screens were black, but someone wearing a helmet and padded body armour ran past a camera before aiming a gun up at it, turning another screen dark.

Shoving through, Gracie leaned closer to the monitors. "You think that's him?"

"It has to be." Nick pointed at where he appeared next. "It

makes sense, dressed like that, how he got the diseased into the bathroom that ki …" He glanced at Hawk. "Well, you know?"

Another camera went dark. Gracie jabbed her finger against the glass, the dead camera turning it into a black mirror. "We should go to him now before he blinds us."

"We can't."

Gracie turned on Olga.

"Not now. We need to wait. We're safe here, and he's already blinded us. Do we really need to be going on a wild goose chase after someone we can't see and don't know where they are? I don't know about you, but I'm not even sure we could track which cameras he's putting out to follow his trail."

"I refuse to fear him, Olga."

"It's not him I fear, but what about the diseased we might encounter? Us running after him exposes us all. This room is about as safe as it gets. Maybe we need to accept we won't have the cameras, but we have each other, and we can slowly secure one block at a time. Hunt him down methodically. That way we can maintain control."

Matilda sighed. "Olga's right. It's not like we're going anywhere in a hurry."

"Fuck!" Gracie turned away from another screen as it blacked out. "Motherfucker. I will find him. I promise you I will."

"We all will. Hawk?"

He scowled at Olga.

"I think we should do something for Aggie. In her honour."

His scowl remained unchanged.

"A way to say goodbye, you know?"

Fresh tears cut tracks down his cheeks.

Olga hugged him, and he fell against her, his body

rocking with his heavy sobs. "I wish it weren't so, but I believe her life needs to be celebrated. In the short time I knew her, she seemed like a remarkable woman."

"She was." His voice warbled. "The best."

"And then"—she pulled away—"when we've had a bit of rest and some time to recover, we'll get control of all eight blocks. We'll flush Duncan out like the rat he is. Will make him pay for every single death!"

CHAPTER 68

J oni paused. A moment like many before it. In the shafts alone. Mistress of her own destiny. The escape route she'd had in her back pocket all along. The ace up her sleeve. She could vanish. At any point, she could crawl away from here. Leave it all behind and live underground. Do everyone a favour and remove herself from their lives forever. Take her deceit with her. Her failings. Her baggage. But why did she need that now? With Andy's death and the truth coming out, everything had changed. She now had nothing from which to run.

Turning around in the shaft, Joni hung her feet from the hatch, slid backwards into the control room, and landed on the chair. Every guard in the room bowed their heads like they were in the presence of royalty.

Theresa walked over. A few inches shorter than Joni, but in her stocky frame she held the power to wrestle a bull. "From the day we met, I knew Sarah was an arsehole. She always had an agenda, doing whatever suited her, every time, without fail. And whenever there was drama, you could bet your life she would be at its centre. I say good riddance. And well done for seeing off Andy."

"No." Joni pointed through the doorway at Matt in his comfy chair. "That was all him."

"I think it was both of you. You isolated him and softened the cult. You showed them compassion when many would have gone to war. Empathy has the power to change. Aggression would have only escalated the situation. In your shoes, I can't say I would have acted with such strength and dignity."

"You think we don't have to worry about them now?"

"Who knows for sure, but I think you've given us the best chance at peace." Theresa raised her voice. "But you're right, we owe Matt too. He's been an integral part of this victory."

"If that's what it is. We still don't know how the cult will react, and the price has been too high to claim any kind of win."

"But at least Andy's gone."

Antonia came forwards. She stumbled into Joni, her arms open wide as she flung them around her and clung on. Whatever happened now, that option to run away to her old life had long gone. Whatever happened now, Joni had started anew. A life with a daughter. A life with friends. Part of a community. Something she'd not had for a long time, and something she'd not allowed herself to miss for fear of it being her undoing. Nothing quite breeds madness like putting a sociable creature alone in a damp hole in the ground.

Ralph approached with Mary beside him, his baritone voice like a landslide. "Thank you." He called back into the observation room, "And to you, Matt. I'll never get over what happened to Warren. Ever. But by making sure Andy paid for what he did, I think I'll manage to let go of the bitterness with time. With no one left to punish for what happened, I can focus entirely on the loss. Feel it for what it is and find a way to live with its burden."

Mary held an open plastic box filled with black origami swans. About twenty to thirty in total. She held the box towards Joni, who took one and turned the delicate creation to view it from all sides.

"One for every person whose passing we want to mourn. A way to say goodbye. To send our love. Also, a way to draw a line under what this place once was and to look forward to what it could be. We're going to throw them from the roof, but wanted to wait for you to come back."

Antonia took Joni's hand and led her toward the door leading from the control room. But she held her ground, an anchor against her daughter's progress.

"Matt needs to come with us too."

The old chair squeaked with Matt's turn. "Huh?"

"You need to come. You're one of us. We can't do this without you."

"But I made you tell everyone the truth."

"No, I made that choice. I gave you a burden too heavy to bear. I should have seen what I'd placed on you. On Antonia and Ralph too. Thank you for giving me that clarity. In expressing how you felt, you did the right thing and helped me do likewise."

"You both did." Many of the guards nodded along with Theresa's assertion. "You were also right to keep it from us when you did, Joni. We needed to stay focused at that point. We needed to end the cult. It came out at the right time."

"You've forgiven me for the lie?"

"There's nothing to forgive. You're a wise woman. You made the right call and were brave enough to carry that weight for us. I, for one, would like to say thank you."

Oswald cleared his throat and elbowed his way to the front. "I'd like to say thank you, too. And sorry. That footage we saw was a lot to take in. I turned my hurt on you, and that wasn't fair."

Nods passed around the room again, which Joni mirrored herself. Her voice weak, she reached out to Oswald. The man gripped her hand and squeezed.

"Right!" Mary raised her box of black swans. "Let's do this, and then we can work out how we deal with the rest of the cult."

Oswald said, "And head south."

Mary raised an eyebrow. "You're still going?"

"After I've rested for a while, yes. I have family there. If they're still alive, I want to find them. There's nothing for me in this prison, so until I know for certain, I'll live in hope there's something more in the south."

Joni said, "And we'll help you get there."

A tight-lipped smile. Oswald pressed his hands together as if praying. "Thank you."

Joni returned the gesture and waited for Matt to join them. She put her arm around him, and his entire frame softened at her contact. She leaned close so only he heard. "They see you, Matt. They know the kindness in your heart."

MARY RESTED the box of swans on the wall around the building's roof. The wind strong and sharp. The bright moon hung in a cloudless sky, and Joni shivered. They overlooked the plaza filled with diseased. A hundred or more, they were aimless in their wanderings. Many wore guards' uniforms. None of them as well as Joni. A perfect fit. She'd been desperate to lose it, but it represented something different now. Belonging. Something she'd wanted for so long.

"Oh, what's this?" Matt leaned on the wall and peered over.

Joni leaned over next to him, her stomach lurching. One hundred and fifty feet to the hard ground below. A cult member ran from the block much like they had when they took down the antenna. Another followed, and then another. Four, seven, ten … she lost count. Twelve? Fourteen? Not enough to win a war against the diseased. She winced as the first creature slammed into the first cultist, tackling them both to the ground. It landed on top of the woman and bit her face, latching on while she writhed and kicked.

Several cult members avoided the first wave, but many more fell. The plaza alive with screams from the diseased and members alike.

It took about twenty seconds for the creatures to take down every cultist bar one. A short woman with a tight ponytail. She weaved through the madness, twisting and turning, darting left and right. And she nearly made it. Nearly. Joni sighed when a diseased tackled her from the side. The woman's solitary scream buried beneath the roar of diseased.

After a brief pause, the final woman snapping and twitching, scrambling to her feet and joining the diseased, the guards formed a queue behind Mary. One at a time, they took a swan or two and threw them from the top of the block. Many cried. Many lingered as the paper animals rode the wind and finally came to rest on the prison's concrete ground.

Ralph kissed his swan. He wailed as he set it loose and fell to his knees.

Antonia ahead of her, she took two and lifted them close to her mouth. Her lips moved with her whispers, the buffeting wind keeping her words private. Words that were only meant for Rose and Carly. She set them free. But where the other guards had thrown their swans, waited for them to

363

land, and moved on, Antonia paused at the box. She turned to Joni while biting one side of her bottom lip.

"It's fine." Joni smiled. "Despite everything, he was your father."

Antonia took another swan, and with less ceremony than before, sent it after the first two.

Many had been lost. Many who didn't deserve to die, and many who did. Death everywhere, and no doubt more to come. The labyrinthine prison stretched away from them. Roads and tall steel walls. Glass lights and white lines. Enforcement from a previous life. A regime toppled with no hope of revival. Like Joni, this prison had abandoned its old ways. Like Joni, it would change for the better. It would get there. Eventually. She lifted a black swan from Mary's box. One wing bent from where it had been on the bottom, discarded, forgotten, underground. Broken. Not anymore.

Mary offered Joni a different one, but she shook her head. "It's the imperfections that define us." While many had died and many should be mourned and remembered, this bent swan represented a life once lived. She dropped the paper bird. The wind picked up and carried the swan farther than any other. It passed over the plaza and the diseased heads. It passed the broken antenna trashed by the cult, and over the wall beyond. It had served its purpose. Half mad because that was easier than feeling the past twenty years, but now it was time for Joni to tend to that broken wing.

CHAPTER 69

The orange glow of the flames turned into a blur as Hawk stood over Aggie's burning corpse. The fire feasted on the wooden base and swaddling of blankets around her body. The heat combatted the night's chill up on the elevated walkway, but did nothing for the frozen grip of grief on his soul. The frostbite in his heart. He hung his head, tears dripping from his face, Ethan's arm around his shoulder. "She should have been harder to burn."

Ethan snorted a humourless laugh. "I know what you mean. That woman was made from granite. The best and toughest of us all."

But at least the flames would sear away what she'd become. Scorch the monster that had taken her over. Drive off what remained of the disease that flooded her veins. But never the image of her final moments. That would be tattooed in Hawk's mind forever. The very last time she looked at him, she did it with hatred. Revulsion. Disgust. Absurd to think she could ever love him. He clapped a hand to his chest. No matter what happened from this moment forward, and no matter how he rationalised that the disease had her by then, he'd never forget her final glance.

Turning from the flames, the heat at his back, Hawk leaned on the walkway's handrail and squinted against the cool wind. It turned his tear-streaked cheeks cold and burned his already stinging eyes. Diseased stared up from the blinking red plaza. The body of the fallen woman still on the ground like a landmark. It could have been worse. Aggie could have gone out alone. Fallen from a great height. Pregnant and with no one left in her world. But she went out surrounded by those who loved her. Who cherished her. Who saw her magnificence and held her in that light.

He gripped the handrail tighter. Maybe he should follow in the steps of the pregnant woman. A life without Aggie seemed like no life at all.

Knives rested a hand on his back. "She really loved you, you know? She's never been like that with anyone else. She held her cards close to her chest, but you brought something out in her. And for that, I'm grateful. I will always think of her as someone in love. Someone happy. You gave her genuine joy."

His eyes on fire, the lump in his throat damn near suffocating, Hawk dropped his head and sobbed all over again. "She left too soon."

Knives' lips buckled out of shape, and she rubbed his back. Her usually strong delivery weakened. "Way too soon. Look!"

Hawk rubbed his eyes, tracking where Knives pointed. Light in the distance. Vehicles barrelling along a road. "A convoy?"

"Yep. It's late for them to be out."

"Why do you think that is?"

"Maybe they're trying to get all their supplies to the shining city before anyone else can get them."

He tracked them across the dark landscape. Eight to ten vehicles. Tanks and chain bikes escorting a large truck and trailer. A road train. How many supplies did they have? Enough to make them a target? There would be time to think about it in the future. His love aflame behind him, he turned back to her burning corpse. With time, the wind would scatter her ashes over a landscape that had once been her home. A life of want and need. A life of struggle.

Rowan stood with his arm around Ash, the pair of them crying. A life they'd never have to live again, because of Aggie and her leadership. A life the baby would never know. If nothing else, Hawk needed to remain on this planet to make sure their kid had something better. Never knew the struggles of those before it. Never wanted for anything. And understood the true legend that was their aunty Aggie.

END OF BOOK FIFTEEN.

Thank you for reading *This World of Corpses:* Book fifteen of Beyond These Walls.

Support The Author

Dear reader, as an independent author I don't have the resources of a huge publisher. If you like my work and would like to see more from me in the future, there are two things you can do to help: leaving a review, and a word-of-mouth referral.

Releasing a book takes many hours and hundreds of dollars.

I love to write, and would love to continue to do so. All I ask is that you leave a review. It shows other readers that you've enjoyed the book and will encourage them to give it a try too. The review can be just one sentence, or as long as you like.

If you've enjoyed Beyond These Walls, you might also enjoy my other post-apocalyptic series. The Alpha Plague: Books 1-8 (The Complete Series) are available now.

The Alpha Plague - Available Now

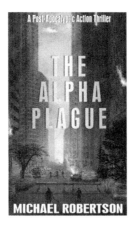

Or save money by picking up the entire series box set HERE

ABOUT THE AUTHOR

L ike most children born in the seventies, Michael grew up with Star Wars in his life, along with other great stories like Labyrinth, The Neverending Story, and as he grew older, the Alien franchise. An obsessive watcher of movies and consumer of stories, he found his mind wandering to stories of his own.

Those stories had to come out.

He hopes you enjoy reading his work as much as he does creating it.

Contact
www.michaelrobertson.co.uk
subscribers@michaelrobertson.co.uk

THE ALPHA PLAGUE:

The Alpha Plague: A Post-Apocalyptic Action Thriller

The Alpha Plague 2

The Alpha Plague 3

The Alpha Plague 4

The Alpha Plague 5

The Alpha Plague 6

The Alpha Plague 7

The Alpha Plague 8

The Complete Alpha Plague Box Set - Books 1 - 8

BEYOND THESE WALLS:

Protectors - Book one of Beyond These Walls

National Service - Book two of Beyond These Walls

Retribution - Book three of Beyond These Walls

Collapse - Book four of Beyond These Walls

After Edin - Book five of Beyond These Walls

Three Days - Book six of Beyond These Walls

The Asylum - Book seven of Beyond These Walls

Between Fury and Fear - Book eight of Beyond These Walls

Before the Dawn - Book nine of Beyond These Walls

The Wall - Book ten of Beyond These Walls

Divided - Book eleven of Beyond These Walls

Escape - Book twelve of Beyond These Walls

It Only Takes One - Book thirteen of Beyond These Walls

Trapped - Book fourteen of Beyond These Walls

This World of Corpses - Book fifteen of Beyond These Walls

Blackout - Book sixteen of Beyond These Walls

Beyond These Walls - Books 1 - 6 Box Set

Beyond These Walls - Books 7 - 9 Box Set

Beyond These Walls - Books 10 - 12 Box Set

OFF-KILTER TALES:

The Girl in the Woods - A Ghost's Story - Off-Kilter Tales Book One

Rat Run - A Post-Apocalyptic Tale - Off-Kilter Tales Book Two

Masked - A Psychological Horror

CRASH:

Crash - A Dark Post-Apocalyptic Tale

Crash II: Highrise Hell

Crash III: There's No Place Like Home

Crash IV: Run Free

Crash V: The Final Showdown

NEW REALITY:

New Reality: Truth

New Reality 2: Justice

New Reality 3: Fear

~

Audiobooks:

Go to www.michaelrobertson.co.uk to view my full audiobook library.